Soldier, Lily, Peace and Pearls

or

La Galaxie des lumières tardives

A Novel of Kindness

Soldier, Lily, Peace and Pearls is a work of fiction. Names, characters, and incidents are products of the author's imagination, are used fictitiously and are not to be construed as real.

Deux Voiliers Publishing

To Jade
A Novel of Your Inspiration

Soldier, lily, peace and pearls,
All together in one world,
When the owl comes out at night,
He will make everything all right.

Chapter One
Coffret à Souvenirs

The small wooden box lay on the teak commode. A boat tipping under the weight of too many passengers was sketched in India ink on its lid. The container was a gift from Quan when the Thieus had left Pulau Bidong for Canada. In it were her treasures, her memories. Dr. Han Thieu opened her *coffret à souvenirs* and gazed upon its contents—a photo when she had brought Minh Chau back from the hospital. Voang, her husband—her beloved other, was dressed in his best suit, holding Minh Chau's sister An in his arms under the green papaya tree in their garden. She proudly stood at his side, with Minh Chau, a flyspeck against her white *ao dai*. Han savoured in her mind the papaya's sweetness, the fragrance of Saigon, the scent of the country that they had lost.

The box held other treasures—the UN laissez-passer which brought them to Canada, Mathieu's measuring tape sweet, forgetful Mathieu. He had lent her the tape to measure scarves cut from an old wool blanket so that Voang, An and Minh Chau could brave the bitter Quebec winter. She kept inviting Mathieu for tea in order to return the measuring tape. Each time, he would put the tape on her kitchen table as they talked endlessly about Canada and Vietnam, and invariably, he would forget it when he left. After a while, she just tucked away the tape in *her box,* but kept inviting Mathieu back for more tea and pleasant conversation. She looked at Mathieu's tape one last time and thought of his immeasurable kindness when they arrived in Canada. He had assuaged her longing for Vietnam and instilled in her children a love of their new country.

There were other nick-knacks in the box, but of all its treasures, Jing Zi's green potion was the most precious. It had brought Minh Chau back to life. It would now seal her memories and spare her family the pain of the last vicissitude of her existence.

***

Dr. Dominic Leblanc shuffled the test results before him. He had never adjusted to this part of his job, and now it was even harder with a colleague and friend. He straightened the files and handed them across to Han. Leblanc was one of Montreal's top oncologists. "I am sorry, Han. There is not much we can do. The cancer has spread too far. We could try chemotherapy, but I am afraid that it might give you only another six months, and your quality of life would suffer tremendously."

Leblanc shuddered at his own words. He looked deeply at Han's face. She had just turned fifty, and was still a very beautiful woman, but the disease had taken its toll, and she looked ten years older. Her skin was pale and her normally small physique now looked microscopic. Dr. Leblanc had battled for a year to prolong Han's life. He had tried all known remedies and had worked with Han to test traditional and new Chinese cures, assembled from the potions that Quan had left behind. Twice unknown to her family, Han had undergone surgery for the cancer. The first time, she told them that it was only cosmetic surgery for the removal of a mole. The second time, it was supposedly an emergency appendectomy.

"Dominic, I thank you for everything that you have done. I only ask of you one thing more. Do not tell my family of my condition. I do not want to worry them. Death comes to all of us. I wish mine to be without fanfare. I have already chosen the day that I will bid farewell to this sweet world."

Leblanc leaned back in his chair. Surely, Han could not be suggesting... He stared at her. Leblanc was a devout Catholic, and attended Sunday mass at the same church as the Thieus. He had always thought that she shared his views on the absolute sanctity of life. "Han, you can't be saying what I think that you are. It is for God to decide when life ends."

Han smiled at the pious doctor. Although she was baptized as a child in the Catholic Church, deep inside she also cherished the Buddhist beliefs of her mother. The ambivalence of Buddhism on suicide gave her more comfort than its absolute condemnation in Catholicism. In Vietnam, she had witnessed as a child the self-immolation of a Buddhist monk in a quest to end religious discrimination. She knew that a prolonged death from cancer would thrust her family into deep emotional trauma. Had they not lived through enough? They had lost their country and witnessed the baseness of human nature.

Still, for many years in Canada, they had also experienced peace and kindness. This had helped heal Minh Chau's torn soul, even after

Quan's disappearance had ripped her apart again. Han would not let her own death put her daughter through that hurt. She believed in the forgiveness of her Christian god, and the wisdom of her mother's religion. If the quietness of her exit from this existence would reduce the pain of those she would leave behind, it was far better than their months of anguish as they witnessed her wither away in pain from a drawn-out death in a hospital ward.

"Dominic, you have been my friend and my colleague for three years. When I die, I would like you to make out the death certificate. I would like you to put on it that I died peacefully from a sudden stroke. Can you do that? Would you do that?"

Dr. Leblanc looked at the tiny woman, his colleague and indeed his friend. He had admired her dedication to her patients. He knew only too well of her love for her family. She was now asking him to do something that his medical ethics and religion forbade, but his inner higher morality agreed with. He knew that no one would question his signature on the medical certificate. No autopsy would be performed, but he needed confirmation that this was what Han really wanted.

"Han, if this is what you wish, then I will do it for you, and only for you."

Han nodded silently, and then took his hands in hers. She had never touched him before, not even a simple handshake. She slowly lowered her face into his open palms and moistened them with her tears of gratitude.

***

Minh Chau packed her bags. She could not believe the generosity of her mother. Airfare to Europe and four thousand dollars to spend, just for graduating from university. She had planned her itinerary for two weeks. It would take her over the next three months from Paris to Madrid to Rome, Florence and Venice and then onto Germany and Scandinavia. She was a bit confused about the suddenness of her mother's generosity, but she wasn't complaining.

An was equally confused when her mother offered her and her new boyfriend Marc a two-week cruise in the Caribbean. She did not even think that her mother approved of Marc. After all, her parents had wanted her to date only Vietnamese men. Her father Voang even had a number of willing suitors lined up. Despite her promise to be raised as a Vietnamese woman, at the end of the day, she had given her heart to a somewhat introverted Montreal carpenter who treated her as a queen.

It took Han a month to put her affairs into order. She had to return to Dr. Leblanc twice for him to change her pain killers, each time upping the potency. Still she could barely make it through a day without bowing over with crippling pain. She had, unknown to husband, referred all her patients to new physicians. In the final days, she had entered all her hand-written notes into the computer for her research on Jing Zi's natural medicines and had sent an article to the Canadian Journal of Homeopathic Medicine on her principal findings. She had added Dr. Leblanc's name to hers as a last act of gratitude.

Han reflected on her life. She had always tried to be a good person. In Vietnam, she had been apolitical before the Communists took over. She abhorred war and had named her first child, An—*Peace*, in the hope that peace would come to Vietnam. She never turned down a patient who could not afford to pay. Yes, she had been raised in a rich land-owning family. Her father had made millions from leasing his lands to international rubber companies, and he had provided his family a luxurious lifestyle while at the same time driving off his lands peasants who were too old to do the back-breaking work of collecting rubber sap from the trees. When one of his foremen complained that a worker was a Viet Cong sympathizer, her father had willingly passed on this information to his contacts in military security. How many he had delivered? Han had no idea.

Han thought of her life-long love for Voang. He had been the only man whom she had ever intimately known. Her parents had looked down on her young suitor from the North, but she had convinced them finally that either they agree to their marriage or she would never marry and bear them grandchildren. Voang was not an angel. She knew that he had had at least one affair with a young dental assistant. However, his devotion to his two children was never in question, and Han had felt his love for her since the first day that they met. Despite the scores of men who paid special attention to her beauty and intellect, she had never even been tempted to look at another man.

Why now was God taking her life away? She felt An was safe. Marc might not have the pedigree that she wanted for her daughters, but he was a kind, caring man. He would take good care of An. She worried still about Minh Chau. Inside her daughter was a secret garden that she was letting no one into. She had scared Han after the disappearance of Quan. Her daughter's morning appearances, drunk and drugged, with her clothes barely on, and the reeking of cigarettes had broken Han's heart a thousand times. When Minh Chau would then recoil at her mother's touch, hiding instead in her bedroom, curled up in a fetal position on the floor, Han felt the blade of fear cut away another slice of her being. Other times, her daughter would simply stand by her window the entire night until sunshine washed away the tears from her face.

For the last four years, Minh Chau had been much better, excelling at her studies and showing a crazy passion for life. Han knew that it was often a mask, that her daughter still felt sharp pains whenever someone asked about Quan or how the family had escaped Vietnam. Minh Chau was not just a prisoner of her memories, she was their victim. Now she was leaving Minh Chau to this world, but at least she would not make her feel more pain than was necessary. When she would leave this life, it would be quietly, and her friend, her dear friend Dominic Leblanc, would tell her loved ones that she, Han Thieu, had not suffered in death. Only friendship gives birth to such a beautiful lie.

The morning was grey, untypical of a Montreal spring. Han put fresh roses in a hand-painted vase that Dao had sent her from Saigon. The roses were red—like passion itself—and as soft as Dao's light brown eyes. Han kissed Voang softly on his mouth before he left for work. He was surprised by her intensity as she looked at him one last time. *Seigneur*, he loved this woman more than life itself. He stroked her cheek with the palm of his hand, kissed her forehead and walked to his car. Han watched him move gracefully. He still strutted with the youthful cadence of a young man, despite his 55 years on this earth.

Han took her coat and walked into the light drizzle. She looked up at the twisting metal balconies of the triplexes in her Outremont neighbourhood. She walked down to Saint Viateur Street, stopped at the Bagel Factory to buy poppyseed bagels and cream cheese for her husband. This was the only concession that Voang had made to Canadian cuisine. Two Hassidic Jews, who were her patients, passed her by, wishing her a nice day. She crossed Park Avenue to head back home, sneaking by a group of Haitian immigrants who were studying English at the International YMCA. This vibrant city had become hers. This country of deep snow had taken the place of her lost land across the sea. The warmness of its people had protected her family from the cutting winter cold, and she, Han Thieu, descendant of Vietnam's royal family, had come to love it and everything that it represented.

When Han reached the door of her modest Outremont home, she was exhausted and in terrible pain. But her heart was light. She put the bagels in the fridge for Voang, leaving a note for him on the kitchen table, and went to the second floor bedroom. She took out Jing Zi's green potion from the *coffret*. After years of research, she knew all its qualities—those that gave back life and those that took it away without leaving a trace. She walked softly to the bed, dialed Dominic's number and whispered to him, "You can come now." She heard him swallow, unable to say a word, but she knew that he would protect her secret. She lay on her bed, thought back to the sweetest moment of her life—the day Jing Zi gave her back her Minh Chau, and then took his medicine. A moment of convulsion changed vitality into the emptiness of the human shell.

Chapter Two
Phnom Penh, Cambodia, April 17, 1975

"They have entered the city. Our soldiers are ditching their uniforms and trying to escape," said Hue as she ran into the salon of her father's house.

"Don't worry. They won't touch the Vietnamese. They dare not," her father Van Phoc reassured his daughter. "Always tell them you are Vietnamese!" He turned to his Chinese wife Mei. "Don't go outside without me. The Khmer Rouge hate the Chinese merchants."

Mei began to cry, thinking of her parents in the eastern part of the city. What would become of them? She had urged them to leave Phnom Penh two months ago when it became evident that General Lon Nol's army did not have the resolve to defend the capital without American support.

Mei's parents had refused to leave their daughter and grand-children behind. "What would we do in Hong Kong?" asked Mei's father Hu. "We were born in this country, and even the Khmer Rouge will need merchants to import goods into Cambodia." Her father's naivety reflected his limited knowledge of the political situation.

Mei who had studied with Van in Paris had come to know the radical mix of nationalism and Maoism that permeated the Khmer Rouge ideology. Both had read the 1955 doctoral dissertation of Hou Yuon, *The Cambodian Peasants and Their Prospects for Modernization*, which advocated a need for radical economic self-sufficiency. They knew of the Khmer Rouge's fascination with the notion that Khmer peasants were the true proletariat, untainted in any way by capitalism. Even then, they still could not fathom what the next four years would bring in terms of death and destruction.

Outside in the streets, Mei could hear the cheers of the ethnic Khmers as they greeted the Communist victors. Van and Mei knew that the population was no more in favour of the Khmer Rouge than they had been of the Sihanouk regime or later General Lon Nol's government, but any end to the country's long civil war was welcomed. And were the Khmer Rouge leaders not educated men and committed nationalists? Van and Mei had come to know many of these so-called intellectuals during their studies in Paris. Each attempted to out-do the other by preaching a yet more radical version of communism, and would even criticize the growing Maoist movement in Europe as being weak-kneed. As for Vietnamese Communists, the Khmer Rouge student intellectuals had only the greatest contempt. For them, Ho Chi Minh was a Soviet puppet, unconnected to the new Asian reality.

"Mama, what is happening outside?" asked Mei's eight-year-old son Quan. Hue moved quickly to embrace her brother. "Don't worry, Quan. It is going to be all right." Mei looked furtively between her children and her husband. "Van, we must leave and leave soon," she implored. "We know these people and what they are capable of. Let's go to Saigon."

"And live under the Viet Cong? Saigon will fall any day now. We will be able to deal with the Khmer Rouge. Don't worry! They will need us to rebuild the country," Van reassured his wife.

Van's driver Samnang burst into the house. "They are here. The Khmer Rouge are here!"

Within seconds, five young men with their red *krama* scarves and green Mao uniforms, trampled into the room and seized Samnang and Van, forcing them to their knees. Shouting loudly in barely intelligible peasant accents, the Khmer Rouge soldiers struck Samnang and Van with the butts of their rifles. Quan rushed to defend his father and was grabbed by a young soldier, probably no older than fifteen, who put a knife to the boy's throat.

"Stop! We will give you money, gold, jewels. What do you want?" screamed Mei.

Suddenly, a Khmer Rouge officer stepped into the house. "Mei, Van, your money and gold are worth nothing in the new Kampuchea."

Mei looked at the face of the officer. Beneath the deep scars, the officer's dark searching eyes revealed a familiar face. Mei could not place it at first, and turned to Van, who looked up from the floor, and gasped, "Sary?"

Khieu Sary, the brother of Cambodia's leftist ideologue Khieu Sampan, turned to his soldiers. "Release the prisoners." Turning to Van, he barked, "Van, gather your family's belongings. We are evacuating the city. The Americans are going to bomb Phnom Penh."

"Thank you Sary. We will not forget this," replied Van. "Mei, Hue, Quan—bring your clothes and some food. Quickly please."

La rue principale became congested with tens of thousands of people marching before the guns of the Khmer Rouge. Slowly the capital was emptied of almost all its inhabitants—women, children, men. Four long columns stretched in all directions into the countryside. Furtive glances back toward the city revealed no signs of the dreaded American bombers. Slowly, it dawned on Van and Mei that there would be no attack on Phnom Penh, that the entire population of the city had been tricked into some menacing enterprise. Khieu Sary joined his former classmates and explained. "The new Kampuchea can never be built as long as cities hold economic clout over the countryside. We will start anew. Today is day one of year zero for our country. Money means nothing. Wealth will not separate the people. Love for the nation is the only value that we will know."

Mei looked into the eyes of the man that she had once secretly admired for his passion and youthful beauty. His face had been badly burnt, but his eyes of jade and noisette still could entrance. Sary's words shocked Mei by their irrealism. She realized that she no longer knew the man, but she needed him to survive. She turned to Van to see if he understood. Van nodded at her glance, and began to ask Sary more about the future of the new Kampuchea, as if they were still young students back in Paris.

Khieu Sary accompanied the family as far as the start of the forest. His heart had become hard from the years of fighting in the jungle, but deep inside, the humanist ideals had not died. The napalm that scarred his face had deformed his body and taken away his manhood. Still he walked proudly, but in terrible pain. Van had never liked the ideological side of Sary when they studied in Paris, but he respected his dedication to his cause and found a certain kindness in the introverted but misguided student. Sary's mother was from a rich Chinese merchant family, distantly related to Mei's family. The two families had even contemplated a match between Mei and Sary, but the revolutionary and his older brother Khieu Sampan had forgone a life of luxury to pursue their egalitarian dreams. If all the Khmer Rouge were like them, maybe their dream of a better society could be a reality.

Van could not help notice that the civility of the Khmer soldiers toward the civilians in their charge increased every time Sary looked their way. Secretly, he wished that their old classmate would stay with them to their final destination. As they parted, Van took Sary's hand in both of his and bowed his head in thanks. The revolutionary turned to Mei and her children and said, "Be true to the new Kampuchea." As he limped away, the faces of the guards who continued with the column darkened with pent-up hatred for the city-dwellers.

The jungle path was barely passable. The wet mud clung to Van's shoes and branches scratched his face without relent. The smell of fresh undergrowth was tainted by the stench of urine and feces from those who had marched before them. Thick swarms of bees tormented him as he struggled to cover his mouth to stop what little he had eaten from coming back up. As he walked on, he began to dream to the accompaniment of running water and insects chirping. For a moment, hope replaced fear.

Night began to close in on the column as it entered deeper into the jungle. Older people began to stumble. Sounds of clubbing could be heard from a distance as the Khmer guards brutally dispatched stragglers. Van and his family marched through the night. Only when the sun rose, did the guards allow the column to stop and rest. Systematically, the guards walked among the expelled population, screaming at people wearing glasses and ripping away young babies from frantic mothers. They repeated again and again their slogan "To spare you is no profit, to destroy you is no loss."

Quan looked at the helplessness of his parents. His image of a strong father and confident mother began to vanish as his parents lowered their heads every time the guards passed by. His sister Hue took him by the hand, squeezing it until he yelped in pain. Hue put her hand around her brother's mouth. "Please do not make a noise. The guards will hear you." Quan learned his first lesson about survival—silence is a defence, not a weakness.

The narrow path climbed through the dark forest. The stones blistered the feet of the ragged prisoners. The thirst in their parched throats became unbearable. The despair in their eyes deepened. Some, exhausted by the journey, began to howl in anguish until the guards took them aside and marched them into the forest. The sound of rifle butts crushing human bones imposed silence on the rest of the column.

On the fifth day, they came to a clearing with newly constructed large bamboo buildings. As they entered the farm, the peasants looked suspiciously at the newcomers, barely hiding the anger that they felt at having to share their meager food supply with the city dwellers. What good would these *New People* be for the farm? They would only be a burden. It would have been better to have killed them all in Phnom Penh. The peasants did not like the Khmer Rouge, but had long since bought into the argument that the corrupt inhabitants of Phnom Penh had invited in the American invaders and prolonged the war at the expense of the peasants.

As the column passed by the first bamboo barracks, Quan and Hue were forcibly separated from their parents, along with the rest of the children. Mei broke down in tears until a Khmer Rouge struck her in the back with his rife. She stumbled forward, but was steadied by Van, who pleaded with the guard to leave his wife be.

Inside Quan, an anger swelled as he glared at the guard. He vowed that one day, he would avenge the affront to his parents.

Chapter Three
The Fall of Saigon, April 30, 1975

The thunder of artillery increased during the early morning, awakening the Thieu household in the well-off suburb of Thao Dien. Mr. Voang Thieu shook the shoulder of his wife Han, whispering "Get up. We need to find out what is happening." Voang looked across the room at his lieutenant's uniform. He was only a dentist in the South Vietnamese Army and had not been called to duty for a week. Teeth were a low priority when the enemy was at the gates. He wondered if he would be called on to take a gun to defend the city now. He had never even fired a gun.

His wife Han looked blankly at the wall, trying desperately to fake sleep. She did not want to face what the day might bring. Could this be the end of life as they knew it? Her family was from the wealthy land-owning elite. Dentist or not, her husband was an officer in the army. For the Viet Cong, he was an enemy of the people and by extension, so was she. The family's only salvation would be that she was a highly trained physician. Even the Communists needed doctors. From the door, she heard the soft voice of her daughter An. "Minh Chau cannot sleep because of the thunder." Four-year-old An stood hand-in-hand with her two-year-old sister Minh Chau. Voang and Han looked at their children, with tears swelling in their eyes.

Voang dressed while Han took her daughters back to their room. He descended to the kitchen and turned on the transistor radio, a gift from Colonel Black, the U.S. dentist who had left Vietnam two years ago after the Geneva Accords. Black had called it a gift of peace. Now it brought news of war.

The melodious voice of Binh Nguyen, the Voice of America's announcer, came over loud and clear. "Reports from Saigon indicate that the North Vietnamese Army has breached the defences of General Nguyen van Toan. Eyewitnesses have told us that the flag of North Vietnam is now flying over the presidential palace. All American nationals are requested to proceed to designated evacuation points."

Han approached her husband quietly. "We should go to the American Embassy. Thomas Smith will help us." Her mind flashed back to a month earlier when she drank tea at the Smiths' residence with Marie-Christine Labonté, Thomas Smith's wife. Marie-Christine had been a patient of Han's for over two years. Han had delivered her second child, Andréa. It had been a difficult operation because the umbilical cord had wrapped around the baby's neck, but Han was a skilled obstetrician and had reached inside the uterus to rotate the fetus to free it from the cord. The Smiths' gratitude and the friendship with Marie-Christine flourished after that. In the lonely existence of an American diplomat's wife, Marie-Christine, a French-Canadian found solace in speaking her native language with Han whose education by French nuns in Hue had ensured her mastery of the language of Molière.

"Thomas, chéri, promise me that you will help the Thieus if things get worse here. Je t'en prie mon amour. Please promise me that," implored Marie-Christine, as Han sat quietly drinking her tea. "Of course, darling," her husband reassured her. "Dr. Thieu, you can find me at the embassy at any time. I will do everything that I can. Please come next Tuesday so that I can arrange for a visa in advance for you and your family."

Thomas Smith fulfilled his promise of a visa. Now would he be able to help the Thieus leave Vietnam? Han asked herself. America had abandoned Vietnam. Would he also abandon them?

"Let's go," said Voang. "Trang, get the car please."

Quickly the Thieu family grabbed their pre-packed suitcases and headed for their Chevrolet station wagon. The driver Trang navigated through the crowded streets of the city, skirting the abandoned army vehicles of the South Vietnamese Army. The smoke rising from the northern end of the city heralded the advancing artillery of the North Vietnamese forces. The car turned onto Thong Nhat Boulevard and stopped before a crowd of 10,000 Vietnamese pressing toward the embassy's entrance, only to be stopped by Marine guards who were only letting in a trickle as the CH-53 helicopters landed at intervals of ten minutes.

"Come out of the car now. We need to get to the entrance. Trang, come with us. Saigon has fallen to the Communists," shouted Voang.

"No, sir. I must stay. My family is here. I will be safe," answered Trang, shaking the hands of Voang, Han, An and little Minh Chau.

"May God go with you," said the devoutly Catholic Voang to his equally devout Buddhist chauffeur.

Voang pushed forward through the crowd as others cursed him. It was impossible to approach the entrance of the embassy, so Voang steered his family to the nearest section of the fence. Through the fence, the Thieu family searched for Thomas Smith. Then in a window on the second floor, they saw him. Han shouted, "Mr. Smith, Mr. Smith, we are here." Smith recognized Han and waved back. Han's heart jumped with joy. Voang embraced his wife and waved at Smith.

Thomas Smith turned quickly to the door, just as his superior Warren Simpson walked in. "Thomas, we need to go to the roof. The helicopter is waiting."

"Hold on. Dr. Thieu's family is outside. We have to evacuate them. I promised Marie-Christine," replied Smith.

Simpson grabbed his arm. "No, our orders are clear. No more Vietnamese are to be evacuated."

"But she was your wife's doctor as too!" protested Smith.

"Sergeant, take Mr. Smith to the roof."

Two burly marines took Smith by the arms and frog-marched him up the stairs to waiting helicopters.

At the fence, the Thieus waited patiently for Smith to rescue them. An hour passed. The last of the marines vanished from the embassy's perimeter. Within fifteen minutes, the South Vietnamese Army guards had ditched their uniforms and disappeared into the crowd. From a side street, a tank with a large photo of Ho Chi Minh turned onto Thong Nhat Boulevard and then crashed through the embassy's gate. The crowd scattered in all directions, trampling in the chaos anyone who stumbled, but up every side street marched scores of North Vietnamese soldiers and Viet Cong fighters, blocking the crowd's escape. Those who resisted the soldiers were savagely beaten. Voang held his wife and children close and stood by the fence until the soldiers came and marched them off to the trucks pouring into the boulevard.

As the convoy drove through the centre of the city, Han Thieu watched the crowds cheer the North Vietnamese soldiers. Young children held pictures of Ho Chi Minh, chanting "Down with America." How quickly people change allegiances to the victorious side.

Chapter Four
The Farm

The soil was hard and stoney and the shovels were crudely carved from teakwood. When you broke a shovel, you were punished for two days without food. Quan grew strong as he worked ten-hour days in the steaming heat to clear the jungle of foliage. Hue was put to work in the vegetable garden, allowing her to steal discarded beet leaves for her parents. Their father Van toiled in another part of the camp, breaking large stones with a sledge hammer. Their mother Mei carried water from the stream to irrigate the fields. While Quan and Hue were each given a bowl of rice and a soup of *luffa* once a day, his father and mother were fed only half a bowl of rancid rice. Without the vegetable leaves that Hue smuggled to them every night, they would have died in their first few days on the farm.

"Quan, we have to find an escape for mother and father. I am to be transferred to plant the new rice paddies. I won't be able to bring them any more food," cried Hue.

"Don't worry, Hue! We will find a way," said eight-year-old Quan. But he had no plan, and the days passed quickly. Hue's work detail was moved to the paddies, and from the distance, Quan and Hue helplessly watched their parents grow thinner and weaker every day.

Van died first, collapsing from exhaustion. The peasants wandered over to investigate the newcomer's body. One took his hat. Another his sandals. They would have stripped him completely naked, had not the guards arrived, pushing them aside. They turned Van over and kicked him hard to see if he was really dead.

When Mei returned from the stream, weighed down by buckets of water, she saw Van's lifeless form bunched over the broken stones, amid sneering Khmer Rouge guards. She pushed past them and threw herself on her husband's body. Her tears streamed down, moistening Van's face as she held him gently in her arms. "My husband, my beloved husband, don't leave me please, please!"

"Woman, you have no man now. Come!" bellowed an older guard, who reached for her arm. Mei struck at the man, bowling him over with the force of her anger. Stunned, the guard ordered his companions to seize Mei and take her to the guard hut. They dragged her, cursing, "Chinese whore, we will teach you a lesson!" For three hours, each guard took his turn raping Mei. Whether the violations of her delicate, beautiful body or her grief over Van's death brought about her demise will never be known. They tossed her lifeless body into the field, like night water from their buckets.

An old, kind Cambodian woman came to Hue in the rice paddy. She whispered something to one of the guards, who was known for his fair treatment, then she took Hue by the arm and led her back to the barracks. As they approached the door, she spoke to Hue softly. Hue collapsed immediately and the frail woman lifted the child in her arms and brought her inside the shelter.

Quan did not learn of his parents' death for three days. He had been taken on a work detail into the jungle to cut eucalyptus trees for the construction of new storage buildings. When he returned, he found that Hue was running a very high fever. The peasants were told by the guards to leave her be, but the old Cambodian woman, who had once been a nurse in Phnom Penh, tended to Hue. From a secret cache, the old woman brought out medicine that broke the fever.

When the guards saw Hue return to her work in the rice paddies fully recovered only two days later, they became suspicious and beat her until she told them that she had been treated by the old woman. They dragged the old woman into the centre of the farm and assembled the entire farm population around her. There they decried the use of western medicine and called the woman a traitor to the people. They then took her entire cache of pills and shoved them down her throat. She squirmed in pain as the lethal cocktail of morphine and sedatives rocked her body before it fell quietly to the rocky soil.

Hue ran to the dead woman and wept over her. The guards struck Hue with their rifle butts. Quan rushed them from behind, shoving one forward onto the ground. The other guards grabbed Quan and Hue, forced them to kneel, and ordered two terrified peasants to strike the children with their hoes.

At that moment, a convoy pulled into the farm. A high ranking official with a deeply scarred face stood in the lead jeep and demanded what was happening. The guards replied, "We are going to execute these Vietnamese dogs."

Quan screamed, "We are Chinese."

The official demanded in the Hokkienese Chinese dialect, "Then tell me where you are from?"

Quan replied in Cantonese, "We are from Phnom Penh. Our mother was Mei Lee, from the Chung Lee family."

Khieu Sary, hearing the name of his distant relative, demanded, "Where are your mother and father?"

"They died last week," answered Quan.

"Release these children," ordered Khieu Sary. "No Chinese on this farm are to be harmed."

He then ordered the farm's political committee to convene a meeting, and left the two children to mourn the loss of the courageous Cambodian nurse. As Khieu Sary limped to the meeting, in which he would once again lecture on the beauty of the new society, he wept inside for Mei, whom he had once secretly loved in Paris and for Van, whose intellect he had long admired. For the first time, cynicism took root in the scarred revolutionary. Was this the society that he had given everything for? One where children were executed by farm implements. Where intellectuals were starved to death and raped. And once-prosperous farms collapsed from the mismanagement of incompetent party officials.

Chapter Five
Cousin Dao

The two-year-old Minh Chau ruled the prison. Her bright smile enchanted inmates and guards alike, but life was not so easy for her mother Han and sister An. Han was still a beautiful woman, and did not escape the notice of the guards, but she had also collaborated with the American occupiers and corrupt South Vietnamese regime. Her Catholic upbringing in a well-known land-owning family descended from the last Vietnamese dynasty made her an enemy of the people. An, who had neither her sister's vitality or natural beauty, was shunned by the other children, whose parents warned them against associating with the Thieu family. Everyone was seeking salvation by avoiding *guilt by association.*

One guard, Huynh, was particularly fond of the toddler. He would smuggle into the prison a few hard candies that Minh Chau would share with her sister and other children, gradually winning them over despite their parents' objections. Huynh was harsh on Han. He could forgive her children, but she had collaborated! Huynh came from a peasant family near Danang. One day, the American forces had entered his village, shooting every man that they saw. Huynh, who was only ten, and his brother Hao, who was fourteen, were initially spared by the Americans, but when South Vietnamese troops joined their American allies, one Vietnamese officer shouted "No good! This boy too old. He will join the Viet Cong and kill us." The American officer turned his back and walked away with his men while the Vietnamese officer took out his pistol and shot Hao in the back of the head. Huynh spent the next ten years fighting with the Viet Cong in the jungle. He knew that Han's husband had served in the South Vietnamese forces, and he had no use for traitors. Still, children were different, and he grew to love his adopted little sister, Minh Chau.

One day, as Huynh walked along Chi Bao street to the prison, a beautiful girl of sixteen in a white *ao dai* approached him. "Comrade brother, you work in the prison, don't you? I am looking for my aunt and cousins." Huynh looked at the girl, whose beauty reminded him of the mother he had lost in an American napalm bombing.

"What are their names, comrade sister?"

"Dr. Han Thieu is my aunt. My cousins are called An and Minh Chau."

"Minh Chau is your cousin?" queried the surprised Huynh.

"Yes, do you know them?"

"Of course, but what do you want of me?"

"I want to take them out of the prison."

"That is impossible for Han Thieu. She betrayed us for the Americans, but the children, perhaps I can help."

"Please anything, comrade brother. Anything you can do, please."

"Meet me here tomorrow then. What is your name, comrade sister?

"Dao. And yours?"

"Huynh," replied the shy guard.

As Dao left, Huynh followed her closely with his eyes. Somehow, he knew that Minh Chau and An would be safer with Dao than in the prison. He could not explain his feelings, but just as Minh Chau had brought lightness to his heart, this girl Dao had in their brief encounter calmed the storm raging so long inside him.

Huynh continued to the prison. After his shift, he went to see Commandant Nguyen, who had fought with Huynh and protected him for ten years in the jungle and was the closest thing to a father that Huynh had known since the death of his own.

"Respected Comrade Nguyen, I need your guidance and advice."

"Huynh, my son, what is it?"

"Would it be possible for the children Minh Chau and An to be released?"

"But to whom? Their father is in a re-education camp near Danang, and the mother must pay for her crimes here."

"They have a cousin, Dao. She is ready to take care of them."

"The children can only leave with the consent of their mother. I will ask her."

Dr. Han Thieu listened in horror as the commandant proposed the separation from her children. She felt that she barely knew her niece Dao, who had been raised by her father in Hue province after Han's sister Hien, Dao's mother, had died in childbirth. Yes, Dao had visited them two summers ago and had taken care of Minh Chau and An during her stay, but Dao was still a child. How old was she fifteen or sixteen? Politely, she refused the offer from the commandant.

Huynh met with Dao the next day and took her to a local *Pho* shop where as they ate the rich noodle soup, he explained that Han Thieu had refused to part with her children. Dao pleaded with Huynh to let her see her aunt. He agreed to raise this with the commandant. Dao took Huynh's hand in both of hers, bowed her head, and said in a subdued voice, "Thank you, honourable comrade. My parents are now both dead. I have no one but my cousins. I do not want to be alone. Please help me convince my aunt to let me take them away from the prison." Huynh's heart beat fast, as he looked upon the beautiful form in front of him. He was now twenty, and had never known a woman's touch since the death of his mother. He saw in Dao the gentle radiance that he had discovered in the child Minh Chau, and felt bound to both of them.

"Come tomorrow early to the prison gate, I will try to convince Comrade Nguyen to see you."

"Thank you, brother comrade. I will not forget this kindness."

Dao then turned to walk to her work as a laundry worker in the central hospital. Huynh could not take his eyes off her. Gradually, the crowded street swallowed her up, and Huynh returned to the prison.

As agreed, Dao was at the prison as dawn broke. She was alone. The relatives of detainees had long since learned the dangers of constantly visiting prisoners. The security forces composed of committed Communists from the North knew well enough that their presence in Saigon was unwelcome, and had decided to strike hard at any nascent dissent. Within their first month in power, they had cowed the population. Raids in the middle of the night were particularly frequent in the better-off parts of the city, inhabited by former officials of the South Vietnamese regime.

Dao was oblivious to this danger. She waited in hope. As Huynh walked out of the main gate of the prison after finishing his night shift, Dao's heart skipped a beat. She had never supported the Communists, but this young man had treated her with kindness and respect. At sixteen, she had never known a man outside of her family. She had gone from childhood to womanhood at an accelerated pace when her father died from cancer the year before. She had never known her mother, who had died giving her birth. Living in the old royal city of Hue, she had only infrequently visited her aunts and cousins in Saigon. The fondest memories of these rare visits were those at the house of Aunt Han. She had played every day of her school vacation with young cousin An and had cradled the baby Minh Chau in her arms for hours.

As they approached the commandant's spartan office, Dao quivered in anticipation. She entered the room with her head bowed in respect. Suddenly, a hand reached out from her left and touched her arm. She turned. It was Aunt Han. She looked older and emaciated, but still had the beautiful face that Dao remembered.

"Dao, my child. Is it really you?" asked Han.

"Yes, Aunt Han."

"Is it true that you are here to take An and Minh Chau?"

"Only if you want me to."

Han fell silent as she pondered the situation. An and Minh Chau had been treated well by the prison guards. Huynh made sure of that. But there was no end in sight for her imprisonment. Could she continue to keep her children in this prison, out of her own selfishness?

"Where will you take them?" asked Han.

"I have a small room in Le Thanh Ton Street. I share it with a widow."

"No, that is a street of prostitutes! And how will you feed them?"

"I work in the laundry of the Central Hospital and in the Thuynh vegetable market. The hospital pays me a little money and the farmers allow me to take home unsold vegetables"

"Dao, if you take An and Minh Chau, you must take them to my husband's sisters – Cam and Ly. They live in Thao Dien. Here are their addresses. If you don't find them, then look for my sister Lan. I don't know where she is now, but I know that she fled Hue for Saigon two weeks ago."

"Aunt Han, I will do as you ask. Will you let An and Minh Chau come with me now?"

"Yes."

Han cried inside at what she had agreed to, but the gentle face of Dao gave her hope. Her niece was only sixteen, but she had come to save her children from prison. Her love for Dao suddenly became as great as her love for her own children. Dao would do the right thing. She then noticed Huynh admiring Dao. She hated Huynh for his disrespect toward her, for the daily cursing that he had subjected her to, but she recognized the kindness that he had shown Minh Chau. And now the hardened Viet Cong fighter had that same kindness in his eyes when he looked at Dao, and she smiled back at him. Vietnam, her country, had been savaged by fifteen years of barbaric war. Now the healing had begun. Could love between Huynh and Dao be also possible? She felt reassured that Huynh's protective hand toward Minh Chau in the prison might now extend to Dao and her children outside.

Huynh brought Minh Chau and An candy and then led them to their mother in the commandant's office. Minh Chau was too young to recognize her cousin, but An ran immediately to Dao and embraced her. Quietly, Han told her children what had been agreed to. Minh Chau looked confused while An cried at the imminent separation from her mother. Han told them to be strong, that Dao would take good care of them, that they would all be soon reunited with their father. They just had to wait a little. Minh Chau then danced with joy, shouting "Papa, Papa!" as she followed Dao outside the prison. An looked back at her mother, standing motionlessly at the prison gate. Tears streaked her cheeks as she continued on, walking hand-in-hand with her cousin and sister. The fear of never seeing her mother again surged within her, but she was the older sister and her duty was to obey her mother and look after Minh Chau.

Huynh accompanied Dao, Minh Chau and An down Chi Boa Street to the nearest bus station. Huynh dug into his pockets to find enough *dong* to pay for their tickets. Before boarding the bus, Minh Chau came up to Huynh and took his hand and said, "Huynh, please come to see me soon." Dao softy smiled in agreement, and said to Huynh's delight. "Brother comrade, you would be our honoured guest." An, in turn, approached the guard, who had been so relentless in criticizing her mother, and pleaded, "Brother comrade please look out for my mother. She is a good person." For the first time, since Commandant Nguyen had found him huddled over the dead body of his brother Hoa amid the ashes of his village, Huynh wept. It was just a small tear, imperceptible to passers-by, but Minh Chau saw it, and squeezed Huynh's hand. "Be happy. Don't cry, Huynh. We will see you again."

Boarding the bus, Minh Chau danced to the back window, rubbed clean the dirty glass and waved to her protector who watched the bus pull away and disappear into the crowded streets of Pham Ngu Lao and rumble on towards Dao's humble lodgings in Phuoc Binh.

When the three disembarked from the bus, Minh Chau's face lit up. Prison had been grey—her parents' house had been painted in subtle shades of blue and mauve, but Le Thanh Ton Street was alive in every colour imaginable. Its sidewalks were crowded with young soldiers and party cadres, mostly from the North. The girls, all southerners, in red *ao dais*, leaned against the doorways, flirting with their potential clients. The new Vietnam, whose prisons were packed with former government officials and officers, had yet to crack down on the traditional vices. The city's new Communist rulers were reluctant to deprive their foot soldiers, who had defeated the almighty United States of America, of the carnal pleasures of victory.

Dao led the children through a narrow alley, filled with the smell of cooking oil and the stench of sweat and urine, and then up a rickety staircase to a row of small red doors, the last of which opened to Dao's room. Madame Bao was waiting for them on the porch. She was a woman in her sixties, but her exquisitely carved cheekbones evoked images of past beauty. Madame Bao smiled at the children. "My, my, what precious pearls, you have brought me, Dao! What are their names." Minh Chau strutted forward, put her hands on her tiny hips, and laughed, "Hee, hee, *precious pearls* is my name – Minh Chau." Madame Bao scooped up the small girl in her arms, hugged her and exclaimed, "Yes, you will be my precious pearls." Dao and An laughed, as Minh Chau raised her fingers in a victory salute.

Life with Madame Bao was good, but Dao remembered her promise to Han. She would look for the children's aunts, but not right now. She had just found her cousins and she was overwhelmed by her need to be with them. Besides, this is where Huynh would find them. She looked wistfully out the tiny front window, and her heart beat heavily as she thought about Huynh.

Chapter Six
Conforming

The Khmer Rouge guards remained obedient to Khieu Sary's wishes even after he left. Order returned to the farm. The deliberate starvation of the older people stopped, and as the new crops came in, everyone had more than enough to eat. Rumours circulated through the camp about how the new society was being organized. There was no formal government, but all were required to pledge loyalty to the Angkar, the organization. No one knew who made up the Angkar, but all feared it.

Quan grew strong with the additional rations and the hard work in the fields. Hue grew more beautiful every day, like the *lily flower,* she was named after, and although she was only thirteen, many young men began to court her. She would have none of them, and tended to the rocks marking the graves of her parents and the kind Cambodian nurse. Her heart was heavy with the guilt that she had betrayed the nurse and failed to save her parents. The Khmer Rouge guards, who had come to respect Quan for his courage and feared his connection to the powerful Khieu Sary, taught the young boy how to wrestle and kick-box. The strength that Quan possessed for his young age impressed them, and they began to speak of enrolling him in their ranks. "You will be a *soldier*, Quan. You can fight with us, the Khmer Rouge. We will defeat all the enemies of the people." Quan look at his would-be mentors, thinking of the insanity of their remarks, but mindful of the need for them to continue to ensure the safety of his sister. As long as he was their protégé, the guards would not touch her. He had learned another lesson of human nature – every face has two sides.

Quan quickly learned to meld into the new social order. He memorized the slogans and began to repeat them at the weekly political education sessions for all the farm inhabitants. He mastered the rough peasant dialect of Cambodian used by the uneducated Khmer Rouge foot soldiers and refused to speak Vietnamese or Chinese to his sister, except for when no one else could hear them. One day, he asked one of the guards who was teaching him kick-boxing for a red *krama* scarf, the symbol of the Khmer Rouge.

The young boy was soon taken off farming duties and assigned to bringing messages between Comrade Ieng, the leader of the political committee, and the Khmer Rouge guards. Quan had been good at school, and he soon was entrusted in reading aloud the messages for the illiterate guards. His penmanship was superb and much admired by Comrade Ieng, who had learned from Khieu Sary the story of his parents.

Ieng, like Khieu Sary, Pol Pot and much of the Khmer Rouge leadership, was a Khmer-Chen, a person of mixed Chinese and Cambodian ancestry. Although he despised the Chinese money lenders who had reduced many of the Cambodian peasants to the status of indentured farmers, he still saw in China a proud cultural and political model for the region. Occasionally, he would speak to Quan in Chinese about his own past as a teacher in Phnom Penh. Ieng was supposed to be sent to France for further studies, but when it became known that his mother had been forced to work as a prostitute in a provincial city before marrying his father, one of her clients, his scholarship was cancelled. The hypocrisy of the ruling class drove him into the arms of the Khmer Rouge.

Quan soon learned all the tenets of the Khmer Rouge philosophy. Although only eleven, he already recognized the insanity of it all. He knew enough of commerce to realize that an egalitarian society based only on agricultural production was a pipe-dream. However, he recognized that Ieng truly believed in this model and was committed to trying to make it work. Ieng had come to the farm with Khieu Sary, who had left him in charge of reorganizing it. Ieng was still authoritarian enough to order summary executions for theft or political dissent, but under him the policy of starving the older *New People* was stopped. Punishment of sexual crimes was finally enforced, and Quan was grateful for this, as the beauty of his sister Hue was stirring the desires of many of the men on the farm.

Quan's military training intensified. Although still too young to be a soldier, it was clear to everyone that this was to be his role. Quan led a double life. He had become his sister's protector in many ways. Through her, he still found ways of showing kindness to the *New People*, especially the Vietnamese, toward whom considerable hostility grew as tensions between the rival Communist regimes in Vietnam and Kampuchea increased. When a Vietnamese was to be punished for some misdemeanour, Quan would often step in before the other guards could, and beat, curse loudly in Cambodian and kick-box the accused, while whispering to him at the same time in Vietnamese to lie down and fake screaming in pain. The other guards would move on, leaving Quan to administer discipline.

Word spread among the Vietnamese of Quan's role-playing and each knew what to do to make Quan look credible in the eyes of the guards. But when there were sexual crimes to be punished, Quan did not hold back his punches. Strong for his age, he plummeted the accused into a bloody heap until the other guards pulled him away. Vietnamese, Chinese or Cambodian did not matter to Quan in these circumstances – the images of his mother's death always played in his mind as his kicks became stronger and more deadly.

Quan's association with the guards separated him from the other children in the farm. At eleven, he had already lost his childhood. Only Hue kept him in touch with his gentler side. His sister became his mother. Although the loss of their parents made it difficult for Hue to smile again, her gentle caresses of Quan's head when he could not sleep at night brought them both solace.

Chapter Seven
Freedom through Work

In Chi Bao prison, life improved for Dr. Han Thieu. Huynh silenced the other guards when they began to curse her for having collaborated with the Americans. One day, Commandant Nguyen came to her and asked her to treat a guard who had been bitten by a snake. The guard quickly recovered and in gratitude, Commandant Nguyen allowed Han Thieu to set up a small clinic, stocked with medicine brought in from a local hospital. Slowly, Han's patients' list grew to include the wives and children of the guards. The detainees and guards began to praise their doctor's skills, and provided her with small payments that she would send to Dao for Minh Chau and An.

Dao brought Minh Chau and An to see their mother every Sunday. Huynh always worked Sundays, and Dao would bring him soup and spring rolls for lunch. Tuesdays were Huynh's day-off. He would visit Dao and the children at Madame Bao's. He would bring hard candy and messages from Han Thieu. Minh Chau and An, who had learned to sing from Madame Bao, put auditions on for their favorite comrade brother. Madame Bao would make ginseng tea for everyone. When they had finished the candies, singing and tea, Dao would walk Huynh back to the bus station. One day, a drunken northern soldier made a lewd remark about Dao. Huynh bashed the northerner's head against the side of the bus. When the soldier's two companions came to his rescue, little Dao pulled a knife out and stood defiantly beside Huynh. The soldiers picked up their companion and backed away from the formidable couple. After that, the bond between Dao and Huynh grew stronger.

Dao, as she had promised, began to search for the children's aunts. All had been dispossessed of their main residences and forced by the new government to move into smaller houses. Dao first located Cam, Voang Thieu's older sister. Cam had been married to a cabinet minister in President Ngo Dinh Diem's government. Her husband had died before the Communists had taken Saigon. Cam had strenuously avoided all contact with the families of former South Vietnamese government officials. When Dao and the children turned up at her doorstep, it took her only a minute to decide to turn them away.

Dao then located Ly, Voang's younger sister. Her husband was a Chinese merchant who had fled to Hong Kong, but was cooperating with the new regime by re-exporting to Vietnam American car parts to keep Saigon's taxi fleet afloat. Ly was in discussion with high-level officials in the Ministry of Trade about the possibility of allowing her son, Chinh, join his father abroad. Chinh was about to turn eighteen, and was facing compulsory military service. Ly was torn when the children turned up. She invited them in, fed them and allowed them to sleep the night. In the morning, a senior security official dropped by. Over a cup of tea, he asked Ly about the children, and then asked Ly about Chinh's birthday. Ly understood. She took out a jade bracelet and offered it to the official for his wife. He nodded, but then warned Ly that associating with enemies of the state was a dangerous thing.

Ly sold some of her jewelry, put the money in a thick envelope and called in Dao. She asked her to take the money and the children and leave. Dao finally found a welcome for Minh Chau and An at Aunt Lan's house. Lan had a modest house in the outskirts of Saigon where she grew garden vegetables. Lan had been educated in French and had taught five years at the French lycée in Saigon. Her garden barely provided her enough to eat. She was unmarried and would be unlikely to attract a fiancé while sheltering the children of collaborators, but she welcomed Minh Chau, An and Dao into her modest home and refused to let them leave. Dao gave Lan the thick envelope from Ly and asked permission from Lan to leave in order to return to work.

Life with Aunt Lan was not as nice as with Dao. Lan refused to take the children to the prison to see their mother, but she did let them write letters to Han. She welcomed the visits from Dao, who continued to bring letters from Han, but Lan refused to allow Huynh to enter her house. She implored Dao to explain to Huynh that the presence of a soldier in the house of an unmarried woman would raise the suspicions of her neighbours. She schooled the girls in French and arranged for them to visit the children of all her neighbours. Minh Chau and An became very popular with the working class neighbours, by rendering auditions of the beautiful classic Vietnamese songs that Madame Bao had taught them.

One day, Dao brought the news that Han was to be released on the condition that she set up a small clinic in the Thieu family's second house in a modest neighbourhood of the city. A week later, Han turned up herself at Lan's door. The sisters embraced and wept together. After Lan brought the children out, she went back to her bedroom and returned with the envelope of money from Ly. She insisted that Han take it. Not a single *dong* had been spent. Han thanked her sister and then left with her children who smiled and danced while practicing on their mother the French that they had learned from Aunt Lan.

At first, only indigent widows and young soldiers with venereal diseases came to Dr. Han Thieu's clinic. The first could not pay. The second refused to. Han treated all, payment or not. With Ly's money, she was able to get by. Her old patients, from Saigon's elite, had either escaped the country or avoided her as they ingratiated themselves with Saigon's new rulers. This was fine with Han. She had little appetite for hypocrites. Gradually, paying patients began to come to her clinic, as her patients from the prison clinic told their relatives of her good and kind treatment. Life began to return to a sense of normality as young women started families and sought Dr. Han Thieu's excellent services.

Two years passed, and Han was now able to afford private tutors for her children. An grew studious. Minh Chau continued to blossom bringing joy to all around her. The children rejoiced whenever Huynh and Dao visited them. Huynh had grown fond and protective of Han in prison after the children had left. She had taught him several simple diagnoses and the use of antibiotics for the treatment of common infections. She too had come to like the young man, especially when he one day told her of the death of his brother. After her release from prison, she invited Huynh and Dao to tea at her modest house. When her niece asked her opinion of Huynh as a potential husband, Han did not hesitate to give her blessing.

Commandant Nguyen had encouraged Huynh to pursue his interest in medicine. One day, Commandant Nguyen appeared at the clinic with an old classmate of Han's, Comrade Doctor Tran Phuong, the new dean of the faculty of medicine at the re-opened university in Saigon. For years, Tran had worked for the Americans, but when his parents were burnt to death in an indiscriminate napalm attack on his home village in 1966, Tran became a convinced Communist. For the subsequent two years, he secretly provided the Viet Cong with information on the military base where he worked. During the Tet offensive in 1968, he helped Viet Cong sappers enter the military base. When the offensive failed to drive out the Americans, Tran fled to the north.

"How are you, Han?" asked Tran.

"Fine, Comrade doctor." answered Han respectfully.

"Please just call me Tran like in the past."

"All right. Why are you here?"

"Comrade Nguyen has recommended a young man for training as a doctor. He told me that he had worked with you at the Chi Boa Prison's clinic. His name is Huynh. I would like your opinion of his abilities."

"Huynh is a very good student. He could be a good doctor."

"Thank you, Han. How is Voang?"

"He is now in a re-education camp near Danang."

Commandant Nguyen injected, "Dr. Thieu, if I could do something to help your husband, I would, but I have no influence outside of Saigon."

"I would also help if I could," said Tran. "Be patient."

"Thank you."

With Han's recommendation, Huynh was accepted into the medical school. He then came often to the clinic to seek Han's advice on different treatments. Dao was also accepted into the nursing school, and Han, who was now making good money, sent her enough money to rent a room in a respectable part of the city. However, Dao refused to leave Madame Bao, who was slowly going blind, and returned every *dong* that Han sent her. Her niece explained respectfully that one day, Uncle Voang would return home, and her aunt would need all her money then.

Lan visited her sister often. Through the assistance of Huynh, Lan was able to secure a new job as a French-Vietnamese interpreter for visiting delegations from European Communist and socialist parties.

While on the surface, there appeared to be improvements, Han knew that there would be no future for her husband in the new Vietnam. No officers had been released from re-education camps. Those government officials who were released were banned from seeking employment in the government. Most sat around idle as their wives and children found work to support them. They had become broken men.

When Han began to despair of ever seeing her husband again, fortune smiled on the Thieu family. Before dawn one day, Han was awakened by the pounding on the front door of her clinic. She hurried down to open it to three young soldiers who carried in the blood-drenched body of a senior officer.

"There has been an accident. General Dang is injured. You are a doctor. You must help him!" barked a young lieutenant.

"Of course, of course," answered Han.

The general reached out to grab Han's arm. "I do not want to die. Save me and I will give you what you want!" gasped Dang.

"Comrade general, I am a physician. It is my duty. I will do my best. Please do not move," answered Han.

A sleepy Minh Chau wandered in. "Mama, mama, what is happening? Are we going back to prison?"

"An, take your sister to your bedroom now!"

"Yes, mama. Come, Minh Chau. Stop crying. Mama is taking care of things."

Chapter Eight

Danang Re-education

Voang watched the field rat gnaw at the bamboo wall as he lay in his cot. In prison, Voang's cellmates would have trapped and eaten the rat, their hunger was so great. In the re-education camp, the inmates were now receiving regular rations. Voang had spent one year in prison in Saigon before being transferred to the small re-education camp outside of Danang. Initially, the North Vietnamese jailers had refused to believe that he had only been a dentist in the South Vietnamese Army. When he first tried to explain this, he was beaten savagely, stripped of his clothes and put in a bamboo cage in the prison yard. In interrogating other South Vietnamese officers, his jailers learned the veracity of Voang's story. Although they did not see him as any less a collaborator, they accepted that he did not have blood on his hands.

Voang had tried to convince the camp's authorities to let him provide dental care for the other inmates. They refused. He, like the rest, was there to be re-educated. They had all committed crimes against the people so let their teeth rot out. One day when Voang persisted in his demand before Colonel Phuc Hoang, the camp commandant, a young sentry, who had lost all his teeth from malnutrition while fighting for the Viet Cong in the jungle, grabbed Voang's hand and brought down with full force the butt of his rifle on it. The bones crackled under the weight of the blow. "You will never fix teeth now," sneered the sentry.

The commandant ordered the sentry to be taken to the stockade and punished for ten days. The camp had no doctor, but a medic tried to heal Voang's hand. He regained movement in only two fingers. After that, the apologetic commandant took pity on the dentist soldier, who had been his enemy for so many long years. Colonel Phuc was an educated man and had suffered the loss of his own family during the war. He had been sent to China for military training when the Americans escalated the bombing of Haiphong, where his young wife and three-year-old son lived. For weeks, he worried as news of the daily bombing reached him in Beijing. He sent letters to plead with his wife to leave the port city, but she refused because of her ailing parents who lived there. Arrangements were made for their son Cheng to be sent to Phuc's wife's home town, a small provincial city near the border with China. On August 11, 1966, just as his wife and in-laws were sending off the boy with an older cousin to live with his aunt, American planes carpet-bombed the rail station in Haiphong. No one survived.

Colonel Phuc began to seek out Voang's company to speak of the past. He wanted to come to grips with his own grief and understand that of others. He could no longer stand to see the world painted in black and white, as the party had instructed him to. He asked Voang how he could have worked for a regime that allowed his countrymen to be brutally bombed by the Americans. For the first time in his life, Voang felt a sense of shame. The two men learned of each other's passion for Da' Ngu'a, a Vietnamese variant of Parcheesi. As they played the game, Voang explained why he had decided to enlist in the South Vietnamese Army. Voang had been born in Hanoi, and had fled from the north with his family after Ho Chi Minh defeated the French and took power. His parents were French educated and had worked in the colonial government. His mother was, like Phuc's wife, from the large and wealthy Chinese minority which lived in the main cities of the north. The family had to leave everything behind.

After his father started a small wholesale clothing business in Saigon, the family fortunes improved, but too late for sending Voang to an elite preparatory school. He studied hard on his own and managed to get admitted to medical school. There he met his wife Han, a brilliant medical student. Han came from a very wealthy family, related to the last Vietnamese imperial family in the old capital of Hue. She was a beauty beyond belief and had many suitors, but it was Voang's debonair, confident manner that won her over. When his father died, and the family business faltered, Voang faced an uphill battle in trying to study medicine while keeping the business going. Eventually, he failed in both. It was at that time that the Americans decided to sponsor a dental school to train South Vietnamese officers in this profession. With a failed business and on the verge of flunking out of medical school, Voang jumped at the opportunity to earn a stable income and learn a profession, which, while not as prestigious as medicine, at least gave him a certain standing in Vietnamese society, hopefully enough to allow him to marry Han. After Voang and Han graduated as dentist and physician, they married despite the strong objections of her parents who saw Voang as beneath the family's status.

Colonel Phuc began to see in his Parcheesi partner his alter ego. His family too had contemplated fleeing the north after the Communist defeat of the French. His father had been a lawyer with many wealthy colonial clients. With the change of regime, knowledge of the old colonial laws and of international commercial law had no value in North Vietnam. Phuc's mother was a fifth generation Chinese-Vietnamese who admired the revolution that Ho Chi Minh and Mao Tse-Tung were bringing to Asia. She begged Phuc's father to stay in Haiphong. Eventually, his father found an administrative position in customs at the port, but he refused to join the party despite his wife's entreaties to do so.

The ideological rift in the family strained the marriage. Phuc's mother began to attend party meetings in nearby Hanoi, and there she fell in love with a young Communist cadre, an ethnic Chinese like her. She abandoned her husband to the daily drudgery of a low-level functionary, and took her five-year-old son with her. In his stepfather's house, Phuc mastered Mandarin and learned the theories of Marx and Lenin, those same theories that he later would teach in the re-education camp. When the Cold War escalated in the early sixties, Phuc was sponsored by his stepfather to join the party's youth wing, and then went to the officers' academy. He married a distant cousin who bore him a beautiful son. It was his fluency in Mandarin and impeccable party credentials that earned him a place at the advanced military college in Beijing, where he would later learn of the death of his loved ones during the Haiphong raid.

"Do you miss your family, Voang?" asked Phuc, catching his Da' Ngu'a opponent off guard.

"Of course, Comrade Colonel."

"I received a letter from an old acquaintance, Commandant Nguyen. He tells me that your wife has been completely rehabilitated and is now serving the people as a doctor in Ho Chi Minh City. Did you know that?"

Voang could barely hold back his tears at the news. "No, I thought that she was still in prison. I have had no news of her for three years."

"She was released almost two years ago from Chi Boa Prison where Nguyen is the warden. Apparently, she also worked as a doctor in the

Soldier, Lily, Peace and Pearls   *39*

prison."

"Respected Comrade Colonel, does the letter mention my children?" asked Voang in anxious anticipation.

"Minh Chau and An? Yes, it says that they are both fine and growing up fast."

Voang looked at Phuc in amazement at hearing so much news at once.

"Voang, I have more news for you. Nguyen was asked to track you down by a senior official. I have been authorized to release you if you will sign a confession for the crime of collaborating with the Americans. Will you do that?"

Voang was a proud man, but it did not take him more than a second to make up his mind. If this is what it took to reunite him with Han and his daughters, he would sign whatever was put in front of him.

Phuc took out the paper, put it before Voang and handed him a pen. After Voang signed, Phuc took Voang's hand in both of his, and said, "It does not matter what this document says. It is only ink on paper. I have come to know you to be a good man. I hope that we can meet again under different circumstances."

"Yes, we will, because our Da' Ngu'a games are not finished. And I will beat you next time!" joked a completely transformed Voang.

"Yes, perhaps you will." Phuc then turned to the door. "Comrade Huynh, you may come in." Then turning back to Voang, he said, "This young man will take you back to Ho Chi Minh City. You will be glad to hear that he knows your family well and has just married your niece Dao."

As Voang marched to collect his belongings from the bamboo barracks, he could not believe how fast his luck had changed. He had expected to remain in prison for years. And now, he was returning to Saigon with a new member of his extended family.

It began to rain outside, the soft rain of Danang that for two years had sung on the roof of his cell the notes of hopeful yearning. The same rain would now cleanse his soul as he re-united with his loved ones.

On the long bus ride from Danang to Saigon, Huynh told Voang of the many changes that the country had undergone in the last three years. There had been political reconciliation, but the economy was faltering. Many people wanted to leave. Tensions with China were rising and there was talk in party circles of allowing members of the Chinese merchant class to leave the country, as a gesture of goodwill toward the Chinese government and to avoid the possibility of a fifth column, should the two countries slide into war. The restrictions on ethnic Vietnamese leaving the country were, however, as strict as ever.

Voang asked Huynh how he had met Dao and the Thieu family. He was touched by the warm story of evolution from warder to protector. When Huynh begged his forgiveness for the early harsh treatment that he had meted out as a guard to Han, Voang was taken aback. Here before him was a hardened Viet Cong fighter, who would now become a doctor thanks to the recommendation of his wife Han.

Here was a man who had married his niece Dao. For a short few seconds, he thought if all of the new Vietnam was like Huynh and Dao, why should he and Han seek to leave. Then, just as the bus pulled into a rural town, soldiers entered it. Seeing a Vietnamese woman with a dark-skinned child of An's age, the soldiers approached and ripped the child away from her. "Collaborator whore," they shouted, "we will teach you to sleep with the enemy." They dragged the woman from the bus, and in front of her Afro-Vietnamese daughter and all the passengers, they stripped her naked and shaved her head.

No, thought Voang. We will leave this country no matter what it takes.

Chapter Nine
The End of the Farm

Rumours reached the farm that China and Vietnam were on the verge of war, and then that Vietnam had invaded Cambodia. All the Vietnamese in the farm, except Quan and Hue, were enclosed behind barbed wire. Quan was given a gun and stayed in the guards' hut and Hue was allowed to stay with the Cambodian peasants. One day, a runner came to the farm and informed the guards that the Vietnamese forces were only ten miles away. The guards melted into the jungle, taking Quan with him, but at the first bend, he slipped back to the farm, throwing his gun and krama scarf into the bush.

Within an hour, the Vietnamese forces rolled into the farm, freeing the imprisoned Vietnamese and rounding up the Cambodian peasants. Quan and Hue greeted the soldiers in Vietnamese and were permitted to join the other Vietnamese. The leaders among the farm's Vietnamese came forward and identified Cambodian peasants who had helped the Khmer Rouge guards kill inmates. Ten, then twenty peasants were marched into the jungle, not to return.

After two days, the Vietnamese forces were ordered to withdraw. Quan and Hue joined their march eastward. When they arrived at the Mekong River, the two children spotted a dug-out. They climbed into it and paddled down the river. Passing by the now abandoned rubber plantations built by the French, the river opened into the delta. Sampans passed on either side. The occasional river patrol boat cruised by them, but the two children blended into the local scenery, raising no suspicions. On the river, fishermen cast their nets, hauling in the occasional fish, barely enough to feed their families, but not enough to sell in the market. Malnutrition was slowly afflicting their villages.

The inhabitants of the local villages were all Khmer Krom, the indigenous ethnic Cambodians who had lived in the delta region long before the Vietnamese immigration from the north. As Quan and Hue beached the dug-out, now taking on water from various leaks in its hull, and approached on foot the first village, they addressed the peasants in the rough peasant Khmer dialect that they had learned on the farm. They told them their entire story – the march from Phnom

Penh, the death of their parents, the liberation by the Vietnamese forces. The elders of the village met to discuss what to do with the children. Many had also lost relatives during the long civil war and others had known persecution from successive Vietnamese governments who viewed the Khmer Krom with suspicion. They knew that harbouring the children would only draw suspicion to the village.

"Who are they really?" asked one sceptic. "Maybe they are working for the government to spy on us."

"Nonsense, they are still children," answered the rest.

"The girl is no child. Look at her. And the boy has a violent streak in him. You heard his story," ventured one of the villagers.

"You would be violent too, had you lived what he has lived through. Let's take them in for a few days and help them leave the country."

"We should turn them into the authorities. They are city-dwellers. They belong in Saigon."

"No, let them leave for Malaysia. There are many boats in the gulf taking people to Malaysia. They can reach these boats with their dug-out."

Even with their knowledge of peasant Khmer, Quan and Hue could barely make out the local Khmer Krom dialect as they tried to overhear the discussion. They began to fear that they would be betrayed by the villagers. Quietly, they returned to the dug-out, emptied it of water and paddled it furiously down the delta until it began to sink. At that point, fishermen in a sampan came by and took them on board. They towed the dug-out to their village. The fishermen were also Khmer Krom, but their village was larger and mixed with Chinese and Vietnamese inhabitants. The villagers tried for several days to convince Quan and Hue to stay with them. They fed them well and offered them a little abandoned hut with a large vegetable patch.

In the last days of the war, the village had been caught in a counter-offensive by the South Vietnamese Air Force against the North Vietnamese forces which were trying to approach Saigon from the south-east. A plane had accidentally dropped its payload of cluster bombs on the field where the young women were working, killing large numbers. Now that the young men had returned from military service, there were few brides in the village.

Soldier, Lily, Peace and Pearls   *43*

Hue's beauty and ability to speak all the languages of the village caught the attention of parents eager to marry their sons to someone so refined. After Hue was approached by three families on this subject, she told Quan that they must leave. Her heart longed for the freedom of the city. During the years on the farm, she had learned much from the older, more sophisticated Chinese and Vietnamese *New People*. They had told her of the splendours of Bangkok, Hong Kong, and even of France where several had studied. She knew that she owed it to her dead parents that her brother and she should try to find again the life that they had planned for their children. Although the generosity of the villagers warmed her heart, she knew that their destiny lay elsewhere.

Chapter Ten

An Honourable Man Keeps his Word

General Dang was the number two in the Communist security services in Saigon. With Dr. Thieu's excellent treatment, he survived the serious wounds from the accident. His arm remained mangled and barely useable, but beyond that, Dang recovered fully.

Two weeks later, Voang Thieu was released from prison. Three months later, when members of the Chinese minority in Vietnam were finally being allowed to leave Saigon on small fishing boats, the Thieu family received a message from a young soldier to go the harbour that night and leave. They were told that an honourable man would keep his word. Voang and Han cut Minh Chau's and An's hair and dressed them like boys. Knowing that only the Chinese minority would be allowed to leave, Voang and Han quickly taught them a handful of Chinese words and told the children to pretend that they did not understand Vietnamese. Minh Chau and An rehearsed saying in Chinese to each other "What did the man say? I don't understand." Voang, whose maternal grandmother was Chinese, had spoken the language as a child and later studied Mandarin in school. Han had also studied Chinese as part of her classical education.

When the family reached the harbour, a sentry stepped forward to ask the children in Vietnamese if they wanted candy. Minh Chau and An recited the Chinese phrases they had learned, and Voang spoke to the soldier in Vietnamese but with a heavy Chinese accent. The family was permitted to pass through. As they turned the corner of a building, a second soldier stepped forward. It was dark, but Han recognized his face. It was General Dang, dressed in a simple soldier's uniform. He looked straight into Han's eyes, and then waved the family through. He was their enemy, but he kept his promise to Han Thieu.

As they approached the dock, they saw a long line-up for a Chinese junk. The boat had been purchased by a wealthy Chinese merchant who had fled Saigon in 1975. Now comfortably re-established in California where he was building a real estate empire, he had decided to bring over many of his relatives, and at the same time turn a tidy profit. The boat was a large and sturdy sea-faring junk from Hong

Kong. Its crew was a mixture of recent refugees from mainland China and the usual Hong Kong criminal element. The captain, Tao Tsoa, was as unscrupulous as they come.

As Voang and his family waited in line, other passengers queued up behind them. Apprehension grew among the late-comers that there would not be enough places on the boat. Except for the Thieus, all were ethnic Chinese. One man three down from the Thieus in the line, shouted at Voang, "You there! Why are you here? You are not Chinese!" Voang started to protest in a mixture of child-like Cantonese and school Mandarin, but the man continued. "You lost the war to the north and now you people are at war again with China. Stay here with your Viet Cong brothers! You do not belong in Hong Kong."

Others joined the chorus, muttering that there was no room on the boat, that the Thieus would only bring everyone problems. Han held her frightened children close to her. Voang bowed his head to avoid the angry looks of the other passengers. As the line moved forward toward Captain Tao, who was collecting payment, Voang noticed that each passenger was handing over 100,000 *dong* a head. It was a considerable amount of money, but thanks to the sale of Han's jade, the family had enough cash to just make it. When it came their turn, Captain Tao, who had heard the dissent of the other passengers, said "For you Vietnamese, you must pay 200,000 *dong* each."

Voang went into a state of shock, realizing that he did not have enough money to meet Tao's demand. He protested that all the others had only paid 100,000. Tao sneered at Voang, and said, "You can pay me what you have, and your wife can make up the difference on the boat," as he glared with lust at Han, with Minh Chau and An clinging to her *ao dai*. "Or maybe the young ones can pay for you," Tao whispered with a perverted smile.

Suddenly, out of the shadows, marched up three officers. Voang did not recognize any of them until Minh Chau sang out, "Huynh, Huynh, big brother Huynh!" Beside Huynh was Colonel Phuc from Danang and Commandant Nguyen from Chi Boa Prison. The Chinese captain stepped back defensively as Phuc walked up to his face, and said in Chinese, "You will take the same amount from this family as from the others. And if anything happens to them, we will hunt you down in your Hong Kong brothels and castrate you before we feed you to the sharks." To ensure that Tao understood clearly the message, Nguyen took out his pistol and pushed the nuzzle against Tao's right temple and pulled out a knife that he held under the captain's testicles. Huynh kept his gun trained on the boat crew.

Voang quickly handed Tao the money and raced with his family up the gang plank. From the ship's railing, the family waved to Phuc, Nguyen and Huynh. Minh Chau shouted, "Huynh, come visit us and bring Dao!" Phuc said calmly but audibly, "Voang, return one day so we can have one last game of Da' Ngu'a." Nguyen stood silently and gazed at the face of Han, whom he had come to admire in the prison. He thought of his own wife and two children who had died in the war as he watched the Thieus depart, and he wished them well. In a foreign land, they would have the life that war had deprived him of.

Chapter Eleven
At Sea

Quan and his sister thanked the Khmer Krom peasants for their hospitality. The peasants had patched the dug-out with rubber sap and put in it a small sack of vegetables and a bamboo jar of fresh water. Wading into the estuary, they helped push the dug-out into the gulf.

The first day was uneventful as Quan and Hue paddled south. On the second day, the waters were still placid, but on the horizon, the sky turned orange and purple. In the night, violent winds rose from the northwest, blowing the dug-out farther to the south. The rain battered the two children, who huddled together to stay warm, too tired to paddle. The waves rose and rocked their tiny boat, sweeping away their provisions of food and water, and making both violently seasick. After two days of storm, fatigue overwhelmed them and they fell into a deep sleep. When the storm subsided and the intense rays of the sun began to scorch their faces, they woke to the brutal pain of days without food and water.

On the third day, dehydration set in. Quan tried to drink the seawater, but immediately vomited. Hue grabbed her brother, holding his head tightly against her chest. Then in the distance, they saw a boat appear. They feared they would be pirated. They had heard the horror stories of the Thai pirates from local villagers as they had paddled down the Mekong. The boat approached. Voices in Vietnamese called out to them. They were pulled aboard by refugees heading to Malaysia.

By a stroke of luck, the boat had not been attacked by pirates. The passengers shared with the children their meagre rations of rice, noodle soup and water. Gradually, Quan and Hue regained their strength. On the sixth day at sea, a Malaysian coast patrol intercepted the boat and towed it to Pulau Bidong Island. They were saved or at least they thought as much.

The voyage to Pulau Bidong had been an ordeal for Quan and his sister, but was nothing compared to what lay in store for the Thieu family, who, the day Quan and Hue reached Malaysia, had boarded the ill-fated Chinese junk in Saigon's harbour.

Chapter Twelve
Courage's Reward

As the junk slipped away from the dock, Voang watched Phuc, Nguyen and Huynh fade into the darkness. And for a brief moment, he regretted leaving. He had lived his whole life in Vietnam. He had hated the Communists all his life and believed in capitalism. But when he needed help, it was his former enemies who came to his rescue. Young Huynh had made it possible for his children and later his wife to leave Chi Boa prison. Commandant Nguyen had intervened with his old comrade for Voang's release from Danang and now all three had saved the family again, at the risk of their own security. As he left his beloved country, he also left behind new friends, who despite their hardness, had allowed decency and simple kindness into their lives. Voang knew that he might never return to Vietnam, but he swore that when the time was right, he would ask his children to do so in his stead to thank these men, and play one last game of Da' Ngu'a with Phuc for him.

Exhausted, Han and An slept soundly on the deck of the junk. Voang stood watch over his family, and Minh Chau, too excited to sleep, gazed at her father's silhouette against the star-lit sky. Although only five, she had felt the sense of fear that pervaded the ship. When a dark shape moved toward her family, she tugged on her father's trousers and pointed to the intruder, who was only yards away.

Voang stepped forward in a defensive posture, only to recognize Cong, the nineteen-year-old son of a long-time neighbour from Thao Dien.

"Cong, I did not see you board the boat."

"Dr. Thieu, I was the first to arrive. Is Madame Thieu here?"

"Yes, she and the children are sleeping."

"I'm not sleeping," interjected Minh Chau, once again coquettish as she viewed the handsome neighbour. She had always like Cong. He was the first to visit them, bringing food and new clothes, when her mother had been released from prison. She had once confided to An that she wanted to marry Cong when she grew up because she did not want to steal Huynh from Dao, even if she liked Huynh better. That would not be nice.

"Dr. Thieu. I saw how they treated you. Do not worry! I am strong and will stay with your family." He then brought out from his pocket a revolver. "My father gave this to me before he died. You should stay close to me."

"Dr. Thieu," he went on, "we need to be careful. The other passengers tell me that Captain Tao was once a pirate. Nobody trusts him."

Voang looked at the young man, whose anxiety was palpable. He had known Cong's father, Dai, in the army. He had been a brave officer, who was known for his fairness to Viet Cong prisoners. When the Communists broke through the city's perimeter forces and most South Vietnamese officers surrendered without a fight, Dai had rushed to defend the Presidential Palace and kept fighting until a hail of bullets struck him down. Since then, Cong had lived with his mother not far from the Thieu's main house.

"Cong, how is your mother?" asked Voang.

"She died two years ago just before your wife was released from prison. She caught bronchitis. After Madame Thieu left, we had no doctor who would treat us because of father's military service. When I tried to buy medicine, the pharmacist was too scared to sell it to me."

"Cong, I am sorry for your loss."

"Thank you. My parents respected you and Madame Thieu very much. I sold our house to pay for this voyage, but I still have gold for Hong Kong. Do you need some? I can help you."

Minh Chau listened to the young man's voice. It was full of sincerity and tenderness. It was clear that her father trusted Cong, and so would she. Her eyes became heavy and she laid her head gently against her mother's warm body. Gradually, she entered her dream world, where she played with Huynh and Dao at Aunt Lan's house and sucked on the hard candy that Huynh brought her. An older boy entered her dream. He was strong and wore strange clothes. A red scarf hung around his neck. Huynh turned to the boy and saluted him, and Dao caressed his unkempt hair.

The crackling of gunfire woke Minh Chau and her family from their dreams. The stars in the sky had become bright in the summer night. In their light, she saw the crew separate the passengers into two groups: Chung Fat's relatives and everyone else. Cong and the Thieus were ushered into the second group by machete-wielding sailors. Cong kept one hand on his gun and the other around An's and Minh Chau's shoulders. On the bridge, Tao Tsao passed over wads of *dong* to the ragged fishermen, whose small boats were tied to the junk.

As Tao counted out the money that the fishermen hungrily stuffed into their shirts, he thought of his profits. For 10,000 *dong* a head, he was able to rid himself of most of the passengers, pocketing 90,000 *dong* each for himself. There would be no bribes to pay the Hong Kong officials and he would keep his arrangement with Chung Fat to only transport his relatives.

That the off-loaded passengers would now have to brave the long journey in small boats to Malaysia, instead of the relatively safe journey to Hong Kong, was not his concern. Let them rot in the pirate-infested waters and those who survived could rot in the Malaysian internment camps. Maybe the fishermen would show some initiative and slit their passengers' throats in the middle of the night.

In any event, they would not be his problem. But what of the beautiful doctor and her two daughters? He felt the rush of blood to his loins. If he tired of her, her children, especially the tiny waif, could pleasure him. He contemplated raping all of them in front of Voang Thieu. Where would his Communist saviours be then? Then he remembered the sharp blade lifted up against his testicles. Hong Kong was brimming with Communist spies, including in the local Vietnamese community. Why take the risk? He grabbed a young girl of fifteen, pushing away her brother and barked orders to his crewmen to take the young girl to his cabin. She would do instead.

Cong hesitated, as he contemplated coming to the rescue of the girl and her brother who was being beaten to a pulp by the crew. Only Minh Chau's tugging on his leg reminded him that his first duty was to the safety of the Thieus, who were climbing onto one of the small fishing boats. Cong was then knocked out by an impatient crewman and tossed onto another boat. When he came to, he saw the boat with the Thieus bobbing up and down in the rough waves. Slowly the overcrowded fishing boats moved away from the junk and headed south to Malaysia.

The fishermen soon paid for their avarice. One day out, Thai pirates attacked all four boats, robbing the fishermen and the passengers alike. The next morning, more pirates came. These ones, poorer and more brutish than the first, stole all the food and water. The fishermen would have gladly turned back to Vietnam had not the passengers threatened to toss them overboard. As the refugees began to suffer from delirium induced by dehydration, the third set of pirates visited the boat and began to take people – young girls for the brothels and boys to slave away on the farms.

From the distance, the passengers on the Thieus' boat watched another boat burn on the horizon. The waters were filled with splashing arms as some tried to swim to the Thieus' boat and others struggled hopelessly before succumbing to the sea. As the first swimmers reached the boat, the passengers helped them aboard. When the tenth swimmer arrived, the boat began to heave. The Thieus watched in horror as those who could not swim well died before reaching the boat. Then they saw a lone swimmer moving toward the boat. Those who had minutes before been in the water themselves began to protest, "This boat is full. We will sink if we take him!"

Voang and Han were closest to the man who had only ten yards left to swim. A burly man threw an oar to Voang and ordered him to push the swimmer away. The boat heaved dangerously. Voang dropped the oar and stared into the waves. "It is Cong, our neighbour. We will take him aboard." At that moment, the burly man grabbed An by the hair, pulled her toward him and placed a razor to her throat. "Push him away, I said."

From the waves, came Cong's pleading voice, "Help me! I cannot swim any longer!" A big wave pushed Cong's struggling body closer to the boat. He grabbed the hull, sending the overcrowded boat into turmoil. The burly man pressed the blade against An's throat releasing a small rivulet of red. Voang and Han froze in horror. A bottle hurled through the air struck Cong's forehead, forcing him to release his hold on the boat. As blood burst forward and his eyes rolled back, Cong slipped under the waves. His outstretched hand disappeared under the water one foot away from the boat. A subdued Minh Chau turned to her parents and then to the burly man who released An and smiled at his young accomplice. "Well done, child."

Chapter Thirteen
Pulau Bidong

Quan and Hue watched the Thieus from a distance. The family moved with such grace compared to the other refugees. Voang bore a tremendous resemblance to their father while Han's affection toward her children reminded them of their own mother's soft ways.

Quan and his sister had settled in the Chinese quarter of the camp when they had first arrived two weeks earlier. Although they spoke functional Cantonese, the Hoa Chinese from Vietnam would mock their Hokkien pronunciation. Some Hoa harboured deep resentment toward the Vietnamese who had forced them to sell their entire belongings and flee a country where their ancestors had lived for hundreds of years. The fact that Quan and Hue spoke to each other in Vietnamese provoked strong reactions from some of the early arrivals, who had been humiliated and tortured in the first days of the government's campaign to encourage the Chinese to leave Vietnam. The children's increasing discomfort incited them to look for shelter elsewhere in the camp.

The Thieu family had chosen to build a new hut in the smaller Vietnamese part of the camp. When Quan saw Voang Thieu struggle with his mangled hand to maneuver the bamboo into place, the young boy marched up and offered to help in exchange for a third of the space in the new hut. Voang was impressed by the confident air of the eleven-year-old, and even more impressed by Quan's strength. In no time, they had a basic structure in place. Hue took Han around the camp and the neighbouring forest, showing her where edible roots could be found. The plants were similar to those along the Thai border in Cambodia, which Hue had learned to harvest. For the city-dwelling doctor from Saigon, Hue's knowledge was invaluable in bringing vital nutrients to her family's diet of boiled rice.

An, now eight, became endeared to Hue who took care of her as her own mother sought to administer simple medical care to many of the malnourished camp residents. With Hue's help, Han slowly developed from the jungle roots a nutritional supplement for the most serious cases. With the meagre earnings from those refugees who still had some money, jewelery or gold, she sent Voang to barter with the camp guards for soap to disinfect the lesions brought on by severe malnourishment.

Minh Chau remained distant from Hue, who was just another stranger, another boat person, perhaps another person who would put a razor to An's throat. As night fell, her tiny body convulsed over recurrent memories of the boat trip. Cong's body sinking below the water sickened her with guilt. Her tears would not stop, even as her mother rocked her softy in her arms for hours on end. After nocturnal marathons of trembling, the young girl would succumb to exhaustion in the early hours of the morning.

When dawn broke, Minh Chau would suddenly awake in a state of euphoria. For the rest of the day, she would dance around the camp in the warm Malaysian sun, singing the sweet songs of liberation that Huynh had taught her in prison or hum the gentle melodies of the Vietnamese singer Khanh Ly that Aunt Lan had sung to her as they worked in the household vegetable patch. But Minh Chau replied only laconically whenever her family spoke to her. While her eyes still seemed to sparkle like wedge-like pieces of jade exquisitely placed in dark brown mosaics, a closer look revealed the emptiness of her soul.

Whenever Han or Hue turned their backs, Minh Chau would wander off. Once, they found her tossing small stones on the roof of the Malaysian guards' hut. The guards laughed it off that time. Luckily, one of the guards, Dahan, who was a notorious drunk, was not there at that time. Of all the guards, he was the only one who truly hated the refugees. He had come from a small farming village in central Malaysia. When he was a child, his family had been driven off their farm by a rich Chinese merchant who had acquired the farm and all the surrounding farms through a corrupt Malay intermediary. The merchant did not even live in Malaysia, but had moved to Bangkok in the early years of independence. Dahan's earliest memories were of the Chinese merchant's henchmen torching the family hut, as his mother kneeled crying before it, and his father bowed his head in the shame of being unable to do anything.

Han had heard from others that Dahan had attacked several of the young women in the camp. More disturbing was the rumour that he had been caught fondling a seven-year-old girl. Han spoke at length to Minh Chau and An about the dangers of going too near to the guards and the need to particularly avoid Dahan. An listened carefully to her mother, but Minh Chau remained in her separate universe, and only giggled as her mother spoke to her.

Finally, An came up with a scheme to keep Minh Chau under control. She whispered in Minh Chau's ear that Quan knew where to find unlimited supplies of the hard candy that Huynh used to bring to Chi Boa Prison. Suddenly, to Quan's discomfort, little Minh Chau began to follow him everywhere. Sometimes she walked behind him like a soldier marching off to war. Other times, she would dodge from hiding place to hiding place, keeping always only ten feet away.

Quan felt very protective toward both the Thieu daughters, and had come to love their parents, who took the time to teach him to write in Vietnamese and gave him some lessons in rudimentary English so that he could communicate with the Malay guards. Voang Thieu had even taken him aside one day and spoke to him of the importance of the girls' honour. He then said, "I will give you a secret name. For now on, I shall call you Bao for Bao Ve Phu Nu – the protector of women. You won't let me down, will you."

"No, Dr. Thieu, never!"

However, Minh Chau's constant shadowing of his every move began to wear on his nerves. When he scolded Minh Chau, she collapsed into uncontrollable tears and convulsions. Quan went into a panic. What had he done? He approached Minh Chau and put his arm around her tiny shoulders to comfort her. It was at that precise moment that an intoxicated Dahan stumbled by. "What do you have there, boy? Let me see! Ah, a pretty little thing."

Dahan effortlessly pushed Quan into the dust, grabbed Minh Chau's arm and dragged her off toward his hut. Quan tackled Dahan, but the guard, even in his drunkenness, had the strength of a water buffalo. He again threw Quan against the wall of a bamboo hut. Quan got up and took out a slingshot from his back pocket. No other guards were in sight. He fit a large stone in the band of the slingshot and aimed it at the back of Dahan's head. When Minh Chau screamed in pain as Dahan tightened his grip on her, Quan released the shot. The stone seared Dahan's shaven head. It was just enough to distract the guard, who released Minh Chau's arm long enough for Quan to run up, scoop Minh Chau in his arms and head off to the forest. Dazed, Dahan just shook his head and then sat on the ground and pulled out a small bottle of rice wine from his jacket.

When the community learned of Dahan's latest rape attempt, an emergency meeting was held. It was decided to write a petition to the new UN-appointed camp administrator. After a short investigation and a considerable bribe in gold from a rich refugee who had three young daughters, the new administrator had Dahan transferred. That evening, men and women lined up to shake Quan's hand, and Minh Chau sang out, "Quan is my friend, my very big friend." Then she ran to him and hugged him, singing, "my big, big, big soldier."

After that, the guards paid Quan special respect. Other parents urged their daughters to play with the Thieu girls just to come under Quan's protection. Ironically, one eleven-year-old boy had brought more security to the camp than the collective efforts of the one thousand adult men in it.

After Dahan's dismissal, things improved in the camp in many ways. The UNHCR representatives began to visit the camp more frequently. The locally recruited Malay guards were gradually replaced by regular Malaysian policemen who were stationed just outside the camp and entered the camp only when the local camp committee called on them to do so. The Chinese and Vietnamese inhabitants soon reconciled their differences and started joint night patrols to improve security.

The biggest improvement for Minh Chau, An and Quan was the newly opened school. A young Malay teacher, Abdul Hakim, was sent to teach the children English. He was a jovial type who came to love his young charges. Minh Chau was a particularly bright student, and her first quest was to learn how to say in English and Malay, "Where does Quan hide his candy?" An had told her that Quan did not want to share his candy because it made him strong. Minh Chau was determined to find Quan's hoard to become just as strong as he was. Abdul Hakim, learning of An's prank on Minh Chau, decided to join in.

One day, he brought a big bag of hard candy to the classroom. Distracting Quan for a moment, he slipped a handful into Quan's jacket pocket. He then went off to Minh Chau, who whispered in his ear in English as she did every day, "Where does Quan hide his candy?" Abdul Hakim answered, "If you can also ask me in Malay, I will tell you." She quickly translated her question into flawless Malay, and

Abdul Hakim answered, "Check the left pocket of his jacket." "No, I already did." "Check again." Minh Chau then sneaked over to Quan, who was engrossed in the new Dick and Jane book that Abdul Hakim had given him, put her hand into the jacket pocket and whipped out a handful of candy. "I found it! I found it! Now I will be as strong as Quan!" She then threw candy right and left to other students. Quan looked at her bewildered. Where did she get the candy? Abdul Hakim bowed over in laughter, and the entire classroom became bedlam, as some students jumped up to catch the *treasure* and others surrounded Quan to beg for more candy.

The next day, Abdul Hakim had twelve new girl students in the class, all of whom tried to sit as near to Quan as they could. Minh Chau made sure that she snuggled even closer to Quan, and stared down her rivals. As often as he could, Abdul Hakim would sneak more candy into Quan's pocket when the boy was not looking, and it did not take long before Minh Chau or another girl managed to pickpocket it. Whoever got the candy first, shared it freely with the rest. Quan, who was by nature superstitious, started to believe that a Malay jinn had taken hold of his jacket. How else could this constant supply of candy be explained? Minh Chau and the other students were convinced that Quan had smuggled into the camp a huge store of candy, and after school, not only did Minh Chau stalk Quan, but so did three or four other girls. Only An and Abdul Hakim knew the real story.

While Quan became very popular both with adults for his stand against Dahan and with younger girls attracted not only by his seemingly inexhaustible supply of candy but also by his good looks, he remained a deeply disturbed child. At night, as he slept beside Hue, he was haunted by the brutal death of his mother. The Khmer Rouge guards who had raped her to death had escaped from the farm before Quan could take his revenge. In his quest for survival and protection for his sister, he had also frequented some of these same guards for more than two years as he role-played loyalty to their insane and brutal ideology. As his sister Hue grew older in the camp, she again attracted many admirers. Since leaving Cambodia, her life had stabilized. Now sixteen, she began to dream of marriage and starting a family.

Voang Thieu's words rang in his ears, "You will now be called Bao Ve Phu Nu." Only twelve, Quan was stronger than most of his sister's suitors. Quan would scrutinize each of them, and frighten off most.

Finally, Hue complained to Han Thieu about her brother's interference. Han took Quan aside, and explained to him that his sister was old enough to make her own choices. Quan nodded obediently at his adopted mother, just as Minh Chau who had been eavesdropping sauntered up.

"I am old enough too. Can I marry Quan?" asked Minh Chau.

Quan blushed immediately, as Han Thieu smiled at her daughter, "If Quan wants to, I agree, but not before we all go to France."

"Whoopee. Then I can eat all of Quan's candy!" cried out Minh Chau, as she gave her mother and Quan a little bear hug.

While Dr. Han Thieu had her heart set on resettlement in France where she had cousins, this was not to be. Instead, one day, the Thieu family were invited to meet a Canadian immigration officer. His name was Denis Prud'homme, and he had a flaming red beard. The family put on their best clothes and the children reviewed their French with Han before the interview. Denis was a kind man. He took down all the details and promised to return for a second interview. Did the Thieus know anyone in Canada who perhaps could arrange sponsorship?

"We know no one in Canada," said Voang.

"Wait! Marie-Christine Labonté is Canadian," jumped in Han excitedly.

"Did you say Marie-Christine Labonté?" queried Denis Prud'homme.

"Yes, we knew her in Saigon. Why? Do you know her?" asked Han hopefully.

"Marie-Christine is my cousin! She lives in Bangkok now with her husband. I will see what we can do," explained the immigration agent.

Just at that moment, Minh Chau could not hold back her curiosity anymore and reached to pull hard on Denis's beard. While her parents suddenly saw their dream of Canada evaporate, Denis only laughed and then plucked a red hair from the beard and said, "Little girl, you can keep this as a souvenir."

"I got the magic hair! I got the magic hair! I can go to Canada with my magic hair," chanted Minh Chau, as she ran off to find Quan to show him her good luck charm.

The Thieus profusely offered their apologies for their daughter's impetuous behaviour, but Denis Prud'homme shook them off. "You have a delightful daughter and I hope that the hair does bring you all good luck. We need families like you in Canada!"

A week later, Denis Prud'homme not only returned as promised, but brought along Marie-Christine. Han bowed before her friend from Saigon, and Marie-Christine reached out to her and said, "Han, I am so sorry. Thomas tried to save you at the embassy. They wouldn't let him. They forced him to leave without you. He sends his best. He also says that if you want, he can work on getting you to the States instead of Canada."

Minh Chau stepped forward, "We must go to Canada because I have the magic hair!"

Voang turned to Marie-Christine, "Madame Labonté, you know that I respect your husband and I worked for many years alongside Americans, but I want to return one day to Vietnam. If we go to the States, that will never be possible. Can you help us go to Canada?"

"Of course, that is why I am here. We have found a church in Quebec City to sponsor you."

"Marie-Christine, there are two children that we must take with us. They have no one else," said Han.

"Dr. Thieu, that will not be possible. Our resettlement policy only allows for immediate family members," explained Denis Prud'homme. "I am sorry. I can try to do what I can for these children, but you should not get your hopes up. What are their names?"

"Hue and Quan Phoc," answered Han quickly. "I can bring them now. Minh Chau, find your brother Quan and sister Hue."

Minh Chau raced through the camp like lightning. She knew exactly where to find Quan. It was Saturday morning and every Saturday morning, Quan bartered Chinese medicine with the Malay policemen for cheap novels in English. He had befriended an old Chinese healer, Jing Zi, from Vientiane, Laos, who knew how to transform the roots and bark of the local trees into traditional medicine. Aphrodisiacs were his specialty and especially popular among the Malays. Quan told the guards that the white powder was ground from rhinoceros horns, and tripled the price in doing so. Apparently, the powder had a very helpful effect on the policemen when they visited their wives on the mainland, and demand kept on growing.

Quan was in the midst of an important transaction at the police station. Not only was the Malay sergeant offering a well used copy of Hemingway's *The Sun Also Rises,* but he had thrown in a vintage copy of *Batman Meets Catwoman.* The *Sun Also Rises* would be a gift for Abdul Hakim. Quan had finally realized how all the candy had got into his pocket, and wanted to thank his gregarious English teacher.

Hue was also nearby taking orders to sew the policemen's clothes. Minh Chau saw Hue first. She rushed toward her when suddenly a hand reached out and grabbed her by the neck. It was Dahan, who had returned to pick up some of his belongings. "Little Vietnamese bitch, I will teach you a lesson," he swore, overwhelming the child with the stench of gin. Minh Chau squirmed helplessly as the huge man lifted her by the throat high into the air. Her face turned blue, as her nails dug into the arms of her attacker. "Bitch, breathe your last breath." Hue and a Malay policeman ran toward Dahan and Minh Chau. With two powerful strokes of his backhand, he sent both flying through the air, knocking them unconscious.

Still holding Minh Chau with one hand, Dahan staggered toward Hue, who lay helpless on the ground. He ripped off her cotton pants and spread her legs. As he began to unbuckle his belt, he felt Minh Chau's body go limp and threw her aside, to concentrate on his new victim. Before he could thrust himself into Hue's delicate body, he felt a sharp blow to the back of his skull. He reached up to touch the top of his head, only to discover that he could feel his brain. He turned around to see Quan holding the police sergeant's service pistol. A second shot struck Dahan through his left eye. Hue woke just in time to avoid being crushed by the weight of Dahan's huge body. Quan calmly walked up and put two bullets in the dead man's scrotum. Within seconds, the children were surrounded by the other policemen. All had come to hate Dahan, but Quan had stolen the sergeant's gun and committed murder. They took him to the makeshift jail and debated what to do with him.

Hue and the young policeman whom Quan had knocked out raced with Minh Chau in their arms to Dr. Han Thieu. For ten minutes, Han used every medical artifice that she knew to revive her daughter. Nothing worked. Her guests, Denis Prud'homme and Marie-Christine Labonté, looked on with horror at the frail immobile body of the child who had enchanted both of them. Finally, Jing Zi came to them with a green potion. With Han's permission, he poured it into Minh Chau's mouth. Within seconds, the child convulsed violently and her heart began to beat again.

With Minh Chau now breathing, Han asked Hue what had happened. Hue described the attack by Dahan and how Quan had killed the former guard.

"We must tell the police to release Quan," said Han. "Monsieur Prud'homme, can you help us?" Han stayed with her daughter as Voang, Hue and their visitors marched down to the police station. Denis Prud'homme spent hours trying to cajole the policemen to release Quan. The sergeant whose gun had been stolen was sympathetic, but the killing of a camp guard, even a former one who was known to be a drunk and rapist, was something that could not be swept under the carpet.

For the next three months, Denis Prud'homme worked hard to get the Thieu family accepted into Canada and find a sponsor for Quan and Hue. Each time it seemed that he was close, the sponsors balked when they learned that Quan had killed a man. Hue swore that she would not leave her brother's side. Ironically, imprisoned in the Malaysian police station, Quan became good friends with all. The fact that Jing Zi kept him well supplied with magic potions to barter was a plus. Regular delegations from the various groups in the camp came to pay Quan homage, some of them leaving with purchases of Chinese medicine or goods that Quan had obtained in barter with the policemen. The small jail became, through Quan's entrepreneurial spirit, an important distribution centre for the camp.

Back in Kuala Lumpur, Marie-Christine convinced her husband, Thomas Smith, to intervene with the Ministry of the Interior to have the charges against Quan dismissed. Finally, both Denis and Marie-Christine convinced their uncle Father André Hibou to sell his parishioners in New Carlisle, Quebec on the idea of sponsoring Quan and his sister. As New Carlisle was too small a place to receive the children, it was agreed that the money would be transferred to Father André's nephew Mathieu Hibou who studied in Quebec City. Mathieu would be responsible for finding a room for the children and overseeing their integration into Quebec society. The paperwork was complex, and Citizenship and Immigration in Ottawa had misgivings about allowing Quan into Canada. The processing would take at least several months. The Thieu family, Hue, Denis and Marie-Christine held a small conference to decide that the Thieus would go first to Quebec City to take up the offer of sponsorship from the local church. Hue would wait for her brother's release and then follow in three months.

When the time came for the Thieus to leave for Canada, Denis, Marie-Christine and her husband Thomas Smith all came to the camp. Together they went to the police station to say goodbye to Quan. Abdul Hakim joined them, bringing hard candy. The police sergeant made them all tea, and brought Quan out. His face brightened when he looked at how healthy Minh Chau was. She rushed to hug him, and pressed into his hand several candies, and said, "I brought some treasure for you, Quan. I love you!" When Voang's turn came to say goodbye, he caressed the boy's face and said, "Bao Ve Phu Nu, I owe my daughter's life twice to you. We will wait for you in Canada—you are now my real son!" An stroked Quan's hand and bowed deeply, "Honoured brother, we all love you."

Then Minh Chau's face lit up, and she chanted, "I know how to make Quan come to Canada!" The family and visitors looked quizzically at her, as she reached deep into her pocket and brought out the red hair from Denis Prud'homme's beard. "Quan, I give you the magic hair to Canada. You must never lose this. Promise me!"

Quan took the hair and put it safely in his own pocket. He then took out the batman comic and handed it to Minh Chau. "When we grow up, I will be Batman and you, Catwoman."

"Yes," said Minh Chau, "yes, Batman and Catwoman forever and ever!"

With the Thieu family's modest belongings, Denis Prud'homme's Land Cruiser pulled toward the camp's gate. As they passed the police station, Quan, Hue, Abdul Hakim and the entire police contingent waved. If tears could become pearls, the Thieu family could have transformed their grief at leaving Quan and Hue and their joy at departing for Canada into the greatest treasure trove the world had ever known.

The Land Cruiser drove onto the tiny ferry that would take them to the mainland. The boat pulled out into the sea, and Minh Chau quivered as images of the sea voyage to Pulau Bidong flashed before her. Without Quan at her side, her body began to shake. Quickly, An unwrapped a hard candy and put it into Minh Chau's mouth and whispered, "Quan's treasure will protect you from the sea." The sweet taste of the candy drove the dark thoughts from Minh Chau's mind, and she dreamed of playing hide-and-go-seek with her protector.

Chapter Fourteen
Quebec

Mathieu Hibou was not quite sure of what he had got himself into when he agreed to help his uncle André. In any case, the two Vietnamese boat children would not be arriving for another three months, according to his cousins Denis and Marie-Christine. He would have time to prepare, but Marie-Christine had asked another favour of Mathieu. Could he keep an eye out for the Thieu family, who were arriving the next day in Quebec? Although the Thieus would be taken care of by a local church, Marie-Christine wanted someone whom she knew personally to ensure that no harm would come to them. It was never in Mathieu's nature to say no to these kinds of requests, even when he was up to his eyeballs in preparing for exams at Laval University.

The next day, he joined Father Pierre, the local parish priest, to go down to the bus station where the Thieus were arriving after their flight from Montreal. He was taken aback at how thin the entire family looked, especially the youngest daughter who could not be more than forty pounds. Like his cousin Denis, Mathieu had flaming red hair and sported a full winter beard, as did most young men in Quebec at the time. As the priest greeted Voang and Han, Minh Chau darted out toward Mathieu, singing in Vietnamese, "Mr. Lucky Charm, you are here, you are here."

An, embarrassed that her young sister had mistaken Mathieu for Denis, caught her sister just in time before she tried to pluck a new hair from the stranger's beard. In halting French, she said, "Excusez-nous, Monsieur, she thinks that you are someone else."

"Perhaps Denis Prud'homme? He is my cousin."

Han hearing the familiar name stepped forward and bowed, asking, "Are you Mathieu Hibou?"

"Yes, I am."

"I am honoured to meet you. Your cousin Marie-Christine spoke very highly of you."

"Thank you, I have promised my cousin and my uncle André Hibou to help you and your family. Can I get your bags?"

Voang's eyes moistened as the priest and Mathieu carried their bags to the waiting taxi. Voang was a devout Catholic, and believed in the credo *love thy neighbour*, but he had never dreamed that his arrival in Canada would be met with such kindness. Han stroked her husband's arm, laid her head on his shoulder and thought, "We will be safe here. We will be happy here. When Quan and Hue come, we will be one family."

Minh Chau was still puzzled about why Denis Prud'homme was now being called Mathieu. Were they really different men? Maybe all these Canadians had red beards. And what was all this cold powder under their feet. In the bus, her mother had wrapped their shoes with newspapers covered with plastic bags, telling the girls that they would be walking in snow. This snow was all around them and was dropping from the sky, and it was freezing. Was Canada at the North Pole? Were they going to meet Santa Claus here?

The taxi pulled up to rue Hamel in the Old City of Quebec. Their tiny apartment was just down the block from Mathieu's. Across from the apartment was a local convent. The priest, Mathieu and the Thieus carried the bags up to the third floor of the eighteenth century building, owned by Mrs. Lau, a Chinese widow from Shanghai. Mrs. Lau, now seventy, lived with her forty-year-old mentally handicapped son, Lee, above the Thieus. The other rooms were rented to university students.

Compared to the bamboo shelter in Pulau Bidong, the apartment was comfortable but a far cry from the spacious house that they had once lived in in Saigon. There were just two narrow rooms, each with a tall narrow window. The first room served as the kitchen, and the second as a communal bedroom for the entire family. The parishioners had furnished the apartment with discarded furniture, but everything was sparkling clean and the cupboards were full of food—exotic food—*créton, fèves au lard,* maple syrup, peanut butter and dozens of packages of *Kraft Dinner*. There was even something called *Minute Rice,* which would prove a challenge for the Thieus' palates. The bathroom was in the outside corridor and was shared with the only other tenant on the floor, a beautiful blond university student from Vancouver, who was teaching English at night and studying French during the day. Her name was Mary and her smile was infectious. Minh Chau, who had never seen blond hair before, was about to pluck yet another lucky hair for her collection, but An, who had learned to read her sister's mind, intervened just in time. Minh Chau scolded her older sister in Vietnamese, "You no fun! Don't you want us to have luck?"

As their exhausted parents slept soundly the first evening, An and Minh Chau heard a knock on the door. They opened the door. It was the blond-haired goddess from next door. She was standing there with towels and soap. In halting French, she asked, "Would you like a bath?" An and Minh Chau had no idea of what the girl said, but followed her dutifully to the bathroom in the corridor. Inside, there was what looked like a big ceramic bucket full of water. In Saigon, houses only had showers, and in Pulau Bidong, the family would go to the beach every morning to wash in the sea. This was the first bathtub the young girls had ever seen. Mary helped the two girls out of their clothes and put them into the bathtub. She then showed them how to use the soap and put some shampoo in their tousled hair. "When you are done, dry yourself with the towels and then knock on my door. I will make you hot chocolate and cookies." Again, An and Minh Chau, not understanding a word of Mary's French, nodded dutifully as they had been taught by their parents.

The girls began to play joyfully in the warm water. With the soap, they made bubbles and challenged each other to hold their breath longest under the water. Minh Chau then kicked the tap accidentally and water began to flow from it. An tried to push and pull the tap to stop the water, but nothing happened. Finally, the two girls decided that there was nothing to be done, thinking that the water would stop on its own. They got out of the bathtub, dried themselves and knocked on Mary's door. With hot chocolate and cookies, they were in heaven. They chatted away at Mary in Vietnamese, Chinese, Malay and in their limited French and English, hoping their new friend would understand. While the linguistic polyphony bore little result, the universal language of smiles did.

Suddenly, they heard the pounding of feet coming down the stairs, followed by loud cursing in Chinese. "Crazy boat people, they are flooding my house." Mary and the girls, and Voang and Han rushed out to find the entire hallway flooded with water and Madame Lau storming out of the bathroom. "You crazy people, you pay for damage or I kick you out!" Mary realizing what had happened followed

Madame Lau down the stairs, taking responsibility for the accident. Minh Chau looked at the water in the hallway and thought, "Outside, they have snow. Inside, there is a river. This is a strange country." An, understanding now what had happened, walked repentantly over to her parents, saying "My fault, not Minh Chau's. I did wrong. I am the older sister."

The Thieus, who had understood the gist of Madame Lau's threat, quietly borrowed a mop and bucket from the neighbour on the second floor and went to work, not only mopping up the water, but cleaning the entire bathroom, hallway and stairs from the main floor to the top floor. It was 3 a.m. when they finished. The next morning, they made some sweet rice cakes for Madame Lau. The peace offering was well received by Madame Lau, who found that the Vietnamese couple could communicate with her in a lingua franca of camp Cantonese and school Mandarin. After serving them tea, she said to them, "You, good people. You flee Communists like me. You can stay long time here, but turn off the water please."

Chapter Fifteen
Mathieu's Song

In the beginning, Mathieu Hibou's involvement with the Thieu family had been almost coincidental. He had really only agreed to help his uncle, Father André Hibou, to settle in two orphaned refugees —Quan and Hue—and he only had agreed to that after his uncle reminded him that Mathieu's grandfather, Stefan Eule, had also come to Canada as a Jewish refugee from Germany in 1935. When Stefan Eule reached Halifax, he quickly anglicized his name to its literal translation, "Owl." When he met the young Catherine Prud'homme from the small town of New Carlisle in the Gaspésie, he changed his name again to the French equivalent *Hibou* and had a baptismal certificate forged to provide him the Catholic credentials needed to marry his devout bride.

Stefan Eule, or now Stéphane Hibou, came from Saarland, which had been administered by the French after World War I, and only returned to Germany after a referendum in 1935. His family had lived in Saarland for centuries and were fluent in French, German and Yiddish. To escape coming under Nazi control, most of the family moved a few kilometres over the border into France, but the young man opted to put as much distance as possible between himself and the Hitler regime.

Stéphane was a trained engineer and had served in the German navy as a young man. He soon found work in the Halifax shipyards, where Catherine worked as a secretary. Their romance blossomed and after marrying in secret in a local Catholic Church where the priest, sympathetic to the tide of refugees coming from Europe, turned a blind eye to Stéphane's rather dubious baptismal certificate. Through Catherine's father, Stéphane was able to land a job as a land surveyor in the local municipal office in New Carlisle.

In 1937, Catherine gave birth to two red-headed boys, André and François, or Frank, as his father preferred to call him. André, fervent in his father's new religion, became a missionary in Africa and eventually the priest for the local French community which made up half of the population in the town. Frank had little time for religion, and was keen on adventure. He enlisted in the American navy at the age of 18 and travelled the world for three years. When he returned, he brought back to New Carlisle the most gorgeous Korean bride, Tae-Ok. Within a year, the couple gave birth to a red-haired boy, Mathieu. A year later, they gave Mathieu a sister, Susanne.

Surprisingly, Mathieu's European features dominated, hiding almost any hint of his Korean ancestry. Only his high cheekbones and slight and graceful frame distinguished him from his cousins. At the age of ten, he lost his father to disease, his mother to a broken heart, and moved with his sister into Aunt Mathilde's home. He loved living at Aunt Mathilde's house, which was full of young female cousins. His favourite was Marie-Christine, who was seven years older, and had decided early on that Mathieu would be her special responsibility.

The love of all of his uncles, aunts and cousins gradually enabled Mathieu to overcome the loss of his parents. Despite their small-town existence, they were cultured people with a wide knowledge of the world, and they nurtured Mathieu's intellectual curiosity and sense of adventure. This was especially true of Uncle André, who would return from his missionary work in Africa to regal the entire family with tales of lions, elephants and exotic tribal practices, but more importantly, he began to discuss with Mathieu the development challenges that the newly independent African countries were facing. From his grandfather Stéphane Hibou, he learned how war and economic insecurity had scarred Europe and given rise to xenophobia.

If ever there was an extended family of perfect harmony, of tolerance and openness to the world, it was here with the Hibous, Prud'hommes and Labontés in New Carlisle. With his French-Canadian, Jewish and Korean ancestry, Mathieu always distanced himself from the rivalries between the town's French and English populations. With his mother, he had always spoken English and only learned a little Korean. With his father and aunts, French was spoken. In school, he studied in French, but played hockey on the town's English team. He always loved to hear his grandfather, Stéphane, speak in his European French with his slight German accent.

When it came time for university, Mathieu followed in his cousin Marie-Christine's footsteps and attended Boston University where he studied agricultural economics. Marie-Christine had already graduated from university with a degree in translation and had married a young American diplomat, Thomas Smith. The couple were now stationed in Saigon. At university, Mathieu observed with dispassion the daily demonstrations urging the end of American involvement in the Vietnam War. He was of two minds—while he abhorred violence, he remembered the stories that his mother had told him as a child of her flight from North Korea to find freedom in the south. After the armistice in 1953, she had worked as a translator for the U.S. military and it was in a PX in a base near Seoul that she had met Mathieu's father who was on shore leave. Mathieu could not help but wonder what would happen to the people in South Vietnam after the U.S. withdrawal.

America was a foreign land for Mathieu. The racial divide in the city between blacks and whites was still strong. The ideological divide between returning veterans from Vietnam and the anti-war protesters was even stronger. Back in Quebec, a new government had been elected to power, headed by René Lévesque, who had lived in New Carlisle as a boy. After his first year in Boston, Mathieu decided to transfer to Laval University in Quebec City to behind America's foreignness and to experience firsthand the political winds back home.

When the Thieus arrived in 1979, the French-speaking province of Quebec was in the throes of a major political showdown. The Parti Québécois government had decided to put the issue of Quebec's independence to the voters in a referendum. As the campaign progressed in 1980, tolerance of English being spoken diminished. Mathieu who effortlessly switched back and forth between English and French was chastised on several occasions by strangers, who pointedly reminded him that French was the language of Quebec. When he replied with a clear Gaspésie accent, his critics quickly backed off. Mathieu had little sympathy for the narrow nationalism in vogue in Quebec, but nonetheless saw himself first and foremost as a Québécois.

The Thieus' neighbour, Mary, would often take Minh Chau and An for walks. Mary was a true francophile, but not the most gifted student of languages. She persevered in her French studies for non-francophones at Laval, but she could not lose her strong English accent. When the Thieu children soon surpassed Mary in the use of French, they asked her to teach them English during their many walks. Minh Chau, a natural mimic, quickly converted to Mary's west coast accent. An's English, however, remained clearly marked by the soft Malaysian pronunciation of their teacher Abdul Hakim.

One day at a local park, An and Minh Chau asked Mary in English about Pierre Trudeau, the Canadian prime minister and chief adversary of René Lévesque. Trudeau was the country's strongest defender of bilingualism, federalism and a new multicultural identity for his country. While wildly popular in English Canada, young French-speaking Quebeckers had come to despise his efforts to crush their dream of independence. The conversation caught the attention of a disheveled man in his late twenties, drinking beer on a nearby park bench. When Mary explained Trudeau's vision of everyone in Canada eventually speaking both languages, this was too much for the man now on his eighth bottle of beer. He staggered over to Mary and the children and shouted, "Maudite Anglaise, sales immigrantes, do you think that you can take our country from us and make us speak English like you. This is Quebec, you must speak French here!"

Startled by the man's violent reaction, Mary pulled the two girls close to her. Tears poured down the cheeks of the two girls, and Minh Chau began to convulse, like she used to at night in Pulau Bidong. Mary, frightened at the feeling of the tiny body shaking violently against hers, shouted at the man in French, "Go away, go away!"

Cycling along a parallel street on his return from the university, Mathieu recognized Mary's frightened voice. He sped to the park, dismounted and ran up to the man, who by now was more baffled than angry. Mathieu recognized the man as one of Father Pierre's parishioners who had recently lost his job as a waiter over a misunderstanding with an English-speaking customer. The case had caused quite a stir among the parishioners, who thought that the restaurant owner should have sided with his employee.

"Monsieur Boivin, please come and have a seat over here," Mathieu gently said as he guided the intoxicated man back to his park bench.

"I am sorry. I am so sorry. I did not mean to frighten the children. It has been so hard. Please tell them that I am sorry."

Mathieu returned to Mary and the children. An had regained her composure. Mary was desperately trying to stop Minh Chau's convulsions. Mathieu took the young child in his arms, and began to sing the soft lyrics of *There is the Good Wind, the Pretty Wind*, the only song he really knew.

Voilà le bon vent, voilà le joli vent,

Voilà le bon vent m'ami m'appelle.
Voilà le bon vent, voilà le joli vent,
Voilà le bon vent, m'ami m'attend.

Derrière chez nous, y a-t-un étang
Derrière chez nous, y a-t-un étang
Trois beaux canards s'en vont baignant.

Trois beaux canards s'en vont baignant
Trois beaux canards s'en vont baignant
Le fils du roi s'en va chassant.

Le fils du roi s'en va chassant
Le fils du roi s'en va chassant
Avec son grand fusil d'argent.

Avec son grand fusil d'argent
Avec son grand fusil d'argent
Visa le noir, tua le blanc.

Visa le noir, tua le blanc
Visa le noir, tua le blanc
O fils du roi, tu es méchant.

O fils du roi, tu es méchant
O fils du roi, tu es méchant
D'avoir tué mon canard blanc.

An and Mary joined in. Even the man on the park bench began to sing. Minh Chau raised her head from Mathieu's shoulder, stroked his crimson beard and with her jade eyes inches away from the turquoise of his, said, "I want Quan. Where is Quan? He must protect me from bad men. My father told me so."

"Minh Chau, until Quan comes, I will protect you. Will you sing with us a little?" asked Mathieu.

Her body stilled as she took a breath. From her lungs, came the sweet sound of her young voice. Soon she was leading everyone in the refrain. "Voilà le bon vent, voilà le joli vent, voilà le bon vent m'ami

Soldier, Lily, Peace and Pearls   *73*

m'appelle."

Jean Boivin, the unemployed man on the bench, came over and apologized again for his behaviour, and shook Mathieu's and Mary's
hands. An tugged his jacket, and said, "Monsieur, please sing with
us."

Minh Chau shouted, "Yes, sing, sing."

Jean, in a deep voice of tremendous cadence and surprising beauty,
joined in.

A crowd grew around them, curious at the musical spectacle. A couple of American tourists even tossed a coin of their feet. Then Mathieu, Mary, An and Minh Chau marched off, waving to Jean who
stood, bellowing out the song with the beer bottle still in his hand.

Chapter Sixteen
No Visa for Canada

Quan was released from the police station just two weeks after the Thieus left. He and Hue waited patiently for a visa for Canada, but Denis Prud'homme's wife fell ill and was repatriated to Canada. When the doctors diagnosed her with cancer, Denis asked headquarters to transfer him back to Canada. He took the time to brief his successor, John Gibson, on the rather complicated case of Quan and Hue.

Headquarters were still dragging their heels on the idea of bringing a killer to Canada. Gibson was a lazy and unsavory type. He had just served for two years in Hong Kong where he had put aside a tidy sum from bribes paid by rich Chinese desperate to immigrate to Canada and escape the return of Hong Kong to the mainland in 1997. The Vietnamese boat people would not be the cash cow that he had known in Hong Kong. Besides, why waste time on trips to Pulau Bidong when all he had to do was wait in Kuala Lumpur for the United Nations High Commission for Refugees to recommend a monthly list of eligible refugees for resettlement in Canada. An additional irritant was that most of these Vietnamese spoke only French, a language that he barely understood, despite his own government's ongoing efforts to promote bilingualism. The file for Quan and Hue Phoc would be assigned to drawer thirteen, at least until his supervisor noticed that he had not yet visited Pulau Bidong.

Marie-Christine took it upon herself to push her cousin's successor for some action on the children's file. First, she invited him to a supper hosted by her husband for other diplomats. Gibson was fairly low on the Canadian Embassy's totem pole and did not have much in common with the counterparts of the Head of the Political Section at the American Embassy, so Marie-Christine kept him company for most of the dinner. Whether it was the four glasses of wine or the second glass of brandy, Gibson soon found himself inextricably attracted to the slightly older married woman.

After that dinner, he made up numerous excuses to meet her to discuss the children's file. Marie-Christine was only too happy to meet Gibson in the various cafés around town, especially as her husband's own efforts to help the children get asylum in the USA had been met with a resounding no from headquarters. Besides, in Quebec City with her cousin Mathieu's help, the children would be safe. Gibson invited Marie-Christine to come with him to Pulau Bidong. She gladly accepted, looking forward to seeing Quan and Hue again.

When they arrived in Pulau Bidong and met the children, Gibson's fascination with Marie-Christine abruptly ended. While an attractive woman, Marie-Christine held no candle to Hue, who had just turned seventeen. Marie-Christine and Hue were both oblivious to the attention that Gibson was paying to the young girl, but Quan immediately became suspicious. An Australian immigration officer was known to request sexual favours from young women in return for visas, why would this Canadian be any different?

It did not take long for Quan's fears to be well founded. When Gibson returned to Pulau Bidong after two weeks, this time without Marie-Christine, he requested an interview alone with Hue. Quan waited nearby within earshot. When Gibson made his move and Hue rebuffed him, Quan was on top of the immigration officer like a jaguar on his prey. When he was finished, Gibson was alive, but barely. Realizing that this act closed definitively any chance of joining the Thieus in Quebec City and would not go unpunished by the camp authorities, Quan calmly walked over to the police station, greeted the policeman on duty, whom he had come to know very well, walked into the sergeant's room and stole his spare uniform. In this disguise, he and Hue boarded the next ferry for the mainland.

Chapter Seventeen
Goodbye Saigon

Mathieu Hibou soon found himself to be the tour guide and social worker for the Thieu family in Quebec. The parishioners were generous in their financial support for the Thieus, and Father Pierre had arranged for a scholarship to the Ursulines Convent School for the two girls, once their French was good enough. However, on a day-to-day basis, neither the parishioners nor the priest had time to help the Thieus wade through the formidable challenge of establishing oneself in Canada. Mary was willing enough to pitch in, but it was the heyday of Québécois nationalism in Quebec City, and her halting French was more of a hindrance than a help. Mathieu proved to be a godsend though.

After much effort and with considerable help from Mathieu, Dr. Han Thieu convinced the Ministry of Health officials that she should be given the chance to qualify to practice medicine in Canada. They gave her an extensive list of books to prepare herself for certification. Mathieu took out as many books as he could on his university library card and accompanied Han to a used book store to look for the others. When the cashier ran up the exhorbitant amount of two hundred dollars, Han froze. She only had sixty dollars in the entire world. Without hesitation, Mathieu produced a cheque to pay for the difference, and then unbeknownst to Han, spent the next month eating only macaroni while waiting for his next bursary cheque to come in.

While Han pored through the books, Voang, who had given up on any hope of resuming dentistry with his crippled hand, worked cleaning the local church. He did it with such zeal that Mr. Dupuis, a parishioner who owned a small supermarket, asked him if he would also clean his supermarket once a week. Before long, Voang was hired on to run the cash register on the day off of the regular cashier, Marie. When Marie got pregnant, Voang found himself with a full-time job. One day, Voang asked the owner, Mr. Dupuis, if his daughters could stay with him in the supermarket when they finished school. Soon Minh Chau and An were practically running the supermarket, showing customers where to find pork and beans, watering the produce and sweeping the floor.

For a year, Quan and Hue regularly wrote to the Thieus, enchanting them with accounts of the everyday life of the camp's residents—family squabbles, new schemes to make money, spring love among the young people, the success of Jing Zi's potions, and the new and imaginative ways of Abdul Hakim to motivate his students. They also wrote of the illness of Denis Prud'homme's wife and the visits of Marie-Christine. In their last letter, they wrote of an impending visit by the new immigration officer and of the reassurance from Marie-Christine that they would soon be accepted in Canada. The Thieus were overjoyed. When they read the last letter to their children, Minh Chau and An danced around their tiny apartment, singing "Soldier, lily, peace and pearls, all together in one world."

The next week, there was no news from Quan and Hue. After the second week with no news, Denis Prud'homme arrived with his cousin Mathieu at their apartment. They explained to the Thieus that Quan had attacked Denis' replacement, John Gibson, in Pulau Bidong. Both Hue and Quan had then vanished from the island. According to Gibson, Quan had gone beserk when he had explained to the boy that could take a little longer to process the application because a psychiatrist's examination might be necessary to assess the impact on the boy of the killing of Dahan. The Thieus were in a state of shock, and chose not to tell their daughters.

It took two years for Han to qualify for her medical certification. Shortly before she did, Mr. Dupuis, who was now seventy, asked Voang if he would like to buy the supermarket. Voang's eyes lit up. As a dentist and army officer in Vietnam, he had been respected. Even the Communists had respected his professional status. It had been hard for him to sweep the floors of churches and stores to survive in Canada. Here was a chance to regain social status as an independent businessman, but where would he get the money to buy the store?

Voang could not sleep that night. The only close friend that they had in Quebec was Mathieu, but he was just a university student from a middle-class family in the Gaspésie. Marie-Christine was married to a well-off diplomat, but she had little money of her own. Would Thomas Smith, her husband, accept to help them? They had already asked so much of Marie-Christine and him, and then the brutal beating by Quan of John Gibson had embarrassed both Marie-Christine and her cousin Denis Prud'homme. It was Voang and his wife who had insisted that Quan be helped. He thought of the boy, still only fifteen, with so much blood on his hands. No one had witnessed the beating of John Gibson. They only had the immigration officer's version of the event. Why would Quan have beaten John Gibson so badly? It did not make sense.

Voang decided that he could not ask anyone for the money. The next day, he told Mr. Dupuis that he would not be able to take up his offer because of the lack of financing. Mr. Dupuis took Voang aside, and explained that he would act as a guarantor if Voang wanted to borrow the money from the *Caisse Populaire Desjardins*, the local credit union. Voang did not understand. Why would a bank give him such a large loan without collateral. Dupuis asked when Dr. Thieu would be able to start working as a doctor. Voang explained that she should have her licence in six months if all went well.

"That's fine," answered Dupuis, "I can wait until your wife starts to work. She will make a good salary as a doctor and I know the manager of the Caisse Populaire very well. He will be happy to give you a loan, but first, we need to have you open an account at the Caisse Populaire."

That afternoon, Voang accompanied his friend Dupuis to the Caisse Populaire and proudly deposited the three hundred dollars he had saved up, obtaining his first deposit book.

Voang and Han discussed the plans to purchase the store with An and Minh Chau. They would call it *Supermarché Thieu et famille.* An was already twelve and keen on working in the store. So was Minh Chau, but Han put down her foot. "Minh Chau, you are too young. Wait two years, and then you can join An. For now, you must study."

"Okay, mama, but I have one condition," said the nine-year-old girl.

"Yes, what is that?"

"Mama, we have lived in Canada for three years. Now I speak French better than Vietnamese. I know that we will not return to Vietnam. Quan and Hue will never join us in Canada. I know that now. I am a big girl, and I want to be raised as a Canadian. I want to marry a man from this country when I grow up. Will you let me be Canadian and not Vietnamese?"

Han looked stunned at the clarity of her daughter's request. For one year in Malaysia and three years in Canada, she had never thought of herself as being anything but Vietnamese living abroad. She had imagined that her daughters would always share that point of view. And now Minh Chau, her youngest child, was turning her world upside down. She looked into the wide jade-brown eyes of her daughter, and saw in them images of Chi Boa Prison, the escape by sea, Cong's outstretched hand, the camp and the snowy arrival in Quebec. She took a deep breath, and answered, "yes."

Han then turned to An, "And you, do you wish to be raised as a Canadian, not Vietnamese?" An heard the remorse in her mother's voice, and it changed the answer that she wanted to give. Her mother had everything in Saigon, and now had to start over in a tiny apartment. The sacrifices that both she and her father had made for her and Minh Chau weighed heavily on her decision. "Mama, I will love this country, but Vietnam is in my heart. I want you to raise me to be Vietnamese like you and papa." She then took Minh Chau's hand in hers. "Minh Chau, don't worry you can be the Canadian rock star in our family, and I will be a Vietnamese star."

The two sisters spent the rest of the evening singing along to cassettes of Céline Dion and Vietnam's superstar Khanh Ly. Voang and Han watched their children sway their bodies to the beat of the music, and engraved in their memories that evening their daughters' mellifluous voices as they sang "Goodbye Saigon."

Chapter Eighteen
Bangkok

While the Thieus seemed on the point of starting a charmed life in Canada, Quan's and Hue's paths took a very different turn. With the stolen police uniform traveling through Malaysia had been no problem, and Quan had amassed a considerable amount of money through his medicinal trading business. Hue was proud of her young brother, and felt safe in his presence. They decided that their best chances would be in Thailand. In Pulau Bidong, they had heard of the extensive human smuggling operations run out of Bangkok. If they could obtain new identities, maybe they could still find a way to Canada and reunite with the Thieus. Both desperately wanted to see their adopted family again. Quan caressed the red beard hair given to him by Minh Chau, and wished upon it that he would see his little sister once again.

For a price, the border with Thailand was as porous as could be. It took Quan only half an hour to locate an official who was ready to look the other way for fifty Malaysian dollars while he and his sister quietly walked across the border.

In Bangkok, Quan sought out the local Chinese medicine market. There he exhibited his store of Jing Zi's remedies. These remedies surpassed anything that the local medicine makers could offer, and there was clearly a profit to be made. As Quan was negotiating with one shopkeeper, a tall, muscular Chinese man entered the shop with two beautiful Thai girls. The shopkeeper, who knew the man well, brought out local aphrodisiacs for re-sale to the girls' clients. Quan sneered in Cantonese, "I have much better than that."

Chiang looked at the boy, whose broad shoulders and height did not match the young age of his round face. "What do you know of such things, boy?"

The shopkeeper, who knew of the potency of Jing Zi's medicines and had long heard of the master when he was still practicing in Vientiane, interjected, fearful of losing one of his best customers. "Boy knows nothing. He just boat people. You buy from me. I sell you strong medicine."

Quan folded up the medicine in a cotton scarf. "As you like. You can let your customers buy directly from me."

The two Thai beauties smiled at the cocky boy who was almost their age. Quan blushed. He was used to being admired by young girls in the camp, but these girls were professionals. One whispered in Quan's ear, "I have very rich, fat customer. He will pay me big money if he can stay hard with me all night. Can your medicine do that?"

"Yes," replied Quan. "Two hundred baht."

"Two hundred baht! That is a lot of money. I give you one hundred, and if you want, well … ," replied the girl, stroking Quan's arm.

Chiang looked amused at Quan's uneasiness. "Are you really boat people?" asked the Triad gang leader this time in the rough Teochew dialect of the Chinese community in Bangkok. "Where are you from?"

"Phnom Penh, but my father was Vietnamese and my mother Chinese."

"And where are these medicines from?"

"They were made by the master Jing Zi in Pulau Bidong camp in Malaysia."

Chiang took an immediate interest. He had been in the *business* long enough to know the name of Jing Zi.

"How do I know that you are not lying?"

"I will give you one dose of this potion, made of rhinoceros horn, for this girl's fat rich client. Then you can ask him what he thinks."

As Chiang and Quan arranged a time and a place to meet the next day, Hue entered the shop and said in Vietnamese. "Quan, I found a room for us!"

Chiang was flabbergasted. He had many beautiful girls working for him, but none compared to Hue. She immediately reminded him of his Vietnamese mother from Haiphong, who had died just two years earlier.

"This girl work for you?" asked Chiang in a voice low enough so Hue could not hear him.

Quan tightened his hand around the knife in his pocket, pondering whether to gut this big Chinese asshole. He breathed deeply, and answered. "No, she is my sister, but if you think that again, no potion will help you ever be with a woman again."

Chiang immediately liked the boy's spirit. He was drawn even more to his sister. Chiang had not always been the brutish type common to the Chinese Triads. His mother Kieu had been a language teacher in Haiphong, fluent in French, Vietnamese and Mandarin. She had married a French officer who was going to take her from Vietnam to France after the fall of Dien Bien Phu in 1954. By the time their ship reached Bangkok, the officer had succumbed to yellow fever. His mother was unceremoniously put ashore in a land where she knew no one, and her money and belongings were confiscated by the ship's captain.

She found work in a laundry and after a year agreed to marry the owner's son, Chiang's father. The son was a lazy man, who soon found more profit in occasionally selling heroin to sailors than in doing laundry. After his parents died, the laundry became a front for the local drug trade. The middle-class customers were soon replaced by the thuggish henchmen of the Chinese-Thai underworld. Still, at home, Kieu taught her son the manners of high society and tutored him in the literature of Vietnam, China and France. In business, Chiang followed in his father's footsteps, but his heart secretly glowed in the elegance of his mother's upbringing.

Chiang turned to Hue, and asked in French, "Do you understand me?"

She replied softly in the beautiful French that Han had taught her in the camp. "Oui, monsieur."

"I like your brother. You are new to Bangkok. I would like to help you. What is your name?"

"D'accord, monsieur. My name is Hue Phoc and my brother is called Quan."

"Quan, hmm," said Chiang approvingly. "That is a good name for him. He has the temperament of a warrior."

After Chiang and his girls left, Quan pressed Hue to know what the Chinese gangster had said in French.

"Do not worry, Quan," said Hue. "He may be a tough man on the exterior, but I feel that we can trust him. He has a cultivated soul."

Quan shook his head. This cannot be. Surely his sister cannot be attracted to a gangster. Still, she was right. They were new in Bangkok and having a little help from someone well connected would not be a bad thing. Besides, he wanted to sell Jing Zi's medicine at the highest price possible, and he would soon be fifteen, and would not mind seeing the two Thai girls again. This Chiang could possibly make both happen.

Quan's business with Chiang turned a healthy profit, and Quan came to reconcile with the fact that Hue appreciated Chiang's attention. When the first potion did its trick, Mali the prettier of the two Thai girls, stuffed two hundred baht in Quan's shirt pocket, kissed his cheek and whispered in Thai, "Customer gave me big, big tip. Thank you." Quan did not understand what the girl had told him, but smiled back at her. It was not long before Mali became Quan's sleeping Thai dictionary.

When Quan's stock of Jing Zi's medicine ran out, Chiang offered to take him into the Triad. Chiang was deputy head of his Triad. His boss, who lived in Hong Kong, wanted to expand into direct heroin smuggling to Europe. They had tried to use Thai girls as mules, but the European authorities soon caught on, and began giving body searches to every young Thai woman. Ten of thousands of European tourists visited Bangkok every month. There were always a few who ran short on funds while on vacation. The trick was approaching them. Even the most adventurous western girls balked when the heavily tattooed triad members approached them. Except for Chiang, none of his crew spoke foreign languages.

Quan was the perfect candidate—multilingual, too young to look threatening, but old enough for a quick romp in the sack, and clean-cut enough to avoid garnering suspicion from the Thai police. Chiang bought a tricycle taxi for Quan's cover. What better way to make contact with the young girls. The plan was carefully laid out and executed. Quan would start as a taxi driver / tour guide. Then he would give his young customers small gifts of local marijuana, and for the wilder customers a pipe of opium. Inevitably, one girl in five would fall for Quan's boyish charm and muscular body. One day, a thief would steal the girl's handbag or ransack her hotel room, stealing her cash and return air ticket.

Quan would come to the rescue by offering a little money to tide the girl over, but not enough to buy return airfare. When the girl's defences collapsed, Quan would propose a one-time smuggling of some local marijuana. Instead, the bags would contain top grade heroin. Some of the girls made it through, others did not, but then heroin was cheap in Thailand and the Triad could afford to lose a few shipments. Quan's heart grew cold when he thought of the young girls. The girls did not matter—at most, they would spend a few months in a first-class European prison.

In exchange for Quan's services, Chiang had arranged for new identities for Quan and Hue, and eventually even Thai passports. Quan, first with Jing Zi's medicines and then with the heroin smuggling, made more than enough to support his sister and pay for her studies at the English-language St. John's University, where she enrolled in a computer science program. Quan's own education remained limited to what Abdul Hakim had taught him in Pulau Bidong and the smattering of European languages that he picked up through pillow talk with young tourist girls.

Mali, his talking Thai dictionary, had long since stopped charging him for her services, and would wait impatiently for his weekly visits. The bedroom encounters slowly transformed themselves also into long walks in Sanrarom park. She was only one year older than Quan, but had been in the business of servicing men for six years, after her impoverished farming family sold her to pay off debts. Mali told Quan of how the Triad dealt with abusive customers. When one hurt a girl, he was visited by a Triad member, who left him in various states of injury according to the customer's offense. There were just two rules. The customer was always left alive—killing a customer was bad for business, and Thai policemen and high-ranking officials had a free pass, provided that they did not disfigure the girls.

Quan one day volunteered to Chiang to mete out punishment to offending johns. Chiang was baffled. Why would the boy get his hands dirty when he was already making a small fortune with drug smuggling? Quan insisted. When Kanya, one of Mali's best friends had her arm broken for refusing to service a customer with a sore on his penis, Quan was dispatched to the customer's home. It was a large house in an affluent neighbourhood of Bangkok. Quan climbed the garden wall and snuck into the house through an open window on the second floor. He found the man smoking opium in a drawing room furnished with colonial teak furniture. The man reached into a drawer for a revolver. The kick-boxing that Quan had learned on the collective farm proved of use. With two quick kicks, he broke ten ribs in the man's body. As Quan was about to break his right arm, the man shouted, "Wait, I am a policeman!" With his free hand, he threw his police ID on the floor. Quan, hesitated, remembering rule number two. Then he crashed his foot on man's outstretched arm, which snapped like dry wood.

When Chiang learned what had happened. He chastised Quan. "Now we will have to pay a big bribe to make this go away."

"Or I can go back and finish the job," said Quan defiantly.

"Quan, there is rule number three. When you work for me, you do what I say, or I will send you and your sister back to Pulau Bidong."

Quan knew Chiang well enough to hear the hollowness of his threat. Besides, Chiang's affection for Hue was an open secret. Quan had made Chiang promise though that he would never meet Hue alone. Hue had more than once tried to ditch her brother on group outings to be alone with Chiang, but Chiang kept his promise.

Although the bribe set Quan back a bit, his star among Chiang's girls rose considerably. The young Thai girls would bring him small gifts of flowers and food. Whenever a police official got rough with them, they only had to mention Quan's name to stop unwanted behaviour. Quan also convinced Chiang to provide condoms to all the customers and girls, even if it did harm sales a little. When new girls from the north arrived, the older girls would bring them to Quan to ask him to break them in. Quan had slept with most of the girls, they all knew his gentleness and wanted the new girls to know it too. But Quan refused to comply, as most of the young girls were barely thirteen. Some were as young as eleven. Quan raised this with Chiang. Why were the girls so young? Chiang explained that the girls had three years to pay off their parents' debts. After that they had only about five years to earn enough to find a man to marry in their village or in Bangkok, before they would be considered too old for marriage. It was a matter of social economics, according to Chiang, who had attended two years of university before taking over as the number two in the Triad. Besides, the brothel owner in Hong Kong, Tao Tsao, personally visited the north every six months to buy the new girls, and Tao liked young girls, often tasting the merchandise before sending it onto Bangkok.

Occasionally, Thai pirates would bring young Vietnamese girls to Chiang. He drew the line at buying them for the brothel. Instead, he would approach the local Vietnamese community leaders for donations to ransom the girls, tacking on his own commission whenever he could. It was not good for business though—and some of the girls still ended up working for Chiang's competitors to survive, but at least Chiang's memory of his own mother remained honoured.

Hue's studies at university progressed well, and she got a job at an international accounting firm to help pay for them. Quan was making more than enough money for the both of them, but she wanted to be independent of her brother, and definitely wanted to see more of Chiang. Hue's love for Chiang grew. She knew of Chiang's business ventures, and pondered if she could convince him to leave his criminal life behind him. She also knew many of the girls he managed, and learned from them that he treated them fairly. After paying off the debt of their parents, all were free to leave, but most stayed. Unlike Quan who slept indiscriminately with all the older girls, Chiang had become celibate shortly after he met Hue. It was not something that he spoke about, but Hue learned from the girls that many were complaining that Chiang had stopped visiting them.

Whenever they could, they would converse in French. Chiang would send her the latest French novels and videos, and paid for her course at Alliance française. Through a French diplomat, who was a regular customer, he arranged for Hue and him to be invited to the receptions at the French Embassy. True to his word to Quan, Chiang would never speak directly to Hue at these receptions, contenting himself to watching Hue attract around her most of the younger diplomats and Thai officials. Hue always knew that Chiang was watching her, and she liked that very much.

Chiang knew that with Quan in Bangkok, he would not have any chance to make his love known to Hue. He had come to believe that she too loved him. One day, he dreamed up a scheme to get Quan out of the picture for a few weeks. The European smuggling operations were going well, but the bigger market was in North America.

The Triad had made a number of contacts in L.A. and New York, but direct smuggling into the United States was almost impossible. Not only were the airports teeming with D.E.A. agents and drug-sniffing dogs, but rival drug smugglers—Colombians, Cubans and Mexicans —were keeping a close eye on the expansion of Chinese Triads into North America, and worked hand-in-hand with the D.E.A. to point the finger at possible mules coming out of Bangkok. Canada was the answer. Chiang asked Quan to undertake a mission to Montreal to assess the security controls at the airport and set up onward distribution into the United States. With the increasing number of naive French-Canadian girls taking direct flights from Montreal to Thailand and the growing immigration of Triad members to Canada, the prospects of successfully penetrating the lucrative North American market were promising.

Quan thought over the proposal. He was now twenty, and he had long since given up on the prospects of immigrating to Canada. When they had left Pulau Bidong, he and Hue had agreed that they would never contact the Thieus in order to protect them from the repercussions of the beating of John Gibson. Quan was convinced that the Canadian police read every letter going from Southeast Asia to Canada. Still, why not? He had a new Thai identity and five years had passed since the beating. Even if he could not see Voang, Han, Minh Chau and An on the trip, it would do him good to see the country.

"Here is the plan," said Chiang. "First, you will fly to Sydney with the passport of a Thai customs official. One passed away recently and his boss is kindly lending us his documents. It will only take a couple of days to modify the passport with your picture. Your Thai is now perfect so no one will suspect you. In Sydney, you will change your identity to Paul Nguyen, a Vietnamese-Australian, who, like you, lived in Pulau Bidong before being resettled in Australia. You will stay there for three days with Cindy. You remember Cindy, don't you?"

Quan smiled. How could he forget Cindy, the tall blonde Australian who had been more than willing to be his lover and his mule. She had come back to Thailand twice more to do drug runs, and when the Triad deemed that another run was too risky, she came back anyway to see Quan. Her sexual appetite was enormous, and both enjoyed this last visit beyond imagination.

"From Sydney, you will fly to Vancouver and then Montreal. You need to check out security in both airports. In Vancouver, you will meet Tao Tsao, the head of our Triad, who is going to bankroll the North America operation. In Montreal, we will have a contact meet you. We have a man there who is willing to do anything to get his brother out of Pulau Bidong."

"We can get people out of Pulau Bidong?" asked Quan, surprised at the reach of the Triad.

"Of course," answered Chiang.

"Then I am willing to pay to bring Jing Zi here to Bangkok."

"We already thought of that when you ran out of the Chinese medicine. Jing Zi died four years ago."

Quan paused for a moment. It was Jing Zi who had really saved Minh Chau, not he. And the sale of his potions had allowed him and Hue to start a new life in Bangkok. But not once had he tried to help Jing Zi leave Pulau Bidong. The image of Jing Zi's chiseled features raced through his mind. The soft Szechuan Mandarin that Jing Zi spoke so beautifully echoed through his ears, as the old master taught the young boy how to mix the ground powders from roots and dried leaves into the sought-after potions. "Quan, this one big power. It makes little man look like tiger, and madame smile a lot."

Although aphrodisiacs were the mainstay of Jing Zi's income, he also made other traditional medicine that cured illnesses that western science was only just discovering. These medicines, like the potion that he had used to revive Minh Chau, were secrets that he had certainly taken to his grave. Quan remembered that Han Thieu had once tried to convince a visiting World Health Organization official to meet with Jing Zi. The official just scoffed, "Dr. Thieu, the WHO is not interested in hocus pocus."

When Quan's trip was completely planned, Mali came to help him pack his bags. "Quan, you will not forget me if you don't come back, will you?"

"What are you saying? Of course, I am coming back."

"But if you don't, you will not forget me, will you?!"

"Of course not."

"Quan, I have earned enough money now, and can start my own bar. I am not going back north like the other girls. When you come back, can we talk? You are a good man. Maybe, we can …"

Before Mali could finish her sentence, Quan came over to her and kissed her gently on the lips. She touched his young skin as tenderly as the first time she had done so when he was barely a man. In the five intervening years, they had made love a thousand times. She had taken his money at the beginning, but for her, it had never really been about business. In his arms, she had abandoned herself to dreams of being free from the shame of prostitution. She had never objected to his many other lovers, and had in fact encouraged the other girls to sleep with him. He had never looked down on her when he saw her with one of her customers. His happiness was her happiness. His acceptance of her filled her with reassurance that blunted the pain of the life that her parents had sold her into.

Sometimes, after long love sessions, she would watch him sleep. Quan never slept quietly. He was rigid as if to strike out at any minute at an aggressor. In his sleep, he would whisper names—Minh Chau, An, Abdul Hakim, father, mother. Once he screamed in the night, "Dahan, go away. I killed you. Leave us alone!" She then enveloped his shaking body in her flesh and woke him with the dampness of her excited womanhood.

As Mali lost herself in the pleasures of her mind, Quan ran his hands down her back. The soft curves of her spine gave way to the hardness of her buttocks. He slipped off the ankle-length skirt of her Thai *Ruean Ton* and unbuttoned her blouse. He ran his hand across her firm nipples down the flatness of her stomach toward the dampness between her legs, and heard her softly sigh in his ear. She shivered at his touch, and he felt his manhood grow stiff and strong. Eagerly, she sought his lips, thrusting her tongue deep into his mouth, tasting him like she had never done before. He raised her light body with his muscular arms and penetrated her with gentle but deep thrusts. She gasped, opening her eyes wide to gaze into his. All the shame that she had felt in life vanished like the dust on Bangkok's streets in a monsoon. Mali knew that she loved Quan and knew that she would never see him again.

Chapter Nineteen
Rwanda Calling

With the Thieu family comfortably set up with projects of prosperity—Voang proudly running the supermarket and Han beginning practice in a matter of weeks at a local family medicine clinic —Mathieu felt that he had successfully acquitted himself of his promise to Marie-Christine. It was at that point that another human being entered his life. He met her through Mary who was dating a Rwandan medical student, Antoine Bikindi. Antoine's cousin, Denise Hakizimana, was studying translation in Montreal, and she was the most beautiful being that Mathieu had ever met. While the affair between Mary and Antoine lasted only through the summer, Mathieu's and Denise's love grew ever deeper in the two years that they dated. Almost every weekend, he would drive down to Montreal. Minh Chau and An complained of course that he had abandoned them. Finally, he brought Denise up to meet the Thieus. At first, Minh Chau, now twelve, revolted. How could Mathieu love this African woman? She was at least three inches taller than him and was built like an Olympic athlete.

Minh Chau confided in her sister An, "We will never find a Canadian man like Mathieu. We are too small and skinny. We have to stop eating all this rice."

An, who was now fifteen and was secretly dating a young boy from the neighbourhood, laughed back, "Don't worry Minh Chau, the Canadian boys like skinny girls too."

If kindness had a name, it would have been Denise Hakizimana. It took only minutes for the entire Thieu family to take to her. Her soft melodious voice enraptured her audience in vivid images of Africa as she spoke of Rwanda, her country. Voang and Han were saddened that they themselves could not bear to speak about Vietnam in the same way. The day they left on that Chinese junk, pride in their homeland had vanished behind a wall of pain.

Minh Chau gazed at Mathieu Hibou and thought about Quan. It had been six years since she had seen him. Was he alive or dead? Soon she would become a woman. If she met Quan again, would he see her as a woman and not just a silly child? Would Quan lose himself in looking at her like Mathieu was now doing with Denise? Minh Chau had known many forms of kindness in her short life, from Huynh and Dao to Aunt Lan, from Quan to Mathieu. It seemed that someone was always saving her. She had a loving family, many friends at school and kind teachers, but Minh Chau felt deeply alone. Was this the punishment for what she had done at sea? Punishment for her betrayal of Cong? Would Jesus forgive her sin, as the nuns in the school taught her? Would she find love?

Mathieu's words woke Minh Chau from her trance. "Mr. and Mrs. Thieu, my little sisters An and Minh Chau, Denise and I have news to share with you. I have found a job in Rwanda. As soon as I hand in my thesis, we will get married and move there."

Suddenly, there was ecstasy in the Thieus' tiny apartment, as Minh Chau and An beamed at each other and broke into a traditional Vietnamese love song - Mai Yeu Nguoi Thoi (Love well forever!).

Been a long time they say
That you do not truly love
Silently each day is a lie ...
Love him
Then you go away
His own helplessness to stay

The young children who were now blossoming into beautiful teenagers took Denise's hands and danced with her around the tiny kitchen. Mathieu contentedly looked at the dancers, thinking of the pleasant years that he had spent with his *Vietnamese family* in Quebec City. Suddenly, Madame Lau appeared at the door. Immediately, Han rose to apologize for the noise, but Madame Lau signaled her to sit and began to clap her hands to encourage the singing dancers to continue.

Within two months, Mathieu Hibou and his beautiful bride Denise Hakizimana were on the long flight to Nairobi and then onward to Kigali. They had celebrated the wedding in Uncle André's church in New Carlisle. The entire Hibou-Prud'homme-Labonté clan had turned out for the wedding, including Marie-Christine and her husband, Thomas Smith. The Thieu family had come down from Quebec City, and An and Minh Chau danced with several of Mathieu's young red-haired cousins. Minh Chau asked each for a strand of hair and then twisted them with strands of hair from each of her own family members into a thin wrist band. She then presented the thin red-black bracelet to Denise. "Wear this and you will be protected by the love of all of us." Denise picked up Minh Chau in her arms as if she was a feather, and kissed the surprised girl on both cheeks. "I will wear it until the day I die."

Mathieu first worked for a Canadian NGO, the Canadian University Services Overseas (CUSO). The pay was not much, but the NGO gave Mathieu a free rein to introduce crop diversification and land use planning to the rural peasants associations that benefited from CUSO funding. At first, the peasants were sceptical that his young Canadian knew what he was talking about. All they really wanted was subsidized seed and farm utensils. They had never planted fava beans and carrots. Why would they? No one but foreigners ate them. It was only when Denise turned up to translate into Kinyarwanda and the manager of the Mille Collines Hotel offered to buy all the carrots and fava beans they could grow that the peasants took notice. After all, if this foreigner could have a wife as beautiful and charming as this Rwandan woman, and at the same time pre-sell their entire harvest at top dollar, he could not be all bad.

Mathieu's success at convincing farmers to try new things soon caught the attention of the United Nations Development Program (UNDP), which offered him a job as a consultant to the Ministry of Agriculture. Soon fava beans and carrots were flooding the markets of Kigali, and Mathieu moved on to showing peasant cooperatives how to build ponds and put in Mark IV India pumps. As the rural population migrated to the city, Mathieu convinced the city authorities to put aside land in each bidonville for collective vegetable gardens. If Rwanda was going to remain poor, Mathieu was determined that its agricultural production would increase and the urban poor would have enough to eat.

Chapter Twenty
Vancouver Jade

When the Boeing 747 landed in Vancouver, Quan was exhausted. He had not slept a wink during the 15-hour flight across the Pacific. This came after three days of bickering with Cindy in Sydney. His last hours with Mali had cut Quan's appetite for sex with other women, or so he thought. Cindy was furious that her Asian stud was rejecting her advances during his three-day stay in Australia. Cindy was handsomely enough paid for arranging the forgery of Quan's new identity, but it peeved her that Quan's sexual drive had evaporated. It did not really matter to Quan that Cindy's sexual wants had not been met. He was tired of western girls who acted so prudish in their own society and came to Bangkok to screw every young Asian man in sight. At least, Chiang's girls had the dignity to distinguish between sex and love. He admired how quickly these girls, when they had made enough money, left their lives in Bangkok behind them and started new family lives in the north. Western girls carried a lot of sexual baggage with them, and it always shocked him how quick they were to compare his sexual prowess to the lackluster performance of their boyfriends back home.

The view coming into the airport was spectacular. He had never seen mountains so high. It was remarkable how they plunged into the water. The city was immaculately clean and modern. He had heard that Vancouver had become the new pearl of the Orient. He also knew it harboured great wealth, an almost insatiable demand for heroin, and the Triad was growing stronger in the city.

As instructed, Quan made mental notes of every aspect of immigration and security procedures that he went through at the airport. Surprisingly, the turbaned immigration officer at the airport did not blink an eye at the fact that he was an Asian Australian. Why would he? As Quan scanned the airport, he noted that almost a third of the employees were either from South Asia, the Far East or black. He had heard how Canada was promoting a new policy of multiculturalism, but the extent of this took him by surprise. When he exited from the customs, he saw a sign for Paul Nguyen raised high by a young Chinese girl. He approached her. "I am Paul Nguyen."

"Come with me, Mr. Nguyen, Mr. Tao is in Vancouver. He would like to meet you."

The name of the Triad's heavyweight from Hong Kong sent a shiver down Quan's spine. He had never met Tao Tsao, but knew of his cruel reputation and penchant for very young girls. Human smuggling was his specialty, but now, he was investing in the Bangkok Triad's plan to flood North America with the incredibly cheap heroin grown in northern Thailand's Golden Triangle.

"What is your name?" asked Quan.

"Melissa. Melissa Wong."

"Nice to meet you, Melissa. Do you speak Chinese?"

"Of course. I speak both Cantonese and Mandarin."

Melissa was a very attractive girl, although rather bookish—certainly not the type that you expected would be working for a Chinese Triad, but looks can be deceptive.

They took a taxi to Chinatown. The wide and relatively empty streets on the way in from the airport soon became congested and noisy but, unlike Bangkok, there was not a scooter or motorcycle to be seen, nor did a single vehicle honk on Hastings Street. When they arrived at the Pink Pearl Restaurant, the city had become more Chinese than Shanghai. Even downtown Bangkok had more Europeans than this Chinese enclave.

Tao Tsao waited inside the crowded restaurant surrounded by local Triad members. Here he was a guest, but one to be watched. The Vancouver Triad boss, John Wong, wielded tremendous power not just in Vancouver but throughout the Pacific Rim. The pretty Melissa was his daughter and he had sent her to spy on Tao Tsao and now on Paul Nguyen. If there were deals to be made, John Wong wanted his cut from day one. Tao Tsao motioned Quan to the table, as Melissa withdrew to the kitchen.

"Chiang tells me that you are smart, Quan. Is that true?" asked Tao Tsao.

"What wisdom do you wish from me?" answered Quan.

"How can we smuggle heroin past the Canadians?"

Soldier, Lily, Peace and Pearls   95

"We should not do it here in Vancouver. I saw too many dogs. Nothing gets past the dogs. The Canadians expect that shipments from Asia will come first to Vancouver. They will be more lax in other parts of Canada. Charters are now flying out of Toronto to Bangkok, but those will be watched as well. Fewer flights leave from Montreal, but we do not need so many flights to bring in the goods. Once a month should be sufficient. Let me see what I can find out about security in Montreal." And now it was Quan's turn. "What can you tell me about onward smuggling to the States?"

"It is easy enough. At the border, they only ask if the driver is Canadian and then wave him through if he is not Asian. Wong's organization here has many willing blue-eyed whores who will smuggle the goods for us. They just need to flash their eyelashes at the border guards to get past. Now let's eat. Do you want a girl tonight? I have asked for a young plump blonde. I can get you one as well, or do you stick to Asian pussy?"

"No, I am fine."

"Good. Let's eat then."

The waitresses in their embroidered Q*i Pao* dresses began to bring around trays of the most varied *dim sum* that Quan had ever seen. Tao had an insatiable appetite for all things, but especially for food. Quan tried hard to keep up with his host, but was soon overwhelmed as the small plates of *wu gok* taro turnovers, *char siu bao* steamed pork buns, shrimp dumplings wrapped in seaweed and topped with salmon caviar, and a multitude of other delicacies kept coming. After two hours of gorging, Tao Tsao offered again to take Quan to a Triad whorehouse which specialized in teenage girls. Quan politely declined, hiding how much Tao's mere presence turned his stomach.

As Tao exited the restaurant, Melissa returned and told Quan, "I will accompany you this afternoon. Where do you wish to go?"

Quan looked at the girl, and asked if she could take him to shops selling Chinese medicine.

"Yes, but we must go now before the shops close." And then she nodded to two of her father's thugs. "No need for you to come with us. Please send Mr. Nguyen's bags to the Pan Pacific Hotel."

The two men instantly obeyed. After all, she was John Wong's daughter.

Quan asked how far the shops were, and then proposed that they walk the twenty minutes needed to reach them. It had been cold in Sydney, but in Vancouver, it was late spring and the city was alive. The streets of Chinatown were lined with vegetable stands and the air reeked of fish. Old women in silk blouses scurried around carrying shopping bags full of bok choy and white radish. When they came to the first shop on East Pender Street, Quan was sceptical. There were no pails of roots, dried leaves and powders, only packaged goods and bottles with Chinese characters. The next two shops were the same. The rich heritage of Chinese medicine had been homogenized by marketing firms in Hong Kong and Taipei. Quan was about to give up when he noticed a green door in an alleyway with the spirit of the dragon horse, a traditional symbol for good health, painted on it. He led Melissa to the storefront. In a dirty window, a small sign said, "I speak Mandarin, Cantonese, Laotian and Vietnamese, Sorry no English—Dr. Kang."

As they entered the shop, wind chimes announced their presence. A very old man in a faded *Tangzhuang* jacket came out of the back and addressed them in Szechuan Mandarin and then in Cantonese. Quan immediately responded in Szechuan, asking for a rare herb that Jing Zi had often used in Pulau Bidong.

"You know this herb?" asked the old man suspiciously.

"Yes, I want it to help a friend with rheumatism."

"How do you know that it is good for rheumatism?" asked the shop-keeper in an astonished tone.

"My friend Jing Zi taught me about it."

"From Vientiane? You know Jing Zi from Vientiane? I too from Laos. Jing Zi was my friend."

Melissa spoke good Mandarin, at least for a Chinese-Canadian, but she had difficulty following the conversation in Szechuan. She moved away to examine some old pieces of jade jewelry, similar to some that her mother used to wear.

The shopkeeper, Dr. Kang summoned both Quan and Melissa into the backroom, a small warehouse piled up with roots of every colour and dimension, buckets of dried leaves, large glass bottles of multicoloured powders and vats of fermenting liquids. On the shelves were large leather-bound volumes written in Chinese and the Chu Nho script of old Vietnamese. There was even one written in the old Abugida Laotian script.

As all the other shops closed, Quan and Dr. Kang continued an animated discussion of the benefits of each of the ingredients. Dr. Kang had amassed a treasure of barks and shrub roots from forests that had long since disappeared from Indochina and Malaysia. Quan learned from Dr. Kang that after Quan's departure, Jing Zi had found a way to smuggle some of these rare ingredients from Pulau Bidong to Vancouver through the steady flow of resettled refugees from the island to Canada. It would seem that the immigration officer John Gibson had mended his ways and had begun to work hard at reducing the waiting lists of those wanting to come to Canada.

So that Melissa could better follow the conversation, Quan and Dr. Kang switched to Cantonese. Gradually, Melissa's view of Quan began to change. She had assumed that he was just a courier for her father's business, but as she listened to the young man's fascination with Chinese medicine and the deep knowledge that he already possessed, she felt a tiny tremour in her body.

Melissa Wong was 21 and a pre-med student at the University of British Columbia, and she was very pretty. Normally, she would have had scores of young suitors, but she was also John Wong's daughter. Most of her male Chinese classmates knew the ruthless reputation of her father and kept their distance. For the other Canadian boys, she was perhaps too thin and small to attract them, or at least that is what she thought. Little did she know that on several occasions, an interested Caucasian boy had been taken aside by one of her father's thugs and given a blunt warning. When her mother had died ten years earlier, Melissa had been enrolled at the Convent of the Sacred Heart. Most of the other boarders were the daughters of rich Latin American businessmen, who wanted their children far away from the scourge of kidnappings in Colombia, Peru and Mexico. At twenty-one, she had never known a man, but was determined that she should put an end to that soon.

Her gaze fixed on Quan as he chatted away with Dr. Kang. This young stranger moved with feline grace despite his muscular build. His Chinese-Vietnamese features brought together large eyes, a broad but noble nose and full lips, like those of a young girl. When he smiled, there was a radiance in the room. When he listened seriously to Dr. Kang, a brooding intensity took over.

After Quan bought two thousand dollars worth of various herbs, roots and potions, Dr. Kang came over to Melissa. You are Lin Wong, aren't you? Melissa was never surprised when people recognized her. Her father was well known in the Chinese community, but it startled her that he used the Chinese name that only her mother had called her by.

"Yes, how did you know?"

"You have your mother's face. She used to come here often, and even brought you along when you were a child."

Melissa looked around the dusty shop and breathed in the strong aromas. Suddenly, she had a flashback to a moment, long ago, when she had stood, holding her mother's hand, as Dr. Kang explained new herbal medicines.

Dr. Kang led Melissa to the assortment of jade jewelry that she had admired earlier. He picked out a chain with a miniature jade-covered flask. He put in the flask some white powder and handed it to Melissa. "I am sorry about the death of your mother. She was a good woman and gave birth to you. Now you should also be a good woman. Lin, take his gift of jade from me. The medicine in it will make any man strong and love you. Maybe even this man Quan from Pulau Bidong. He is a good man, but his heart also needs to heal through love."

Melissa was stunned by the directness of Dr. Kang's remarks, but dutifully put the chain around her neck. How could she do otherwise? If her mother had trusted the doctor, why shouldn't she? And besides, life could be worse than being loved by this young handsome stranger who knew so much.

Quan was ecstatic about his purchases. In Bangkok, he could make a ten-fold profit with them. Moreover, he had learned from Dr. Kang where in Laos many of the plants and trees grew. Even though Laos was under the Pathet Lao Communists, the government in Vientiane was eager to trade with Thailand. With his Thai passport, he could easily go there. He began to dream that perhaps he could leave behind him his criminal life and even convince Chiang to do the same. He knew that marriage between Hue and Chiang was inevitable and that Chiang would be a good brother-in-law, but he wanted Hue to live in honour not disgrace.

"Why did the doctor call you Quan?" asked Melissa.

"Because that is my real name, and I told him so."

"Does your name have a meaning?"

"Yes, it means soldier."

Suddenly, Melissa jerked back. What was she thinking of? This guy was only a foot soldier in her father's Triad. No matter how handsome and cultivated he was, no good could come of a relationship with him. Pulling herself together, she focused on doing what her father had asked of her—ensuring that Mr. Paul Nguyen or Quan or whatever his name was put safely in his hotel and made the flight the following day to Montreal.

The Pan Pacific Hotel was one of the most beautiful buildings in the Pacific Rim region. Twenty stories high, its rooms opened onto the sea-faring vessels and sportscraft in Burrard Inlet and beyond to the majestic mountains of the coastal range. Quan's room was a suite on the tenth floor. The Triad had spared no expense. Quan's mission was an important one for them. If he succeeded in discovering a reliable route for cheap Thai heroin into the United States via Canada, the Triad could dominate the world's largest drug market and then finance a recruitment campaign to muscle out their competition. Canada was being flooded with legal and illegal Chinese immigrants, many of whom had past Triad connections. Finding new foot soldiers was the least of the Triad's problems.

When Quan asked if Melissa would like to see the suite, she wanted to say no, but the polite gentleness of his request overcame her hesitation. Besides, foot soldier or not, she still felt intensely attracted to the young man.

Despite his wealth, John Wong worked hard to avoid attracting the attention of the authorities. He did have a few legitimate businesses, but none could produce revenue statements to justify an ostentatious lifestyle. Back in Hong Kong, he had already build a sumptuous compound for his retirement. In Vancouver, he lived in a modest East End home with Melissa, his only child, and drove an old Lincoln Towncar.

For Melissa, the luxurious hotel was a welcomed distraction from the otherwise spartan lifestyle that her father's caution imposed on them.

The elevator to the tenth floor was made completely of glass, even the floor and ceiling. It was like ascending to the heavens on a platform of air. From it, they began counting the lights coming on in North and West Vancouver as the sun set over the ocean. Melissa looked again at Quan. Was he really like her father's henchmen?

Hardly had they arrived in the room when room service brought them a sumptuous meal of crab, shrimps and lobster, courtesy of the hotel manager who had a tidy side-business going with the Triad in providing Asian escorts to rich hotel patrons from Japan.

"Melissa, would you do me the honour of joining me for dinner? There is more than even the two of us could eat."

"Yes, but on one condition. Over dinner, you must tell me how Quan became Paul Nguyen, and how you learned so much about Chinese medicine."

"Sure, but will you tell me the difference between Mclissa and Lin Wong? And why Dr. Kang gave you the jade flask?"

"Okay. Let's trade our secret lives. What have we got to lose?" laughed Melissa, who had no intention of telling Quan what was in the flask or who her father really was.

They ate on the balcony where the late lights of far-off galaxies carpeted the sky as the night advanced. Quan chose to skim over much of the last five years in Bangkok and talked instead about Pulau Bidong and how Hue and he had arrived there from Cambodia. As Quan struggled to gloss over the most violent episodes, especially the death of his parents, Melissa felt a deep sorrow emanating from within him. She had grown up in complete safety in Canada, and only been to Asia once, to improve her Mandarin. She had never seen anyone die, not even her mother who had slipped away peacefully in a hospital bed after her fragile heart had given in while Melissa was visiting an aunt in California.

Melissa went to the mini-bar and poured two glasses of champagne. She fingered the flask around her neck and then poured its contents into Quan's glass before joining him under the stars.

Dr. Kang's potion was more potent that Melissa had imagined. Quan took her tender body and made love to her zealously for hours. After years of pent-up desire, she responded hungrily, exploring every corner of his strong body and yielded to her deepest fantasies. He was not only an ardent lover, but a skilled and gentle one. No moment of pleasure was rushed, no tingling of her body cut short. She lost count of her orgasms, which came quicker and more intensely after the first one. Exhausted, she finally melded her body one last time into his, tenderly kissing his neck goodnight.

She had not slept long before she felt his body stiffen and grow cold. The gnashing of his teeth and the shaking of his head frightened her. She saw him ball his fists, as if ready to strike out at an invisible adversary. Melissa's eyes darted around the room in the fear that Quan had sensed a real danger, but they were alone. Alone with Quan's pain. Alone with Melissa's incredible attraction to the young man.

Melissa was perplexed. Should she wake her new lover from his nightmare or leave him be? From his contorted face and twisted mouth, she could hear him speak in Cantonese, Mandarin, Vietnamese and other languages that she did not recognize. Then the shaking and sweating began. Melissa rose from the bed and brought a towel dampened in warm water. She wiped away the sweat from his forehead and then from every part of his body. She kissed him all over and touched with the tips of her fingers his genitals. Quan finally awoke, and looked at the beautiful savior of his nocturnal ordeal. He kissed her hard, exploring every cavity in her mouth with his tongue, turned her around and thrust hard and long into her until the dawn broke.

Melissa ordered coffee and muffins from room service, as Quan showered. Her heart was racing with joy. She had always feared that her first time would be awful, awkward and with the wrong person. She looked at the ceiling as if to praise God, although she believed in none. Life was beautiful. This man that fate had brought from across the ocean was beautiful. It did not matter that he would soon be on a plane to Montreal. She was certain that she would see him again, and relive the ecstasy of the last night, over and over and over again. If happiness had a name, it would have been Melissa Wong that day.

Chapter Twenty-One
Reunion

Minh Chau was now 14 and at the top of her class at the Ursulines School in Quebec City. She had even skipped a grade and was only one year behind An, who plodded along at school, but never brought home the spectacular marks that Minh Chau did. It was obvious that her younger sister was headed for better things. While Voang, Han and An never managed to pick up the local Québécois accent, Minh Chau was an expert at speaking *joual,* the increasingly popular street slang. And she liked boys! Even if there were few to be found hanging around the convent school. The young girl had progressed beyond Céline Dion to Michael Jackson and dressed up like him whenever she could, but mostly when her mother was hard at work in the clinic and her father worked late at the store.

In her painted-on jeans and tight-fitting jean jacket, she would hang around the esplanade in front of the Chateau Frontenac, flirting innocently with young American boys who were vacationing in Quebec with their parents. She had grown her hair long, very long and wore five-inch heels to make herself seem taller than five-foot one. Each day, she stood on the scale to see if she had topped eighty-five pounds and stare in the mirror to see if the tiny protrusions on her chest had grown enough to merit a bra. One day, she found a perfect padded bra, which almost gave her father a heart attack when she dropped by the supermarket in it. François, the delivery boy, also took note and smiled crookedly at his boss's daughter. Despite the boy's extensive acne and bad teeth, Minh Chau did not mind. At least, it was a start toward a social life.

Voang was beginning to worry about Minh Chau's behaviour and decided to visit a cousin in Montreal, who had immigrated to Canada after practicing psychology for many years in Paris. Maybe cousin Leyna could help. He put An in charge of the store and took Minh Chau with him on the morning train to Montreal. He tricked Minh Chau into thinking that this was just a social call on her father's very sophisticated cousin, who had an amazing collection of shoes! From Bonaventure Station, it was just a short walk to the Saigon Pho

Restaurant where they were to meet Leyna. They entered the restaurant at the same time as a muscular young man, who excused himself in English for almost bumping into Voang. Immediately, Minh Chau recognized the Malaysian accent that Abdul Hakim had ingrained in all his students of English. She tugged hard on her father's jacket and said, "It can't be!"

"What can't be, Minh Chau?"

"Just look ahead. It's Quan!"

Voang turned to scrutinize the features of the young man who had joined two other older men at a booth by the window. Could it really be Quan? Why wouldn't he have written? He physically restrained Minh Chau from throwing herself at Quan. "Wait. We must be sure. It has been seven years since we saw him last."

Voang and Minh Chau sat at a nearby table and listened to the men's conversation. It was not Vietnamese, but a rough form of street Cantonese or Teochew, with various Thai words thrown in. Voang looked puzzled at his daughter. Had Quan changed so much or was this just someone who bore him a resemblance? When the waitress came to take the men's orders, Quan spoke in fluent Vietnamese. It was a deeper voice than he had as a child, but it was definitely his voice. At that moment, Quan turned and looked at Voang and Minh Chau. All three stiffened in their moment of mutual recognition. Like a shot, Minh Chau's arms were around Quan's neck, much to the bemusement of his two companions, and Voang marched up with tears in his eyes and an outstretched hand to welcome Quan back.

It was just at that moment that cousin Leyna walked in. She greeted Voang and Minh Chau who introduced her to Quan. Quan quickly introduced his business associates, two tough-looking Chinese who leered at Leyna. The two men then excused themselves after making arrangements with Quan to see him that night.

Quan was reluctant at first to explain what had transpired over the last five years, but when Voang told him that they had heard about the beating of John Gibson, Quan gave them a detailed account about what had really happened. After the lunch, Voang asked to speak to Quan alone, and Leyna offered to take Minh Chau shopping for shoes. Minh Chau revolted at the thought of leaving Quan, but he took her hands in his and promised that he would not disappear.

Voang had sensed that something was terribly wrong. He patiently waited for Quan to piece together the last five years in Bangkok. Quan left aside his role in beating abusive johns, but admitted his guilt in drug smuggling. Voang loved Quan so much and owed so much to him, that he could find no blame in him. Instead, he reached over to hold his shoulder. Your life does not have to be like this. You are in Canada now. You can live with us. We have money. We can give you work. Please come with us to Quebec City and start a new life—the one that you always wanted. Quan thought of Hue. Would she be all right if he did not return? Would Chiang be angry? He decided then and there that Hue would be fine. She was almost finished with her degree and he had bought her an apartment. She could work full-time for the accounting firm. And besides, it was only a question of time before Chiang would marry her.

"But what about Gibson? My beating him will bring you trouble."

"No, Quan. It can't. We are now Canadian citizens. We have rights. And you will too. We will talk to Denis Prud'homme about how to get you refugee status."

It was as if Quan's entire life was turning on a dime. He had rescued Minh Chau and saved his sister Hue. He had tried to save his parents, but failed. In his entire life, no one had ever saved him. Now this bespectacled former dentist from Saigon wanted to rescue him from an existence of perpetual crime. A life that only promised a cycle of violence and shame. Voang was right. Yes, he would miss Hue, but she would be all right. In Quebec, he could be with the rest of his family: Han, An and Minh Chau. He felt a weight lifted from shoulders that had been there ever since he had struck down John Gibson.

Voang and Quan agreed that they would tell no one else in the Thieu family of the drug smuggling nor of the brothel. Instead, Quan would have earned his living in Bangkok from the sale of Chinese medicine that he learned to make from Jing Zi. He was now in Canada on a business trip, and Hue was going to get married in Thailand to a local Chinese-Vietnamese businessman. The beating of John Gibson would still be the explanation for the five years of silence. Now Voang would find a way to solve that problem.

When Minh Chau returned with cousin Leyna and listened to the story that Voang and Quan had concocted, she asked if she could take a walk alone with Quan.

Walking past the outdoor cafés on Saint Denis Street, Minh Chau said, "Why are you lying to me, Quan? I understand that you were frightened when you beat Gibson, but that does not explain everything. I waited for you. I am still waiting for you. You know that!"

"Minh Chau, you are my sister and will always be so. I will always love you, An and your parents."

"Quan, I do not want to be your sister. I am now 14. I am not a child, do you understand?!"

Quan took Minh Chau's hands in his, and said, "No, you will always be my sister, and I will protect you with my life, but you must do one thing for me."

"Yes, what is it?"

"Teach me about this country. Help me learn its language. You are the most intelligent person that I know. I need your help, little sister."

Minh Chau could not refuse. Without Quan, her life would have ended in Pulau Bidong. She could wait for his love, but for now she would help him become a Canadian.

Chapter Twenty-Two
Separation

Quan and Voang decided that they should depart that night for Quebec City, without leaving an explanation for the Triad. The Triad would not agree to such an abrupt end to Quan's mission. There was really only one way to leave the Triad, feet first. Quan checked out of the hotel and loaded his suitcases full of clothes and Chinese medicine onto the train. They bid farewell to Leyna, who promised to mention Quan to no one in Montreal. When they arrived in the small house in Sillery that the Thieus had recently bought, the entire family stayed up talking the whole night.

They decided that Quan should call Hue in Bangkok to tell her that he would not be returning. He caught her at the accounting office. He could hear the tears in her voice.

"Quan, you made me a good life in Bangkok. Now you should make a good life in Canada for yourself. Do not worry about me. I have everything that I need, but I must tell you something. Please do not be mad."

"Yes, Hue?"

"Chiang has asked me to marry him."

"What did you say?"

"I said that if he left the Triad and ran the laundry, I would, but Chiang told me that no one can leave the Triad. Quan, you are my brother. Tell me what I should do!"

"Hue, you must follow your heart. I know your heart is with Chiang. I have known Chiang for five years. He has changed and he is a good man, but he has no choice."

"Then I will marry him, and love him for all my life. And I will love you always, my brother."

Quan's sadness at leaving his sister was soon replaced by the euphoria of his new existence in Quebec City. Voang gave him work in the supermarket, and Minh Chau taught him French every day after school. Under her direction, he was soon quite fluent in French, which proved to be easy after learning Thai, Malay and several Chinese dialects. At night, he would mix his Chinese medicine and Dr. Han Thieu and cousin Leyna would sell the medicine through their contacts in the large Chinese and Vietnamese communities in Montreal. Soon Quan's assets grew. His only struggle was in obtaining permanent residence in Canada. They consulted Denis Prud'homme. Quan had entered Canada with false documentation. There was the outstanding case of John Gibson's beating. It would not be easy.

While the Thieus grappled with a scheme to get Quan refugee status, he became Paul Q. Nguyen, an Australian exchange student, and a distant relative of the Thieus. For all their neighbours and friends, it was very believable. Minh Chau added a twist to the story when she told a classmate, who was teasing her about not having a boyfriend, that she was dating the exchange student who worked at her father's supermarket. Suddenly, the supermarket became a frequent haunt for several of Minh Chau's classmates who agreed that her secret boyfriend was certainly a keeper. At one point, Minh Chau's indiscretion almost scuttled things when one of the classmates told her parents about the twenty-year-old boy dating a 14-year-old. The mother of the classmate made an appointment to see Dr. Han Thieu to explain that in Canada, dating under-aged girls was not allowed, even if it was allowed in Vietnam. After this humiliation, Han called in her daughter and scolded her soundly about lying and calling attention to Quan. Minh Chau acquiesced to her mother's wishes to keep her feelings about Quan to herself.

But as in the best laid plans of mice and men, there was a fundamental flaw. Tao Tsao and John Wong went into a fit when Quan vanished off the face of the earth. Both thought that he had either gone over to the Vietnamese competition or had been killed by the local Italian mafia on orders from the Colombians. Either way, this was a slight that they would not forgive. Word went out to the Triad in Toronto, Montreal, New York, Chicago and L.A. to keep their eyes open for Quan. Under much duress, Chiang was forced to send them a photo of Quan. Without proof that Quan had actually betrayed the Triad, Tao Tsao did not have the power to remove Chiang, but he was deeply suspicious of the man who then married Quan's sister.

Leyna, whose patients included a local Vietnamese crime boss, was able to keep tabs on the effort to get to the bottom of Quan's disappearance. The suspicion that he had gone over to the Vietnamese gangs had caused some tensions in Montreal. The possibility that the Italian mafia had interfered with the Asian gangs' plans to take their share of the drug trade was also worrisome. The Italians, on their own, were anachronistic thugs, certainly no match for the youthful Chinese and Vietnamese Triads. But if they had cemented an alliance with the Colombians and were now cocky enough to take out a Triad member, this was really worrisome. Quan's disappearance came close to triggering a gang war in Montreal.

Quan's downfall came when a Triad member's girlfriend was diagnosed with cancer. He heard from his boss that Leyna had a direct line to powerful Chinese medicine. There was no Chinese medicine able to cure cancer, but the thug persisted in demanding who Leyna's supplier was. When he brutalized her, she gave up the supermarket's address in Quebec City. She phoned the Thieus to warn them, and spoke to An. An rushed to the supermarket, but got there as the Triad member was getting out of his car. Quan was just locking up the store. It did not take the gangster long to recognize Quan from the photo that had been in circulation for more than a year. He reached into his breast pocket for his gun. An threw her arms around the attacker and Quan kicked him in the groin. The gun went off fatally wounding the man. Quan pushed him back into his car and shoved him over to the passenger seat. He ordered An to sit in the back. The man gave his last gasp. Quan turned to look at An. "Where to?" he asked.

An guided him to a small cabin near Mont Ste-Anne, which belonged to some friends of a classmate. From the woodshed, she brought two shovels. Quan and An carried the body into the woods and buried it in a deep grave. They then drove the car into a lake thirty miles away, and hitch-hiked back to Quebec City. When they arrived at the house, An angrily tossed a suitcase at Quan. "You must leave. You have put our family into danger. It was one thing to have beaten the immigration agent, but now you have gangsters hunting you down. Promise me that you will go far away."

Quan looked at An with his heart beating fast. He had indeed put everyone in danger. It was his fault. How could he think that he could just walk away from the Triad. He stuffed the suitcase with his clothes and sought out the large bag of cash from his medicine sales. He offered the money to An.

"No," she said, "keep the money. You will need it. Quan, I love you as much as Minh Chau does and probably more, but I must protect my family. Please understand. I will never forget what you did for us in Pulau Bidong, but please leave."

When morning came, the Thieus looked everywhere for Quan. He was nowhere to be found. Then Leyna phoned. An claimed that when she had arrived at the supermarket, Quan was already gone, but did not want to worry her parents. The only conclusion was that the Triad had kidnapped Quan. The Thieus considered contacting the local police, but feared that this would only make matters worse. Minh Chau took it hardest. For days, she could not sleep or think straight. It was not just her infatuation with Quan, it was the fear that his disappearance had brought back. She had become convinced that only Quan could protect her. She dreamed every night of Dahan. Ugly, vicious nightmares that left her exhausted by morning. Her guilt over the death of Cong resurfaced. All this had happened because of her.

Leyna began to visit Minh Chau in Quebec. Dr. Han Thieu prescribed her daughter anti-depressants and pulled her out of school for a year. Finally, Minh Chau stabilized, but she was never the same. Now at fifteen, she sought out the toughest males in Quebec—bikers and local hoodlums. To her parents' horror, she spent nights away from home, arriving in the morning reeking of alcohol and pot. An tried to talk to her sister, but Minh Chau had become insolent and resentful of An, whom she blamed for not warning Quan in time. When Dr. Han Thieu was offered a job at the Notre Dame Hospital in Montreal, the entire family decided to move.

If anything, Minh Chau was resilient. After her year of grief, she walked into the living room of the family's new house in the Outrement neighbourhood of Montreal and apologized for her behaviour. Quan was strong. Wherever he was, he would be okay. She was convinced that he would return one day. In the meantime, she would resume her studies and make her parents proud. That night, An confessed to her parents the role that she had played in concealing the dead man's body and driving Quan away. They embraced her just as they had embraced Minh Chau earlier that day. Life had again been cruel to the Thieus and to Quan. All they could do was hope for the best.

Chapter Twenty-Three
A Gift of Life from Pulau Bidong

In the first five years in Kigali, life was perfect except that Denise's efforts to have a baby were having no success. They begin to consult with specialists, including Dr. Han Thieu, who had moved to Montreal and began to work as an obstetrician in the prestigious family planning clinic at Notre Dame Hospital. Han took the couple aside and said, "I really shouldn't do this, but there is something that I brought from Pulau Bidong. It is a Chinese medicine produced by the famous healer Jing Zi. I have run various lab tests. I do not know how it works, but I do know that it will not do you any harm." She then took out from her drawer a small bamboo vial with a dragon carved on its lid. "I was given this by Jing Zi before we left the island. He told me that if ever An or Minh Chau had trouble conceiving a child, I should use it. I want you to have it. It might just work."

Before leaving Montreal, Mathieu and Denise dined with the Thieus at the new restaurant that Voang had opened in Chinatown, after selling the supermarket in Quebec City for a considerable profit. The Thieus called their restaurant ironically the Pulau Bidong. Neither An nor Minh Chau were able to join them. An had decided that she wanted to be a teacher and was preparing for her final exams for high school, and Minh Chau was on a student exchange in France. As they discussed the good days in Quebec City, Mathieu could not but notice that Han was looking tired and somewhat haggard. Voang spoke proudly the whole evening about the success that his daughters were having in their studies. Minh Chau wanted to become a lawyer and practice international law. An's passion was to teach art to elementary school students. She had become a gifted artist, like her cousin Dao who was allowed to correspond with them from Vietnam and occasionally sent the Thieus some of her work. They sold Dao's art to Canadian galleries and put the proceeds into a Canadian bank account for her, building up a nice nest egg for Dao's family, should they ever decide to leave Vietnam.

Dao had married Huynh and they had two wonderful daughters. She had recently sent them a stunning painting of a young Vietnamese child. The painting was entitled, "Reviens" (Return!). It was too beautiful to sell to an art gallery. The Thieus depositied three hundred dollars in Dao's account and kept it for a special occasion. With a broad smile, Voang took out the painting. "Mathieu and Denise, when you married, we did not have enough money for a real wedding gift. Now we want you to have this painting. When you see this child, think of all of us because we are all children of Vietnam, and remember its name, "Reviens," because we want you to return to us in Montreal."

Mathieu and Denise cherished the painting, putting it above their bed in their house in Kigali. Then, with the help of Jing Zi's potion or the magic of the painting, Denise conceived, bringing into the world a beautiful baby boy, Étienne Hakizimana-Hibou.

In the Hibous' upper class neighbourhood of Nyarutarama in Kigali, the differences between Tutsis and Hutus were almost non-existent, but until recently, there had been little intermarriage between the two groups. Tutsi oppression of the majority Hutu population in neighbouring Burundi was the occasional subject of dinner conversation and news of the increasing importance of Tutsi refugees in the Ugandan rebel movement led by Yoweri Museveni was also sometimes discussed. More important to both educated Tutsis and Hutus was the seeming inability to move Rwanda forward economically and socially. Population growth since independence was straining the country's natural resources. More and more subsistence farmers were moving into the city in search of work. Tourism which once seemed promising was stymied by the country's image of post-independence instability and corruption.

In Mathieu's own work, he often felt that he was fighting an uphill battle, both within the Ministry of Agriculture and with UNDP. Both organizations had become very self-serving, and there was almost no accountability for achieving tangible results. Mathieu took pride in the success of his projects, but while farmers were benefiting from better water-harvesting and crop diversification, these projects only reached 10% of the rural population. He was constantly campaigning to raise more funds from donors, but Rwanda was a backwater for most donors. The real action was in Ethiopia where millions of people faced famine or in Zambia, Zimbabwe, Mozambique and Angola, all front-line states in the battle against apartheid. There were simply not enough cases of mass starvation or direct connections to global politics to put Rwanda on the front burner.

Despite these frustrations at work, life was beautiful in the Hibou family. A year after the birth of Étienne, Denise had gone back to work, not as a translator but as a radio announcer for a new private radio station *La Voix du Progrès*, financed by Rwandan expatriates in France. Denise not only read the news, but participated in the editorial board decisions on all programming. Increasingly, she took on a political profile as one of the most astute analysts of African and world affairs. When Rwanda Radio and Television decided to start a weekly TV public affairs show, they offered the host position to Denise. Her natural beauty and lyrical voice drew a loyal following from the common people and her insight into politics gained her the respect of her peers in the country's elite.

Being married to a television celebrity was not always easy for Mathieu. They would often receive invitations to embassy receptions addressed to Mr. and Mrs. Hazikimana. Despite his ground-breaking work in revitalizing parts of Rwanda's agricultural sector, most Rwandan politicians greeted him as Mr. Hazikimana. At one point, he suggested to Denise that maybe he should just change his name to hers. After all, his grandfather had changed his name twice after coming to Canada. Denise brushed aside the suggestion, "If you change your name, then who will be the big *Hibou* who watches over us?"

Denise's celebrity increased further after Tutsi refugees formed the Rwandan Patriotic Front and invaded northern Rwanda in 1990, starting a four-year civil war. Although a Tutsi, Denise's objectivity as a media commentator gained her wide respect among moderate Hutu and Tutsi political leaders. Even when her cousin Antoine Bikindi quit his job at the university to join the RPF rebels in the north, this did not rub off on her.

Every month, Mathieu and Denise received a long letter from Han Thieu. She wrote proudly about how well her daughters were doing in their studies and how profitable the restaurant had become under Voang's excellent management. Her own research in fertility was beginning to show promising results. She had been able to isolate an enzyme from Jing Zi's potion. It seemed to stimulate hormonal activity outside of the regular cycle and allowed women to ovulate for longer periods. Of course, the research was still preliminary, but she was earning the respect of her Canadian-born colleagues. Much earlier, Han had written to them to tell them that Quan, the refugee boy that Mathieu was supposed to take care of, had finally arrived in Canada and was living with them. There were several other references to Quan during Han's letters that year, but then he suddenly vanished from the scene.

Gradually, the correspondence from Han became less frequent and her hand-writing more disjointed and at times hardly legible. Mathieu became concerned. Perhaps it was time for a visit to Canada. It had been almost seven years since he had seen the Thieus. An must be about 24 and Minh Chau perhaps 22. Han had written him that An had begun teaching and that Minh Chau who would soon finish her economics degree wanted to study law. Mathieu's most vivid images of the two girls were when they had just arrived at the bus station in Quebec, wearing shoes wrapped in newspapers and covered with plastic bags because the family did not have the money yet to buy winter boots. Once when he was visiting Mary, who was baby-sitting the two girls, Minh Chau began to scream, pointing frantically at the TV where a Godzilla-like monster was munching on his human prey. An, not knowing how televisions worked, shouted, "Don't worry Minh Chau, I will drown the monster," and then poured water from Mary's large flower vase on the set, sending sparks everywhere. Mary had refused the Thieus' offer to pay for the TV, but years later when Mary had moved back to Vancouver to teach French at a local high school, a monstrous colour TV was delivered to her Kitsilano apartment, courtesy of *Supermarché Thieu et famille*, Quebec City. The Thieus always paid their debts. It would be good to see the entire family again, but mostly he was worried about Han. He sensed that something was wrong.

The next morning at the office, the Head of UNDP asked Mathieu if he could attend a conference in New York in two weeks time. He jumped at the chance and requested an additional week of vacation so he could tack on a trip to Canada. When he asked Denise to join him, she declined explaining there were rumours of a regional security agreement between the Rwandan and Burundian presidents, and she needed to be in Kigali to cover it. He took her hand in his and stroked it, touching lightly the red and black hair bracelet that Minh Chau had woven for Denise. "It is okay. We can also go back this summer when Étienne is on school vacation. It is about time that he met his Vietnamese family." Denise smiled. She knew how much the Thieus had come to mean to Mathieu, and how kind he had always been to them. It was not physical or intellectual attributes, or wealth or fame that had drawn Denise to her future husband when Antoine had introduced her to him. It was the kindness in everything that Mathieu did that made him irresistible. She looked into his turquoise eyes, touched with her fingertips the boyish grin on his mouth and said, "Mathieu, I love you and I will always love you."

Chapter Twenty-Four
The Glass Shatters

Had Mathieu not decided to surprise Han, things may have been different. He stood at her door, ringing the bell. He had called Voang at the restaurant, who told him that Han was home. After the second ring, Mathieu was about to leave when a man in a blue wool overcoat walked up the steps. Dominic Leblanc recognized Mathieu from the wedding picture of him and Denise that Han kept on her living room mantel. She had often spoke of the gentle boy from Quebec City who had welcomed her family to this new land, and had kept a protective eye over her children. Dominic never tired of Han's stories, which made him proud of his countrymen and made him regret the emptiness of his own life.

"You are Mathieu Hibou, aren't you?" asked the doctor.

"Yes, I am."

"Then come in with me. I am afraid that there may have been an accident," lied Dominic, as he opened the door with the key that Han had given him for his special mission.

The two men entered the house. Leblanc asked Mathieu to wait downstairs, as he went to Han's bedroom. He pocketed the empty vial beside her, closed her eyes and straightened her body from the distortion of pain in the final movement of her life. He then returned to Mathieu and informed him that Dr. Han Thieu had passed away from a stroke caused probably by an arterial embolism. It was the start of the collapse of Mathieu's world.

***

Four thousand miles away, Minh Chau was walking every canal in Venice. The pastel colours of the crumbling buildings swallowed her up in the ecstasy of the moment. She lived her life as if in constant escape from the scarring of her soul, but this city in its total and unrelenting splendour was a salve more powerful that all of Jing Zi's medicines. It breathed life into her like never before, and made her forget to write her parents on a regular basis.

"Guten Tag, können Sie Deutsch sprechen?"

"Ja, ich spreche ein bisschen," responded Minh Chau in her heavily accented school German to a teutonic giant with flowing flaxen hair. A beautiful specimen of a man.

"Ou bien, nous pouvons parler en français, mon anglais n'est pas très bon," responded the giant.

Relieved to be able to speak in her adopted tongue, Minh Chau asked what she could do for the stranger.

Wolfgang, it seemed, was totally lost in the maze of canals and dead-end alleyways, which stumped sometimes even Venetians. "I was looking for the Ravagnan Art Gallery. There is an extensive collection of Ludovico de Luigi's paintings there. I hear that it is tremendous."

"Absolutely, I was there yesterday. It is a fabulous exhibition. I could take you there if you wish."

"Good. Let's go!"

Minh Chau practically had to run just to keep up with her giant. While not the fastest walker in the world, she had a phenomenal memory and navigated through the piazzas and bridges, as if she had built-in GPS.

"Oh, by the way, my name is Minh Chau."

"Oh, that's a beautiful name. It means precious pearls, doesn't it?"

Minh Chau swirled around in surprise, "What! How did you know that?"

"I watch a lot of Asian films and always like to look up the meaning of names. It inspires me for my own work."

"Which is?"

"I write film scripts. Wolfgang Schwarzfeld is my name."

"Honoured to meet you Herr Schwarzfeld."

"The pleasure is mine, Minh Chau, but please call me Wolfgang."

Minh Chau smiled. There was something hugely charming about Wolfgang's nonchalant French. It was almost flawless, but had a hint of a regional accent, perhaps Alsatian.

"Are you French, Minh Chau?"

"No, Canadian, but I was born in Vietnam."

"In Saigon?"

"Yes."

"Then in the South, your name means radiant jade, I believe."

Oh boy, this was getting a little out of hand, Minh Chau thought. Was he an encyclopedia or perhaps a little creepy?

"You are right, but father is from the north and he chose the name for me. Have you been to Vietnam?"

"Yes, I worked there last year as a consultant for a documentary on the Vietnamese war for Deutsche Welle."

Wow. Maybe this guy is a keeper, thought Minh Chau. Tall, handsome, in the film business. Or maybe it was the Venetian sun and the beauty of the sinking city stirring in her a genuine sexual arousal for the first time. After the disappearance of Quan, Minh Chau had indulged in all sorts of relationships, mostly one-night stands with bikers or punks—anything to help her forget Quan and to punish her parents for not protecting him. When she finally got her act together and went to university, she had less daring relationships with a series of clean-cut young French and English Canadian boys. There was no question of dating a Vietnamese boy. That was for An. And besides, she did not want to be with anyone who reminded her physically of Quan. Wolfgang was certainly the antithesis of Quan, but no, that was not the reason for her attraction to this quiet Berliner.

It did not take Minh Chau to realize that Wolfgang's expertise in art of all forms, particularly the surrealism of de Luigi and de Chirico, was truly exceptional. He saw in a painting the artist's soul and articulated aesthetic journeys through oil or acrylic in such compelling terms that Minh Chau found herself involuntarily hanging on his every utterance. And yet, there was never a moment when she found him pompous or overbearing. Well, maybe a little when it came to the etymology of names. In almost all things, it was as if his knowledge had been acquired effortlessly. On the island of Murano, they visited a glass factory in operation since the fifteenth century. Wolfgang admired an intricate serving glass. It had been blown by the factory's ovens into a boat full of people with some clinging to the side as if on the verge of falling overboard. Wolfgang spoke only three words, "It is humanity." Minh Chau was overwhelmed. She looked at the piece and saw her own family in the boat, and decided to purchase it immediately.

Minh Chau scrapped her plan to head off to Florence and stayed another week in Venice, keeping as close to Wolfgang as she could. She would greet him in the morning at his inexpensive hotel in Campo San Polo with a fresh batch of brioches from a local bakery and fruit from the Rialto market. She fed him and he nourished her soul. Despite her almost unbearable attraction to him, she still felt a little inhibited when she invited him to the Lido for a swim. Wolfgang was six foot seven and perfectly proportioned. Minh Chau at five foot one and pushing 95 pounds looked like a tiny doll beside him. She wore the skimpy bikini that she had bought in Nice, and thought that she looked pretty hot, but Wolfgang did not seem attracted to her. Of course, she thought for a nano-second. She should have figured this out earlier. Wolfgang was gay. How stupid could she be! It was just then as they waded into the warm Mediterranean that he proved her wrong. The massive German reached out to take Minh Chau's tiny hand. She turned toward him, placed her other hand on his shoulders and like a spider climbed up to kiss him passionately on the lips. She opened her eyes to find him smiling broadly. Uninhibited by the other swimmers, she straddled his broad body with her legs. She could feel his manhood grow hard and vibrant underneath her. She then then reached down and undid the strings of her bikini bottom and slid onto him, moving up and down to the rhythm of the waves. Every one of her gracile movements brushed his body lightly against her clitoris and brought him deep into her vagina to touch her cervix. She climaxed in seconds, and then again and again. And when he came, the explosion inside her satiated her.

Sex made Minh Chau the most talkative woman on the face of the earth. She recounted every aspect of her life, trusting him entirely with every secret except the "sea." And she accepted immediately Wolfgang's invitation to go back with him to Berlin.

Wolfgang's four-room apartment was on the fifth floor of a late nineteenth century building in Kreuzberg. He did not own a car and bicycled everywhere. The first day in Berlin, he brought home an old East German *Diamant* one-speed from the flea market in Mauerpark. Minh Chau had never learned to cycle, so the first order of business was to teach her. Like in everything she did, she interrogated Wolfgang on all aspects of how a bicycle worked before agreeing to try it out. They walked the bikes to the path along the Spree River that divided Kreuzberg from Mitte.

It was early on a Sunday morning so they thought that they had the bike path to themselves. Wolfgang chose to follow Minh Chau at a safe distance. Suddenly, a young dark-skinned boy entered the bike path and headed straight toward Minh Chau, throwing her into a panic. Thinking that she was headed for a front-end collision with the boy, she veered sharply to the right and flew through the air with her *Diamant* into the murky waters of the Spree. As she hit the river with full force, Minh Chau went into shock. With her foot caught in the bike, she sank like lead beneath the water. When she opened her eyes, she was in the South China Sea. A hand was reaching toward her. No, no, it was Cong coming to take her with him. She struggled to fight off the hand, which grabbed her waist, but instead of dragging her down, pulled her to the surface. The sun blinded her for a moment, and then she saw him. Wolfgang had dived in to save her. She clung to his body as they swam to shore, murmuring softly in Vietnamese, "Toi yeu ban" (I love you) to the music of water splashing around them.

Unable to release her arms around his neck, Minh Chau allowed herself to be carried through the streets of Kreuzberg to the apartment. Passersby stared at the sight of the dripping giant and his spider-like companion, curled up in his arms. Even for the five flights of stairs, Minh Chau would not let go, but it did not tire the giant, who climbed two steps at a time. Inside, he ran her a hot bath, placed her in it and gently cleansed her body with scented soap. Minh Chau closed her eyes, and thought back to the first bath that she and An had had in Quebec City. Four thousand miles from Quebec and half a world away from the South China Sea, she had been saved once again.

That evening, Minh Chau decided to let the "sea" speak—the glass bottle propelled through air, blood on Cong's forehead, the hand of his kindness vanishing beneath the waves forever. When she had finished, she turned away from Wolfgang in shame and buried herself in his bed. She would have curled up in agony like she had done so often in Pulau Bidong, had not her giant lain beside her and enveloped her in his strong arms. Up to then, she had always taken the initiative in their love life. She loved being the spider on his broad chest. She loved to ride his manhood to attain carnal pleasure. This time, there was no violent abandon. Instead, Wolfgang's fingers wandered gently across her body, bringing to it an energy that she never felt before. There was nothing rehearsed about his touch. It was like he explored her for the very first time. No one had ever touched her like this before. He undressed her slowly, spread her legs and with every beautiful thrust, cleansed her of sixteen years of guilt.

The next morning, she brought Wolfgang coffee and woke him softly from his sleep. Behind her back, she held in her hands the Venetian glass boat. She kissed him tenderly on his lips and then placed the fragile boat on his chest. "I want you to have this because you have given me back my humanity."

Wolfgang had a short assignment in Cologne to advise a TV film crew on a re-make of one of his earliest scripts, and to discuss with Deutsche Welle the possibility of doing a documentary on the civil war in Rwanda. Rumours of mass killings of Tutsis had begun to reach Europe. Wolfgang, who had been born in Namibia to German-speaking settlers and had only returned to Germany to do his university studies, had a strong interest in all things African. He asked Minh Chau to join him—Cologne was a beautiful city—but she decided to stay in Berlin. There were still a few sites that she wanted to see, and in her obsessive attachment to Wolfgang had not had the opportunity to do so. In any case, she wanted to test her ability to go without the man for at least a week.

In Berlin, Minh Chau regained her passion for life—not the artificial comedy that she often played for the benefit of her friends, but a joy that emanated from within her. She even tried out again the *Diamant* that the young boy who had almost collided with her, had fished out of the river and brought to their apartment, along with a huge platter of Turkish pastries from his parents' bakery. His mother had scolded him for his recklessness and insisted that he make amends. The boy, Ahmet, was a little unsure that pastries would do the trick. To his immense surprise, Minh Chau did not just forgive him, but hugged and kissed him profusely. After all, without this accident, how else would she have come to know absolution? How else would she have been really able to confirm her love for Wolfgang?

Berlin was an amazing city, unlike any that she had every seen before. True, the architecture in Paris was more grandiose, and the floating mosaic that was Venice was more captivating, but Berlin was a city of the people—rich, poor, German, Turkish, Arab and to her surprise, a large Vietnamese community. Everywhere she sensed the city's rich, but torrid past. Potsdamer Platz, the old heart of the city, was still the open field created by the allied bombing at the end of the war, and turned into a killing zone between the inner and outer sections of the Berlin Wall by the East German Communists. When the wall fell, only five years earlier, West and East Germans had celebrated there in the tens of thousands.

The city was still alive with the enthusiasm of reunification. The German government, which had decided to make Berlin in 1990 the capital of a re-united Germany, was pouring in billions of *Deutschmarks* to renovate the eastern part of the city. Not everyone was happy though. For many older East Germans, the Communist regime had offered job security, especially for women, free daycare and university studies and predictable lives. Now, they were challenged to adapt to free market capitalism and conform to the ideological allegiance demanded of them by their West German countrymen.

Nothing good could be said of the former East German system without at least the risk of public criticism. The East German managers and employees whose companies that had been purchased by West German investors felt cowed from trying to educate their new employers in a balanced way about the past. And heaven forbid if any of the backward East German workers, technicians and engineers might be able to offer a creative solution to a problem. For the new masters of a re-united Germany, what was from the West was always the best. Most succumbed to regurgitating the condemnation of the old system, which had indeed its many, many flaws, and passively watched as their new bosses proved unable to re-design the factories to produce products that could compete in the market place. Factory after factory closed done. Young East German women streamed to the service industries in the West, leaving a growing population of disgruntled, unemployed young men behind them.

Minh Chau soon tired of the more modern western part of the city, and focused on discovering the East, especially Friedrichshain, a neighbourhood adjacent to Kreuzberg. Friedrichshain with its low rents was home to much of the city's teeming student population and unemployed young people. Together with Mitte and Prenzlauerberg to the north, these neighbourhoods were the heart of Berlin's alternative lifestyle scene.

Friedrichshain was bordered by Karl-Marx Strasse, the massively wide boulevard that the Communists had built as a showpiece to the world. It was there that Minh Chau came across Minh Khai Vinh, a tall student journalist and aspiring actress from Darmstadt, near Frankfurt. Minh Khai was born in Germany of Vietnamese parents and like Minh Chau had decided to embrace her country with a fervent passion. Her one concession to her Vietnamese heritage was the decision to undertake an assignment for a youth TV station to investigate the divide between the Vietnamese in the former West Germany and those in the East.

The two Minhs became the best of friends when Minh Chau discovered that Minh Khai knew Wolfgang from an internship that she had done at Deutsche Welle TV earlier that year. In fact, Wolfgang had recently discussed with Minh Khai the possibility of her helping him on a documentary that he was thinking about doing on Vietnam.

Unlike the Vietnamese in West Germany, who had mostly fled Vietnam to escape communism, the 30,000-strong East Berlin Vietnamese community was composed primarily of former students, trainees and exchange workers who had come under East German-Vietnamese cooperation agreements before the fall of the wall. As their scholarships ended and the factories where they worked closed down in quick succession, these Vietnamese soon found themselves in dire economic straits, and some turned to organized crime. At least six gangs, with memberships of 150, were gearing up to conduct turf battles to control contraband cigarettes, gambling, prostitution, and video and audio piracy in the city. Elsewhere in the East, some Vietnamese had come under attack from the growing neo-Nazi movement. In 1992 in the port city of Rostock, extremists had set fire to a hostel housing 100 Vietnamse asylum seekers. As the Minhs began to contact Vietnamese families in the working-class suburbs of Marzahn and Lichtenberg, they increasingly came under verbal abuse from neighbourhood youths, sporting leather jackets, shaven heads and *Vaterland* tatoos. Minh Chau shuddered to think that it was only a few years earlier during her revolt against her parents that she had willingly given herself to French and English Canadian bikers who bore striking resemblances to these racist thugs.

Minh Khai was, however, no shrinking violet, and hurled back equally ugly epithets at their aggressors in her best working-class German accent. Fuck them! These shitheads! Up to that point, Minh Chau had been happy to believe that all Germans were just kind blond giants like Wolfgang. Yes, indeed just a taller race of Canadians. While Minh Chau was mature enough to appreciate that these youths represented a fringe element in overall German society, she learned in her discussions with Minh Khai that multiculturalism so in vogue back home was seen by the majority of Germans as a threat to their way of life. The growing criminality of the Vietnamese gangs was flaming racist reactions. On the other hand, Germany's youthful Green Party under its charismatic leader Joschka Fischer was rallying many Germans to combat racism and build a multicultural society. Minh Khai proudly showed Minh Chau her party membership, with its sunflower logo, and spoke at length of the Greens' vision of a safe environment, peace, one Europe and a rainbow society of Germans of all origins.

Although Minh Chau had just finished a degree in international relations, she was still largely apolitical. Back home, she had integrated fully into Quebec society and favoured the social policies of the Parti Québécois. She had always viewed the party's founder René Lévesque as a father figure, and had mourned his death seven years earlier. Still, Canada was her country and she could not endorse the idea of full independence for Quebec. This left her in a void, and she was careful to avert debate with her university classmates, almost all of whom were fervent *indépendantistes*. Indeed, the Green Party had interesting ideas, and Minh Chau vowed to take a closer look at its nascent Canadian branch when she returned to Montreal. Wait a minute! Was she returning to Montreal? That would mean leaving Wolfgang. Suddenly, Minh Chau was thrown into a whirlwind of confusion.

"Earth to Minh Chau, where are you?" kidded Minh Khai.

"Sorry, I just came to a sudden realization that I need to think about what I should be doing next for the rest of my life. Tell me, how hard is it to get a job in Germany?"

"It is not easy, but your German is not that bad. If you study at a German university as a foreign student, the government will allow you to work for twenty hours a week. There is a lot of work for students in the restaurants and bars because the owners don't have to pay for the social benefits."

"Really. Hmm, let me think about that."

"You know if you want to work, maybe Wolfgang can help. I know that he is keen on proceeding with the docu-drama on Vietnamese boat people that he is planning to sell to Deutsche Welle."

"On boat people?" Minh Chau was somewhat taken back. Wolfgang had never mentioned this to her. She began to ponder all his questions. Well, that is all right. This film project really was not about her or her family. Wolfgang would never intrude like that. He was simply too kind and considerate.

After the two Minhs finished their second bottle of wine on the Kreuzberg apartment's tiny balcony, Minh Khai decided to call it a night. Minh Chau lay in bed for an hour, but finally curiosity got the better of her and she began to leaf through the notebook, in which Wolfgang wrote every day. She pulled out her dictionary to work through the German. After a few paragraphs into the notebook, she realized that she was reading a screenplay of her own life. The humiliations that the pirates had inflicted upon her mother as they held down her father with a knife to his throat were graphically on display. When she came to the incriminating passage on the boat, the act of murder that she as a child had committed, her heart sank. He had betrayed her. He had stolen her life and was ready to sell it to the world for his fame, or perhaps just for money. She threw the notebook across the room, shattering the delicate Venetian boat on the mantelpiece. She staggered over to the broken glass, sank to her knees, picked up a sharp piece and ran it down her arm stopping just before her wrist. With a rivulet of blood flowing from this superficial wound, she fainted beside her broken *humanity.*

In the morning, Minh Khai dropped by to discover Minh Chau sitting on her packed suitcase in a state of tears and a long bandage on the inside of her left arm. When Minh Chau was finally able to tell Minh Khai what she had discovered, the latter tried her best to defend Wolfgang. He was an artist. He drew from life's experiences to write his films. He was certainly going to discuss the script with Minh Chau before he did anything with it. Minh Chau should wait for his return to discuss things. While Minh Chau had come to respect and like her Vietnamese-German *alter ego* immensely, there was no going back on her decision. Wolfgang could burn in hell for what he had done. There were rules to respect in life. She felt violated by his intrusion into her private life.

Minh Khai accompanied her Canadian friend to the airport. On the bus ride there, the two girls held hands like schoolchildren. Minh Chau, who was exhausted by a sleepless night, lay her head on her friend's shoulder and dozed off. Her sleep brought back the tremours, the cold sweat to her brow. Minh Khai put her arm around her friend and gently wiped away the dampness. She had no sisters or brothers. Her father had raised her alone after her mother disappeared with an American soldier when she was only two. When she was ten, her father was killed in an accident at the Opel factory in Ruesselheim where he worked. Ruediger Werkmann, his father's foreman and friend, took her in. Ruediger's wife Heike became the only mother that she was ever to know. The Werkmanns lived in a working-class neighbourhood of Darmstadt near Frankfurt. There were plenty of Turks, Arabs, Greeks and Italians, but no Vietnamese. Minh Khai was sixteen before she met another Vietnamese. Outside, she looked Asian, but inside she felt German, at least until this beautiful, petite Canadian, her new sister, entered her life only five days earlier.

She did not agree with Minh Chau about Wolfgang. She thought as a German, rationally, and refused to take rash decisions. Minh Chau had made her promise to tell Wolfgang nothing—Minh Chau wanted him to suffer, never knowing why he had lost her. Minh Khai knew that one day, she would probably break that promise. Ruediger had been kind to her, and she intend to maintain her own friendship with him. For the moment, he did not even know that she and Minh Chau had become friends, so it would be easy to keep her promise, at least for a while.

As the bus pulled up to Tegel Airport, Minh Chau awoke with stars in her eyes. Minh Khai smiled at her and helped her through the airport. They did not need to speak. They were sisters.

Chapter Twenty-Five

Worlds Fall Apart

The funeral at Saint Viateur Church was well attended. Dr. Han Thieu's quiet and pleasant manner at the hospital was matched by the ardour of her efforts to cure her patients. Doctors, nurses, patients all filled the pews of the church as did hundreds of Vietnamese-Canadians from Montreal and Quebec City. Father André drove down from New Carlisle to say the mass. Marie-Christine and Thomas Smith flew in from Washington. Only Minh Chau was absent. An and Marc had cut their Caribbean cruise short, flying back from St. Lucia as soon as they heard the news. No one was able to reach Minh Chau. She was overdue in seeing her cousins in Paris. The last postcard that she had sent was from Venice. And then radio silence. The family had put off the funeral for two weeks to wait for word from Minh Chau. Finally, Voang decided to proceed to allow Mathieu to return to Rwanda as he was becoming increasingly concerned about the safety of his own family, amid reports of growing ethnic violence.

After the funeral, An asked if she could speak to Mathieu. They agreed to meet at Le Petit Italien, a nearby restaurant.

"Mathieu, I have wanted to talk to you since I got back. You and Dr. Leblanc were the ones who discovered my mother's body. Was there anything unusual about it?"

"Unusual? No, but I was in a state of shock and do not remember the details very well. Dr. Leblanc just explained to me that your mother died peacefully after a clot from her arteries had traveled to her brain."

"Yes, that is what I do not understand. There has never been a history of strokes in our family. But what worries me more is something that I came across when I sorted out my mother's papers. She was always so meticulous, but there was no medical record for her. I remember her having a very detailed one and she insisted that all of us keep copies of our medical history in case our physicians were to move or suddenly die."

"What are you suggesting, An?"

"I think that my mother and Dr. Leblanc have kept something from us. I was wondering if, perhaps, you could ask him."

"Ask him what precisely?"

"I want to know if my mother took her own life."

"Suicide? You surely don't think that just because of a missing medical file?"

"There is something else."

"Yes?"

"My mother still had title to our house in Saigon. When we left, she insisted that my cousin Dao and her husband Huynh live there. Yesterday, I received a letter from Dao, sent one week before my mother's death. My mother had gone to the Vietnamese Embassy in Ottawa to arrange for the transfer of the house to Dao's name. She did not even tell my father about this. We all would have agreed to it, of course. We love Dao. But mama told us nothing of her plan to transfer the house. It was as if she knew that she was going to die."

"But suicide, why suicide? Han was a successful doctor. Your father's business is going well. Both you and Minh Chau have done well."

"Let's not talk about my sister. She has a lot of explaining to do, and until she does, I do not want to hear her name. Mathieu, I think that my mother was terminally ill. I think that she had cancer. Dr. Leblanc is not a general practitioner. He is one of Canada's leading oncologists. Why would he be acting as my mom's G.P.? And why did he just happen to turn up at her house the morning that she died?"

"Okay. I have thought the same thing. An, we have not seen each other for many years, and I do not know how you will react to what I am about to say, but I will say it anyway. When I knew your mother in Quebec City, she asked me once to go with her to the hospital for some tests, and she asked me to say nothing about it to your father. It was a cancer clinic. Afterward, she explained that it had been a false alarm, but she did not want to burden any of you with worry."

"Is there more?"

"Yes, after the results came back, we went to a café and talked about my father's death. When he was diagnosed with cancer, it was already too late for treatment. The doctors gave him a year. During that year, he wasted away. My mother visited him in the hospital every day. He was the love of her life. It was awful. As the cancer ate away at his body, my mother also became emaciated. There was nothing physically wrong with her, but she seemed determined to follow my father in his final journey. I was ten at the time and I had a sister Susanne, who was nine. When my father finally died in incredible agony, my mother returned from the hospital and asked us to pack our bags to go to stay with our father's cousin, Aunt Mathilde, Marie-Christine's mother. She drove us to Aunt Mathilde's house, and argued terribly her. I remembered Mathilde shouting at my mother, 'This is not Korea!' My mother ran to the car and drove off into the fog. Her body washed up on the coast a few miles from New Carlisle. My sister Susanne never really recovered from the deaths of our parents. When she was sixteen, she pleaded with my Uncle André to find her a convent that would accept her so young. He used his position as a parish priest to do so. She has been a nun ever since and struggles with depression on a daily basis. Sometimes when I go to see her, she turns me away, telling me that she sees our mother's face in mine."

"Mathieu, I am so sorry."

"An, when your mother heard my story, she told me that she would never allow her death to be a burden on her family. If she did end her own life, it was an act of kindness toward you. You should remember it that way. However she died, you should take comfort in the fact that she passed away quickly and peacefully. Your mother only wanted your happiness and that of your father and sister. Let's not go turning up stones. They won't bring her back, and they could cause Dr. Leblanc a lot of trouble. Remember, he was not just your mother's physician, but also her friend."

"Mathieu, you are wise. It's hard not knowing the truth, but I think that you are right. I too have been keeping something to myself for a long time to protect others, or so I thought. I think that it is time that I told my father about Quan."

"About Quan?"

"Yes, he is still alive and I know where he is."

"That has to be your decision, An. I know that your family loved Quan very much, but I do not know what happened to him. I have never even met him and you don't need to tell me what happened. Just do what you think is right. There is one thing though."

"What is that?"

"Before my father died, he told something that I have always to tried to follow. He said, Mathieu, you find in life beauty and ugliness, happiness and despair and at times, it won't be obvious how you should react. The one thing that can guide you through the vicissitudes of life is understanding that kindness is the noblest of actions. When the world falls apart, be kind to those around you. When others want you to join them in punishing someone, let kindness forbid you from doing so."

"An, remember your mother's kindness to you and to everyone she knew. Note every act of kindness ever made toward you, and every one that you make toward another. And An, put aside your anger with Minh Chau. If she is not here today, there is surely a reason."

An thought deeply about the impact of Mathieu's mother's death on his sister Susanne. If their mother had committed suicide, what would be the impact on Minh Chau? She wished that Minh Chau was here to listen to Mathieu. His words, so softly spoken, were not only wise, but the embodiment of kindness. She hoped that her Marc would be just like Mathieu. She then decided that yes, she would tell her father about Quan, but she would turn over no stones about her mother's death.

Suddenly, she felt an uncontrollable desire to pay Mathieu for helping her make these decisions. She reached into her purse for the last piece of jade jewelry that her mother had managed to bring from Saigon. It was a tiny pendant. On the back were the ideograms of the old Vietnamese Chu Nom script "To Han from grandmother Mai, may happiness be yours for now and forever."

An pressed the pendant into Mathieu's hand. "Please take this for Denise."

Mathieu put away gingerly the pendant, stood, embraced An once last time, and left for the airport. As the cab moved forward in the light spring rain, the faces of Han and her family flashed before him, just as he saw them the very first time in Quebec. There was kindness in Han's features, pride in Voang's, the nine-year-old An showed wisdom and reliability, and the face of little Minh Chau waltzed between extreme joy and silent pain.

Mathieu was grateful that so many years ago, he had been given the opportunity to help this family, and vowed silently that should it ever be necessary, he would help them again. He then fingered the jade pendant, closed his eyes and dreamed of holding Denise and Étienne in his arms.

***

As the large jet cut through the clouds over Labrador, Minh Chau's anger finally subsided. She thought of the joy of seeing her family again. In her whirlwind romance with that fucking German, she had neglected to even write to them. She would make amends and seek their forgiveness. First, she would cook for her father his favorite rice and shrimp dish, *Con Chien Voi Thom,* and then show her mother fantastic photos of France and Italy. She had already shredded the pictures of Berlin, and flushed down the plane's toilet every photo of that fucking German. And he would not have his notes to humiliate her in public. She had burned those before leaving, and vowed that if she ever saw a film with her story in it, she would suc him to his last *deutschmark.* She could hardly wait to start her law studies to prepare herself for such an eventuality.

Mathieu picked up a copy of *Le Monde* at the bookstore at Mirabel International Airport. Without even looking at its front page, he tucked it under his arm and headed for the mezzanine restaurant to park himself with a coffee and doughnut at a table overlooking the concourse. He watched the mass of humanity passing each other in attire of all sorts. Sun-tanned tourists arriving back from Mexico in flamboyant cotton shirts. Canadian businessmen in dark, ill-fitting suits. European businessmen in well-tailored light grey suits. Some women of great style and beauty. Others in sweat pants and tee-shirts ushering along kids with chocolate-smeared faces.

One figure stood out in the crowd. It was not just her walk, a quick trot on six-inch heels, or her flowing black hair and dark sunglasses. It was her tiny stature, accentuated by the suitcase on wheels that dwarfed her even as she pulled it along. Or maybe, it was her determination to navigate around all the other passengers to gain a nanosecond in her race to the exit. Suddenly, he heard the figurine spew out two well-chosen Québécois epithets—*hostie, tabernac,* followed a perfunctory German *Scheisse,* a souvenir from her European vaca-

Soldier, Lily, Peace and Pearls   131

tion no doubt. In her efforts to beat the clock, she had broken the heel of her stylish Italian shoe. Falling forward, she found herself suddenly under the full weight of her gigantic suitcase. Two passengers rushed over to help the young woman, who had managed to squirm out from under her luggage and was holding up the heelless shoe. As the others helped her to her feet, she began to profusely apologize for her profanities in the most beautiful French, a delicate blend of international vocabulary framed in a light Québécois accent and with the slightest hint of the lilted Vietnamese intonation. It reminded him immediately of Han Thieu, who had mastered the language of Molière at her exclusive Saigon lycée, and then wrapped it in the sweet rustling of papaya leaves.

Mathieu rose to his feet to get a better look. From the concourse, the young woman looked back at him and removed her large dark glasses. Even from the distance, Mathieu could see that she had a stunningly beautiful face and was indeed from the land of a thousand smiles. She turned quickly away from him, and he felt somewhat shamed by his impetuous display of curiosity. As she hobbled toward the exit, holding her head up high, despite her wounded pride, and pulling once again her monstrous and potentially lethal luggage behind her, he followed her with his eyes before turning to the front page of *Le Monde*.

Rwandan and Burundian Presidents killed, read the headline. *On April 6, 1994, the airplane carrying Rwandan President Juvenal Habyarimana and Cyprien Ntaryamira, the president of Burundi, was shot down as it prepared to land in Kigali.* Mathieu's heart pounded as he read on that the Hutu press was already blaming the killing on the Tutsi-led Rwandan Patriotic Front and UN peacekeepers. His connecting flight from Brussels to Kigali would not arrive until the day after tomorrow. He dreaded what could happen before then, and immediately went to find a pay phone to make a call to Denise.

Minh Chau fished through her carry-on bag for a pair of sneakers as the bus pulled away from the terminal for the hour-long ride to Montreal. Even inside the bus, she kept on her sunglasses. The tear-streaked eyes beneath them were not a pretty sight. The plane ride had been a torment, as her thoughts of Wolfgang re-played themselves again and again in her head. How can someone go from such kindness to such treachery. What she had told him had taken sixteen years to voice. For the first time in her life, she had opened up to someone, something that she had not even done with her own family. She had never even told Quan what had happened on the boat. It was unfair. Life was unfair.

On the plane, a well-intentioned older man had tried to engage her in a little conversation. She listened to him politely, as she had been raised to do, by her parents. He was a journalist, returning from Central Africa. He had just finished an assignment on the UN peace-keeping mission in Rwanda, led by the Canadian general Roméo Dallaire. The ethnic tensions between the Hutus and Tutsis were at an all-time high. For a moment, Minh Chau put aside her own sorrow, and asked, "We have friends in Rwanda. I have not seen them since I was a teenager, but they were very close to us when we arrived in Canada. Did you meet Mathieu Hibou and his wife Denise in Kigali by any chance?"

"Denise Hazikimana?" asked the journalist.

"Yes, that's her name."

"Of course, she is a leading television commentator in Kigali. We spent a lot of time discussing the situation. But her husband has been in Canada for the last three weeks."

"Mathieu is in Canada?" said Minh Chau. "Wonderful. I really want to see him again."

"I am sure that you will."

Yes, thought Minh Chau as she settled in just across from the bus driver. If Mathieu is in Montreal, I am going to ask him to dinner. I never really thanked him for all that he did for our family. Funnily, she thought, the man in the airport who stared at me, he looked a little like Mathieu. No, that can't be right. That would be too much of a coincidence.

"Do you like music, mademoiselle?" asked the bus driver.

"What do you have?" asked Minh Chau.

"I have a beautiful tape that I recorded of a concert of one my favorite singers, Lina Boudreau. She comes from Acadia like me."

"Okay. Let's listen to it."

Minh Chau leaned back, as the bus driver put in the tape. It was great to be back home. Slowly the deep voice of Lina Boudreau filled the bus with images of the Acadian fishing hamlets devastated by the impact of overfishing.

Tous les bâteaux sont amarrés,
Et tanguent doucement,
Devant la mer qu'on a vidée,
Je pense à mes enfants,
Je suis pêcheur, c'est mon métier,
Et c'est celui de mon père,
Et me voilà sur le quai,
Avec plus rien à faire.

"What is your name?" asked Minh Chau.

"Robert Leblanc."

"Thank you, Robert for introducing me to this music. It is wonderful. My name's Minh Chau."

"You are welcome," replied Robert with a broad smile.

"Are you from Montreal?"

"Yes, from Outremont. And you?"

"I live in Plateau Mont-Royal," answered the blond bus driver, "but come from Shediac, New Brunswick."

"Have you been driving buses long?" asked Minh Chau, who began to study the young man.

"For about a year. I only do it on weekends. I study medicine at McGill."

"Another Dr. Leblanc then."

"What do you mean?" inquired Robert.

"No, it's just that our family's doctor is a Leblanc."

"Your last name is not Thieu, is it?"

"How did you know that?" asked a somewhat surprised Minh Chau.

"My uncle is Dr. Dominic Leblanc. I am so sorry about your loss."

"My loss? What are you trying to say," asked impatiently Minh Chau of the now pale-looking young bus driver.

"I am sorry. I shouldn't have said anything. You have been out of the country."

"Robert, tell me what you were going to say!" insisted Minh Chau.

"You really don't know, do you? I am sorry. Your mother passed away two weeks ago."

Minh Chau's heart sank to the bottom of her being. She stared angrily at Robert Leblanc, and then howled at the top of her lungs in grief.

When the bus reached the bus terminal in Montreal, the other passengers disembarked, but Minh Chau who had fled to the back of the bus, did not. Her body was paralyzed and unresponsive to Robert's entreaties. He went quickly into the bus terminal office and called his uncle. Twenty minutes later, Dr. Leblanc drove up in his beige Mercedes. He entered the bus and administered a sedative to its last passenger. With Robert's help, he put Minh Chau into the Mercedes and drove her to the hospital. From the hospital, he called Voang and explained what had happened. Voang and An were at the hospital within half an hour. They waited for Minh Chau to awake from her sleep. Three hours passed. When Minh Chau opened her eyes, she saw the remainder of her family and realized that what Robert Leblanc had said could only be true. She then laid her head back and let herself slip into a catatonic state.

***

The UN Hercules was the only plane that was allowed to land at Kigali Airport that day. The UN peace-keepers had muscled their way into the airport to ensure that its cargo of medicine would not be stolen by the rag-tag Interahamwe militiamen who were trying to take over airport "security." The Hutu militiamen were only lightly armed and certainly were no match for the Belgian peace-keepers, but they were unpredictable. Half of the UN escort kept a close watch over the militiamen while the other half unloaded the precious medicines from the vintage DC-3 to the armoured UN vehicle. Mathieu Hibou was greeted by his friend Major Hans van Eck, a no-nonsense professional soldier who had frequently dined at their home in Nyarutarama. No, Hans did not know where Denise and Étienne were. Yes, the UN had visited their house. It was empty like half of the houses in the neighbourhood. Yes, the Interahamwe were going after Tutsis in Kigali, and many people had fled to safe moderate Hutu and Tutsi villages in the countryside. No, he was not sure whether Denise had done the same.

Mathieu knew that Denise would try to make it to her grandmother in the town of Byumba in the north. They had discussed this scenario many times. The RPF rebels would be able to advance quickly on Kigali, and Byumba would soon be safely out of reach from Hutu extremists.

Mathieu rode into Kigali with Major van Eck. He was anxious to see General Dallaire, a fellow Canadian, who commanded the UN peace-keeping mission. Van Eck did not speak much to Mathieu, during the trip. His only remark was, "We are under orders not to speak about certain things, but maybe General Dallaire can brief you." On the road in from the airport, there were several roadblocks set up by Hutu militiamen. Drunk on beer, they screamed and shouted at the UN peace-keepers as they drove through the roadblocks, but did not try to stop them. Closer to the city centre, the roadblocks were manned by regular Rwandan soldiers who did not hesitate to level their AK-47s at the UN trucks and to carry out lengthy inspections. One of the Rwandan officers, Lieutenant Pascal Kirusu, recognized Mathieu. At first, Mathieu was glad. Pascal came from a mixed Hutu-Tutsi village near Butaré. As a young recruit on home leave in his village, he had helped Mathieu by acting as an unofficial translator for discussions with the village elders over a water distribution project. When the new well and water pipelines were finished, Denise had visited the village with him and met Pascal.

"Hi Pascal. Do you remember me? Mathieu Hibou from UNDP."

"Of course, Monsieur Hibou."

"Listen, have you seen or heard anything of my wife Denise Hazikimana?"

The Hutu officer's face darkened. He leaned toward Mathieu and whispered in his ear, "Forget your cockroach wife. She and her kind have soiled our land long enough." And before Mathieu could react, the young Hutu officer straightened up and waved through the convoy.

The truck rumbled along Boulevard de la Paix, the main thoroughfare of the capital. Mathieu felt a sharp pain in the left side of chest. It was like a stone weighing heavily on his chest. How could he have left Denise and Étienne in such danger? Why did he stay in Montreal so long? He knew that tensions were running high despite the Arusha peace agreement between the RPF and the Rwandan government. The success on the battlefield of the highly disciplined RPF had struck fear into the hearts of Hutus, who under Belgian colonial rule had been second-class citizens under the Tutsis favoured by the Belgians. Hutu extremist parties had increased their support among the urban unemployed and the poorer parts of a growing rural population faced with the scarcity of arable land.

As the truck pulled into the UN compound, General Dallaire came out of his office, flanked by two heavily armed bodyguards. His face was ash-grey. He jumped into an armoured personnel carrier and sped off before Mathieu could reach him, but one of his officers, Captain Jean Boivin, walked up to greet Mathieu in a disciplined military gait.

"Mathieu, you should not have come back."

"Jean, what are you saying. Denise and Étienne are still here."

"Of course, forgive me! We will help you find them. It's just that the situation is extremely grave. The presidential guard assassinated Prime Minister Agathe Uwilingiyimana yesterday along with ten of our men who tried to protect her."

Mathieu looked in disbelief at the captain whom he knew from Quebec and had once helped overcome personal difficulties. Could what Boivin had just said be true? Had the Rwandan military really turned against their own political leaders and against the UN peace-keepers?

"Have the killers been caught?"

"No, our orders are to evacuate foreign nationals, but General Dallaire is trying hard to get more reinforcements to protect Rwandan politicians and other civilians."

"What is happening to the Tutsis?"

"Tutsis and moderate Hutus are being exterminated in the country-side. In Kigali, we are protecting those who have taken refuge in schools and churches. I do not know for how long we will be able to hold out if reinforcements are not sent. It is a nightmare!"

Mathieu reflected on the information. Boivin was never one for exaggeration. "When can I go to Nyarutarama?"

"We will get you there this afternoon. We have a convoy headed for the Mille Collines Hotel at 2 pm. It will pass by your house, but I can tell you already that you will find no one you know. The entire neighbourhood has fled and looters are stealing everything that is not nailed down."

"Then I need to get to Byumba."

"Byumba will fall to the RPF any day now. You won't make it through the front. If Denise and Étienne are there, they will be safe. The Rwandan army is not a match for the RPF. It will only be a matter of time before the RPF takes Kigali."

"I want to go to Byumba."

"I will see what I can do. We still have radio communications with the RPF battalion that was stationed here. It fought its way out of Kigali yesterday, but it has taken up a forward position fifty miles from here. We are still trying to negotiate a ceasefire between them and the Rwandan Army. I know the RPF commander well. Have you maintained contact with Denise's cousin Antoine Bikindi?"

"Yes."

"You may need his help to get to Byumba after you get to the front. My intelligence officer tells me that Bikindi is commanding RPF troops in that area."

"Jean, thank you for doing this for me."

"Mathieu, you helped me pull my life together many years ago in Quebec City when I struggled with alcohol. I only wish that I could do more."

Boivin was true to his word. That afternoon, under the protection of five UN peace-keepers, Mathieu went through his ransacked house in Nyarutarama. The looters had stolen ever stick of furniture and taken Dao's Reviens painting. He went from door to door, but found no one. No one alive that is. Barely twenty feet from his front door behind some mulberry bushes, the bodies of his neighbours Jean and Marie Mujawamariya lay face down with the back of their skulls blown away. Mathieu and his protectors investigated the thirty corpses that littered the neighbourhood. Several were just children.

Many of the women had been raped before being killed. Even more horrifying, half the bodies had been hacked to death by machetes. Even two of the seasoned peace-keepers could not hold back and vomited at the sight of the headless bodies of two young children. Mathieu turned over the bodies to search for the mole on his son's lower back. There was none. Mathieu sighed in relief and then was overcome with nausea as he discovered that one of decapitated bodies had his castrated testicles stuffed in his hand.

At the Mille Collines Hotel, Mathieu went immediately to his friend, François Lasalle, the hotel manager. Lasalle offered to put Mathieu in contact with Colonel Mudenge, the commander of Kigali's special forces. For a price, Mudenge could surely get Mathieu to the northern front. The peace-keepers refused to take Mathieu to Mudenge's head-quarters. It was too dangerous after the cold-blooded murder of the Belgian peace-keepers by the presidential guard. The UN force had strict orders to give Rwandan special forces, known for their Interahamwe sympathies, a wide berth. Lasalle's personal driver had two brothers in the special forces and agreed to take Mathieu to Colonel Mudenge the next day.

Mudenge had been educated as an engineer in Brussels and had immigrated to Montreal in 1982. After a bar fight with Tutsi refugees two years later, he spent one month in prison and was then deported to Rwanda. Unable to find work as an engineer, he joined the army. Despite the deportation from Canada, Mudenge was still favourably disposed toward Canadians. His stay in Montreal had been the most beautiful time of his life. For years, he corresponded with his Québécois girlfriend in the hopes of returning to Canada. One day, he met a Canadian immigration officer, who said he could help for a "consideration." It was enough to start Mudenge on a career of extorting local businessmen, especially Tutsis, to amass enough money for the "consideration." Gibson was transferred before the transaction could be made, but Mudenge kept on extorting businessmen. Mathieu had never met Mudenge, but he knew of his story and his ardent desire to one day return to Canada.

"Hello Colonel Mudenge. My name is Mathieu Hibou."

"Yes, I know who you are. What do you want?"

"I am looking for my family. They have disappeared."

Soldier, Lily, Peace and Pearls   *139*

"Hakizimana, the TV journalist. Yes, I know of her. She is not with us."

"I think that she is in Byumba. I need to go there."

"The RPF already controls Byumba. You can go there when we liberate it."

"I want to go there now. Can you help?"

"Why should I ?"

Mathieu reached in his jacket pocket, pulled out one thousand U.S. dollars and placed them on the Colonel's desk.

"I do not need the money. I can get enough of that any time I want."

"Can you get one of these?" said Mathieu, as he pulled out his Canadian passport.

"What are you offering exactly?"

"My cousin, Denis Prud'homme is the Director General for Africa at Citizenship and Immigration Canada," said Mathieu truthfully. "He can get your case reviewed," embellished Mathieu.

"You are lying."

"And if I am not, do you really want to be here when the RPF takes Kigali?" asked Mathieu.

Mudenge pondered for a moment. "You are full of bullshit, but I will make you a deal," he said, pocketing the thousand dollars. "Give me your passport."

Mathieu realized right away what Mudenge's game was. A local Indian merchant in Kigali was well known for his contacts with top-notch forgers in Mumbai. A quick courier service, and Mudenge would have a perfectly forged Canadian passport. Mathieu did not hesitate for a second. Passports were often lost in Africa and he had his UN special travel document as a back-up until he could get a replacement passport. "Deal."

"It will cost you another five hundred for a guide to cross the front."

"Okay. When can we go?"

Mudenge snapped his fingers. A young soldier rushed up. "Take this

Tutsi-fucking white man to our man in Kinyami and get him across the front."

Turning to Mathieu, Mudenge said, "If you bring your wife back here, you will regret it. They killed our president. My men are hungry for revenge and the taste of sweet Tutsi cunt. Do you understand? Take your family back to Canada."

Ten miles out of Kigali, the Rwandan Army driver pulled over to fill a jerrycan with some river water. The driver came back in a panic. "Monsieur, they are crazy," said the young soldier. Mathieu went down to the river. There were hundreds of corpses floating down a small tributary of the Kagera River, some headless, others without arms. The river was crimson and on its bank, half a dozen bodies rotted as flies swarmed around them. Mathieu cover his face with a handkerchief and inspected each body. Some had single bullet wounds to the head. For most, the killers had used machetes. Sickened by the stench of decomposing flesh, Mathieu nonetheless felt relief to discover that his wife and son were not among the dead.

The young driver sped toward Kinyami, not daring again to stop again. After an hour, the young soldier said to Mathieu. "I want to cross over with you. My mother is Tutsi. Can I come with you?"

"Yes."

Just as they turned the corner, a dozen AK-47s were trained on them. The RPF rebels raced up and dragged the young driver out of the jeep. Mathieu screamed, "Stop," giving just enough respite for an RPF officer to step forward and spare the young driver from an immediate execution.

"Mathieu, brother, you have aged."

Incredible, in the middle of nowhere, Mathieu's old friend Antoine Bikindi appeared. Mathieu vouched for the young driver, who was quickly given an AK-47 and sworn into the RPF. The troops danced around the new recruit and sang *Rwanda Nziza*.

Rwanda nziza Gihugu cyacu
Wuje imisozi, ibiyaga n'ibirunga
Ngobyi iduhetse gahorane ishya.

Rwanda, our beautiful and dear country
Adorned of hills, lakes and volcanoes

Soldier, Lily, Peace and Pearls   *141*

The young driver was happy. He had feared the RPF. He had thought that they would kill him when they found out that he was a soldier. As he too sang Rwanda Nziza, his eyes beamed with hope. Then the bullet pierced his forehead, blowing away the back of his head.

The rebels fanned out with military precision, taking covering behind rocks where they could train their rifles on the open-back truck racing towards them. Ten shots took out the engine and three the tires. Four more shots decapitated the driver. The vehicle went reeling into the ditch. As the twenty government soldiers jumped out of the back, half of them were gunned down in mid-air. The others fell in a hail of bullets before they could reach the forest. Antoine went to each body to see if any could be saved. He was an RPF commander, but he was still a physician. None had survived.

Just then, a second truck came around the bend, carrying machete-wielding militiamen and a handful of armed soldiers. The soldiers realized the hopelessness of the situation, immediately threw away their AK-47s and put their hands in the air. The militiamen followed suit by tossing away their machetes. Slowly, the soldiers and rebels jumped down one by one from the back of the truck, and laid on the ground face down. Mathieu noticed immediately the red stains on the pants of the prisoners. He then walked over to the machetes. Their blades were covered with fresh blood.

Antoine grabbed hold of the militiaman nearest to him and dragged him to the discarded machetes. "Whose blood is this?" he demanded. The militiaman began to reek of urine and feces as his internal organs betrayed him. Antoine asked again, "If you want to die by these machetes, we can do that. If you want to live, tell me now."

"They made us do it."

"Who?"

"The Interahamwe from Kigali, and the soldiers too."

At that moment, one of the prisoners pulled out a pistol from his jacket, and shot the man dead. Other soldiers and four militiamen made a run for it. None made it farther than ten yards before the rebels' bullets cut them down. The man with the pistol was disarmed and forced to the ground.

"Who is this killer?" demanded Antoine.

Two prisoners shouted that he was the leader of the Kigali gang, and then pleaded for their own lives. Suddenly all the other prisoners were pleading for mercy. They were just farmers, they said. Those who had refused to kill had been killed themselves. They had no choice. The excuses flowed like diarrhea.

"Which village did you just attack?" demanded Antoine. The prisoners named a small village only ten miles away.

"When were you there?"

"Thirty minutes ago." The rebels suddenly realized that there could be survivors. Antoine ordered half his men onto the captured truck. He then turned to his second-in-command. "Tie up the prisoners and march them north to Byumba."

"What about this one?" asked the second-in-command.

"Castrate him and make him eat his testicles," said Antoine coldly. "But keep him alive."

"Stop, Antoine. You can't do that!" argued Mathieu, tugging at this arm.

Antoine turned to his friend and pulled out a Polaroid photo of hacked corpses. "We took this photo yesterday ten miles from here. You can come with us or stay."

"For the love of God, Antoine, do not do this to this man."

Antoine hesitated and then ordered his second-in-command, "Wait until I return, and don't touch him until then. Let's see what they did first."

The Interahamwe leader suddenly grabbed a machete from the ground and slit his throat before anyone could stop him.

"God's justice," said Antoine, as he climbed into the truck.

Mathieu looked back at the dead man, and glanced at the rest of the prisoners still lying face down on the ground, some quivering, others stiff as if already dead. "Will they be safe from your men, Antoine?"

Antoine raised his rifle and shouted to his men, "Today, we will liber-ate another village in Rwanda. The men we have taken prisoners today belong to the justice system of our new Rwanda. Until they are judged by our courts, by fair judges and juries of their peers, no harm shall come to them. Murderers cannot build a country, only free and just men can. Like you, I have suffered at the hands of Hutu extremists. Like you, my family members in the south are now threatened. I know your thirst for revenge, but God created the RPF to free Rwanda from killers and reunite its people, both Tutsis and Hutus, through re-establishing justice for everyone, including these men. Do you understand me?"

"Yes," shouted the rebels.

"Then God save Rwanda!"

"God save Rwanda." cheered the rebels.

Mathieu jumped aboard the truck and sat beside Antoine. Two miles down the road, Antoine offered him a half a bar of chocolate. From the direction of the group that they had left behind, they heard the crackling of AK-47s. Mathieu turned to Antoine in disbelief. Before he could say anything, Antoine softly said, "When you see what is surely awaiting us at the next village, you will understand why even the dreams of men cannot control the anger and sorrow of this war." Mathieu looked at his friend, a man of medicine, an individual of culture and compassion, and saw in his eyes the torment of a deep moral dilemma.

Chapter Twenty-Six
Through the Window

When Voang came to bring his daughter home from the hospital, his heart was as heavy as a stone. Since Han's death, he had eaten almost nothing. From his usual small but well proportioned stature, he had become a mirror image of his daughter Minh Chau. The two skeletal beings walked invisibly past the doctors and nurses to the exit and onward to Voang's new Renault sedan. He opened the door for his daughter, sat in the driver's seat, shifted into gear and began the 20-minute drive home in total silence. Neither was capable of beginning a conversation. Their thoughts remained mired in the fog of grieving and the absence of beauty.

An and Marc were waiting for them on the doorstep of the Thieu's house. After the funeral, An had asked her father's permission to live with Marc, and reluctantly, Voang had agreed. Reluctance not from his dislike of the young carpenter, whom he had come to admire, but from the fear of his now empty dwelling. Inside, Voang was happy that Minh Chau would be able to alleviate some of the sense of deep isolation that he had felt since his wife's death, but his worries about his daughter's health were taxing his reserves.

"Papa, let me take care of Minh Chau at our place," said An, as Marc nodded in agreement.

Minh Chau, lost to the world, did not even acknowledge what was being said about her.

"No, An, I am her father. It is my duty to protect and bring her back. It is what your mother would have wanted me to do."

An and Marc took Minh Chau by the arms and led her up the stairs, into the dark hallway and to her bedroom with the large bright window which gave onto the park across the street. They had bought new bright-coloured bed linen and a wonderful green duvet, and had even painted the walls in a soft shade of light green. Green was Minh Chau's favourite colour in all things. An tried to help Minh Chau into bed, but she refused and wandered over to the windowsill. She pulled apart the curtains and stared across at the empty park where crocuses were in full bloom. In seconds, the blue sky darkened and rain pelted against the window. Minh Chau did not even flinch when the rain turned to hailstones and played on the glass like a drum.

"Cousin Leyna will arrive shortly. She will know what to do," said An. As soon as Minh Chau had been hospitalized, she had called her psychologist cousin. During the two-week hospital stay, Leyna had worked closely with Dr. Leblanc and the staff psychiatrist to start Minh Chau on some new anti-depressant drugs. It would still be a week before the impact of the anti-depressants would be felt. Leyna had tried to engage Minh Chau in the hospital, but the young woman was totally unresponsive. Leyna reassured Voang that this was not unusual in the first weeks of post-traumatic stress. Once the anti-depressants did their work, it would be possible to try the therapy again.

Leyna knocked on the door and was greeted by An who led her immediately to her father. Like all the Thieu women, Leyna had been remarkably beautiful, but the vicious beating by the Triad mobster seven years earlier had left hideous scars and a deformed eye on the right side of her face. She had not given up Quan's whereabouts easily, but still felt deep guilt about what had happened to him. Greeting Voang in the customary two-handed shake, she then put her arms around his neck and held him tight for a moment until his tears soaked the collar of her blouse. She then helped him to the kitchen chair and seated herself across the table from him.

"Voang, do not worry. Minh Chau will have the best of medical attention. Many of Han's colleagues have offered to serve as consultants, and Dr. Leblanc is continuing Han's research on Jing Zi's medicines for depression. But you have to realize that it will not be easy. This is the third time in your daughter's life that she has endured serious psychological trauma. I treated her for the last episode, but I need to know how she recovered from the first episode in Pulau Bidong."

"It was Quan. It was always Quan who saved her." Voang explained the incredible role that the boy had played in Minh Chau's life, in all their lives. He spoke of his own grief when Quan disappeared, and was probably later killed by gangsters and buried in an unmarked grave or tossed into the Saint Lawrence. When his voice began to choke, An interrupted him. "Papa, Quan is not dead."

Voang looked at his older daughter. "How do you know that?"

Before An could answer, Leyna intervened, "Voang, let me tell you what really happened seven years ago." She nodded to An, with whom she had kept the full story a secret for seven years. An returned her glance, lowered her eyes in agreement. Leyna proceeded to tell her cousin how she had betrayed Quan to the Chinese gangster. An finished the story with how she had helped Quan bury the gangster and what she had made him promise. Voang took his cousin's hand at the end of the story. "No, Leyna, anyone would have done what you did. I am sorry for you. It was because of me that you came to know Quan." He stroked gently her scarred face—something that he had never done before. His touch healed Leyna's wounds, inside and out. He turned to An, and said, "I know that you meant well, but you should not have forced Quan to leave. We could have worked it out. Now we will never see him again."

"Papa, I know where Quan is."

Voang and Leyna looked up at her. "How?"

"It was part of our agreement that he should write me once a year. He has never failed to honour this agreement. I have his address in British Columbia."

Voang sat pensively for a minute. "Give it to me. I will bring him back. Only he can save Minh Chau."

"Wait Papa. Do you think that is the right thing to do?"

"Voang, we should talk about this," said Leyna.

"No, God gave us Quan to protect our family and for us to protect him. We are one family."

"Papa, Quan has his own life now. He wrote me about a beautiful woman he has lived with for seven years now. We should leave him in peace."

"If Quan tells me no, I will accept it, but first I need to speak to him. Do you have his telephone number?"

"No, but I have his address," replied An.

"An, will you stay with Minh Chau for a while. Tomorrow, I will fly to Vancouver."

Voang had never been so resolute. The quest to find Quan removed the weight from his heart. Han would be happy in heaven that he would bring Quan to save Minh Chau. He would not take no for an answer.

The sun was setting and Minh Chau still stood by the window under the watchful eye of Marc who had been asked to stay with her until the return of the others. The room grew dark, but Marc did not turn on the lights. The twilight through the window illuminated Minh Chau's silhouette as the shadows drew close around her. Had it not been for the incredible joy that An brought him every day since he met her, he would have been inextricably drawn into the web of Minh Chau's sorrowful allure. Minh Chau then turned her jade eyes toward him and unexpectedly crossed the floor and buried her tears into his chest before collapsing unconscious to the floor.

Chapter Twenty-Seven
Dom Bosco

After the first village, Mathieu threw his lot in with the RPF. He would not carry a gun—this was not in him to do, but with eleven years of rural development experience, he knew every inch of Rwanda. He guided Antoine's men through the mountain paths to surprise the Rwandan army and Interahamwe from directions that they never anticipated. Sometimes they arrived in time to prevent a massacre, but more often they were too late. For three months, Mathieu inspected the corpse of every woman who even slightly looked like Denise and every boy of Étienne's age. With an old Leica he photographed every victim. When he ran out of film, Antoine and his men would break into the general store of a local town in the middle of the night to steal new film. Often they were obliged to fight their way out when larger groups of Rwandan troops were alerted to their raids. Five rebels had given their lives for this film, but all were agreed on the necessity of photographic evidence of the genocide. In villages that had escaped the massacres, the rebels would escort the Tutsis and moderate Hutus into the mountains where they would be safe. Local Interahamwe leaders were executed as a warning to the others not to participate in the massacres. In July, they arrived on the outskirts of Kigali. The push of RPF from the north was crushing the Rwandan military and the Interahamwe had little stomach for fighting real combatants. Antoine's troops were the first to reach the Dom Bosco school.

The 2000 victims of the massacre at the school were murdered on April 17. This was in the first two weeks of the genocide and just after Mathieu had left Kigali. This reassured Mathieu. Had Denise and Étienne been in the school under the protection of the UN peacekeepers, Van Eck would have known about it. Mathieu was clinging to the hope that they had gone south instead of north. Most of the Hutus there supported parties in opposition to Habyarimana's Hutu power movement. Several of the Hutu prefects and Burgomasters, local mayors, had actively resisted the Interahamwe campaign against the Tutsi. Several had paid with their lives, but their bravery had encouraged the population to hide large numbers of Tutsis from the army and militiamen sent down from Kigali.

A Belgian missionary accompanied them to the school and recounted the story of what had happened—much of it compiled from the confessions of devoutly Catholic Belgian peace-keepers just before Brussels withdrew them in protest over the refusal of the UN to reinforce the mission in Rwanda.

Senior UN officials had ordered the peace-keepers protecting the school to withdraw to the airport, and this despite the presence of beer-drinking Interahamwe militiamen with machetes just outside. When the refugees inside the compound realized they were being abandoned, they began to crowd around the UN vehicles to stop them from leaving. Some even pleaded with the Belgians to shoot them in order to spare them from the machetes. The soldiers had to fire in the air to open the path for the last vehicles. The shots alerted also the Interahamwe in the neighbourhood that the Europeans were abandoning the refugees. As the Belgian soldiers drove away, the killers moved in.

Dutifully, Mathieu helped to photograph and document the corpses in the Dom Bosco School. The putrid smell of three-month-old decaying bodies was overwhelming. What the rats and insects had not eaten away, left little for identification. As Mathieu was wrapping up his work, he saw Antoine staring at him from the other side of the school's meeting hall where a small number of the remaining corpses lay. The lids of Antoine's eyes dropped, as he motioned Mathieu over. At Antoine's feet were a woman and a small boy, their faces rotted off and the rest of their bodies full of maggots.

"Did you find identification papers, Antoine?" asked Mathieu, refusing to acknowledge what could be the only reason for Antoine to call him over.

"They are not necessary, Mathieu," said Antoine, as he crouched down and picked up the hand of the female body. Around its wrist was a thin bracelet caked in dried blood. Antoine scrapped away the blood to reveal intertwined strands of red and black hair.

Mathieu froze. Denise, Étienne, it could not be possible! Here in Kigali! They were here under the protection of the Belgian peace-keepers while he was still in the city. He cursed Van Eck. Why hadn't he known that Denise was here at the school. Why hadn't the Belgian peace-keepers taken them with them when they left. His thoughts whirled in anger and confusion. And then, an inner peace prevailed. He reached down to lift up in his arms what remained of his wife's body and, without asking, Antoine did the same for Étienne. Together they marched outside into the sunlight and laid Denise and Étienne onto the back of a truck.

The young *Twa* in Antoine's group rushed up with a bed sheet and asked deferentially if he could cover the bodies to protect them from the swarm of flies and give them some final dignity. Mathieu held his hand up to stop him. He gazed upon the bodies, and their bodies became whole again. He saw them there in their incredible beauty, gently smiling as if they were just sleeping. He bent over and kissed their foreheads and then put An's jade pendant around Denise's neck. He could feel Antoine's hand on his shoulder. "Mathieu, my brother, I promise you that I will arrange the best funeral possible for my cousin and your son. But now, I have to leave. We must liberate Butaré. We must end this killing, once and for all. You should stay here until I return. Remember this life is but a passage to the next, and Denise and Étienne will wait for you in God's kingdom."

For the first time in his life, Mathieu looked angrily at Antoine and said, "Denise and Étienne are too good for a god who allows this!" He then slipped the hair bracelet from Denise's wrist and put it on his own. He sat on the back of the truck among tens of corpses and interlocked his fingers in the hands of his wife and son. As the truck pulled away, he sang softly the song that he had first learned to calm Minh Chau down and had sung countless times since to put Étienne to sleep.

Voilà le bon vent, voilà le joli vent,
Voilà le bon vent m'ami m'appelle.
Voilà le bon vent, voilà le joli vent,
Voilà le bon vent, m'ami m'attend.

Chapter Twenty-Eight
Bao

Quan woke at Melissa's side. For seven years, her body had given him comfort and diminished his nocturnal journeys into the darkness of the past. He did not love with the same intensity that he knew she loved him, and he reproached himself for that. Their love was certainly the best kept secret in the small community of Cultus Lake where they lived in a modest cottage that Quan had bought with the proceeds from selling Jing Zi's medicines. Without proper documentation to work in Canada, Quan had worked under the table in construction for the first five years while he developed a small clientele for the medicines that he bought from Dr. Kang and re-sold in the surrounding communities of Chilliwack and Abbotsford.

He was careful to stay away from Vancouver itself, and never went to Richmond, which had become a majority Chinese suburb. He kept his head shaved and wore glasses, which he did not need, to alter his appearance. He never spoke Chinese. Instead he would speak only English but with a distinctive French accent. Through Melissa, he had obtained a new identity—that of Paul Marois, an immigrant from Réunion, a small French possession off the coast of Madagascar. His false papers would not hold up to scrutiny at an international airport, but they were good enough for Quan to get a Canadian driver's licence.

Today was one of the most important days of his life. Voang had tracked him down and left a note on his door for the two to meet at the local coffee shop that morning. Quan was happy. He had faithfully kept his promise to An, but he missed his adopted father, mother and sisters, Minh Chau and An, almost as much as he missed his real sister Hue still in Bangkok. Life with Melissa was beautiful, but they were never able to have common friends. After he had returned to Vancouver and to Melissa, she told him who her father really was. It shocked him, but by then their relationship was sealed and he accepted the risks associated with being with the daughter of the head of the Triad that was actively looking for him. Melissa kept tabs on the search through cultivating some of her father's henchmen. It was easy enough, given her looks and her status as the daughter of the crime organization's boss. John Wong had called off his own search for Quan after a couple of months. Tao Tsao, on the other hand, was dogged in his hunt for Quan and had put up a $50,000 bounty on Quan's head. No one made a fool of Tao, and the gangster killed in Quebec City was the brother of one of his three wives. But Melissa was also convinced that it was just a matter of time before Tao gave up. Quan was not so sure. There was only one way out of the Triad, and Tao kept on increasing the bounty year after year.

Melissa was now practicing medicine and had just set up a small clinic in nearby Chilliwack. Soon they would have enough money to move elsewhere—somewhere safer, far away from the Triad. Perhaps in the B.C. interior or far off in the Maritimes, where the Triad had no presence.

Quan's meeting with Voang was scheduled for 10 am. Quan shaved and put on his track suit for his daily five-mile run along the lakefront. It was only six and the path was empty in the tiny community with its mainly pensioner year-round population, who were never in a rush to get up in the morning. Quan watched the bright red-orange sun reflect in the placid water and light up the evergreen mountains. Cultus was the most beautiful place that he had ever known. He particularly liked its colourful residents. Mrs. Wilson, who had, at 95, just returned from her first visit to China, a three-week tour to Beijing, Shanghai and Hong Kong. Mohammad Najib, the Syrian pizza owner, who had escaped the Hama massacre which had claimed the lives of three of his brothers. And then there was Pablo, the computer software designer from Chile whose programming was revolutionizing something called the Internet.

Quan had never expected to find such serenity. He could not have done so without Melissa. Why was it then that he felt that he was also holding back? Was it the fear that if he gave in completely, he would no longer be able to protect her? Quan reflected on his life. He had loved his parents, his sister, the Thieus, but he had never completely loved a woman, not Mali, not even Melissa. Still, Melissa made him feel whole and maybe that was what love was.

Quan decided to cut through the forest on the way back. The Douglas firs were all 100 feet tall, still young trees by British Columbia standards, but they cut out the sun. Quan enjoyed the magical darkness of the woods between the village and the golf course. His feet pounded the forest floor, as he picked up the pace, jumping over fallen trees. The chirping of wrens, chickadees and jays filled the air, and Quan felt invigorated.

Voang waited patiently at the coffee shop. It was almost 10 a.m. It was hard for Voang to imagine that Quan had spent seven years in this tiny community. Yes, it was beautiful, but what was there to do here? Voang had only known living in cities. He could not imagine spending more than a week in this lakeside community.

"More coffee, sir?" asked the buxom, blonde waitress.

"Yes, please." Voang had never seen so many blondes before. It was like being in Scandinavia. As the waitress moved across the floor, he watched her with his eyes. He felt guilty. Han was only two months dead, and already his hormones were taking over. At 56, he was in excellent shape and knew women were attracted to him. He had had affairs during his marriage to Han, but all were well kept secrets and they had been spaced far apart—just the occasional relapses. It was not that he had not loved his wife. He certainly had, but he had been married since his early twenties and at times, he felt he had missed his youth. Now, he was alone and yearned for companionship.

"Would you like some pie. We just made a blueberry pie," smiled the waitress. She was probably no older that thirty. Far too young for Voang, but there was a glint in her eyes that betrayed a definite interest. He smiled back at her, and could see a slight blush come to her cheeks.

A hand on his shoulders brought Voang back from his lapse into flirtation.

"My God. It really is you," said Voang, jumping to his feet to embrace Quan.

"It has been a long time, father."

"Seven years."

"How did you find me?"

"An told me."

"An? Has she changed her mind?"

"Yes, we all want you to come back."

"But my life is here now."

"Quan, I have bad news for you. Han died two months ago."

Quan drew a long breath as the soft image of his adopted mother passed through his mind. "I am sorry, Voang. How did Han die?"

"A stroke. It was a quick death. She did not suffer, but the impact on Minh Chau has been serious. She is in a deep depression. Quan, we need you to talk to Minh Chau."

"Of course, father, I will come as soon as I can."

"Sit Quan. Tell me about your life."

Quan told his adopted father of the seven long years hiding out in Cultus Lake. He spoke of Melissa, but avoided telling Voang who her father was. He then noticed a heavyset Chinese man sitting two tables down. At the point, Quan realized that he was speaking in Vietnamese to Voang. The large man got up and passed directly by Quan, giving him a long look.

"Voang, did you find my cottage right away?"

"Well, I had to ask a few people, but no one knew you by the name of Quan. The owner of the Chinese convenience store here told me where you were when I described you."

A shiver went up Quan's spine. He knew the store owner was deep in debt to the Triad. To date, he had managed to avoid suspicion. There were a lot of Asians in Réunion, and up to now, no one had ever heard him speak Chinese or Vietnamese. Quan watched as the stocky man got into his car and picked up a large mobile telephone. "Voang, we have to get out of here. Follow me," he said, as he pulled Voang toward the rear exit.

"Where is your car, Voang?"

"Over there."

They climbed into the compact rental. Quan directed Voang to the road toward the Columbia Valley. There they would be safe.

Twenty minutes later, they pulled up to the Fa Yu Buddhist Monastery hidden away from the main road deep in the woods. The monastery had been founded only a few years earlier by mainly Chinese Buddhist nuns, seeking solace in their adopted land. The nuns greeted Quan warmly. He asked for sanctuary for a few days. Of course, he was their friend and co-religionist. They covered the rental car with branches, and Quan explained to Voang the danger that they were in. That night they would return to the village and see if Melissa was under surveillance. He would ask Mrs. Wilson to visit her. She would do so for him. She was always there for him, and loved Melissa as if she was her own granddaughter. Mohammad Najib would also help. He feared no one, and was well connected with the local bike gangs should they need some muscle. He was also tight with the RCMP detachment.

Sister Chenda took Quan and Voang to a small hut 200 yards behind the monastery. Chenda was originally from Cambodia and had discovered by accident Quan's real identity three years earlier. Quan, who had been hired to help build an extension, had made the mistake of swearing in the rough peasant Khmer that the guards had taught him, after he dropped a beam on his foot. Chenda was at first discreet, but eventually she won his confidence and invited him to confide in her. Quan's parents had only been nominal Buddhists and died before they had been able to pass on to their son even the most rudimentary notions of their religion. Besides, the Khmer Rouge had ruthlessly repressed all religion on the farm. Chenda took him on a spiritual journey of re-discovery and raised his self-understanding through meditation. Together with Melissa's unconditional love, Chenda's guidance helped Quan leave behind the nightmares of the farm and realize his own coincidental existence in the vastness of the universe.

"Brother Quan, how can we help you?" asked Chenda.

"Can you drive us back to the village tonight when it is dark? It is too risky to use Voang's rental car."

"Of course. Is it the Triad?"

"Yes."

Quan had told his spiritual guide his entire life. She too was a survivor of the Khmer Rouge reign of terror. Raised in Angkor Wat, she had been a civil engineer before becoming a nun. It was the restoration work on the city's temples that had brought her back to religion after her rebellion as a student in Phnom Penh. Like Quan, she had tasted the carnal pleasures of the world, but had renounced them forever. Still at fifty, these desires would come back to test her. She looked at Voang's handsome face. His virility attracted her, and at the communal evening meal, his quiet manner captured her attention. There was neither weakness nor arrogance in his tone. Although he was a devout Catholic, his respect for the Buddhist nuns was beyond question. He too felt comfortable with Chenda, and soon recounted the purpose of his journey. He described Minh Chau's condition, and what Quan had done for her in the past. Chenda promised to help however she could.

That evening, she drove them to Mrs. Wilson's house. It was a pleasant one-storey bungalow with climbing roses covering its exterior. Mrs. Wilson took a stroll and ten minutes later came to inform them that Melissa was gone, but had left a note for Quan. She would be visiting her father for two days. He had phoned her to ask her to return to Vancouver because he was ill. Quan realized that this was a ploy by the Triad. They did not want Melissa around when they dealt with him. He decided that his only option was to leave right away. Through Mrs. Wilson, he would get in touch with Melissa and they would complete their plans to leave. He did not fear for Melissa. No harm would come to her from her father, but when they would be finally re-united, she would have to break forever with her family. There was no other way. They had discussed this a hundred times. First, he and Voang had to return to Montreal. There was no question of taking a plane. Quan's fake identification would never make it through airport security. He decided to see Mohammad Najib.

"Marhaba Habibi," said the affable Syrian who gave Quan a big hug. "Who is your friend?"

"Mohammad Najib, this is Dr. Voang Thieu. He is my adopted father."

"Pleased to meet you, Dr. Thieu."

"And for me."

"What can I do for you, Paul."

Although Mohammad Najib knew that Paul Marois was just an alias, he had never learned his friend's real name, nor did he care too. After all, Mohammad Najib was also just a name that he had picked out of a hat when he fled across the border into Lebanon in 1982.

Quan explained their dilemma, for the first time trusting his friend with the full story. Then he asked Mohammad Najib for the cash that he always entrusted him with in case of emergency and for the old Ford Focus that Mohammad Najib kept licenced, but never used. Without hesitation, Mohammad Najib gave Quan both. He then asked Mohammad Najib to return the rental car for Voang. Again he agreed. Quan would miss the Syrian's unconditional friendship.

The wrens were wakening the forest with their broken melodies as Quan and Voang rose the next morning. It was too dangerous to return to the cottage for Quan's belongings. Quan had no doubt that the Triad was already staking it out. Mohammad Najib had lent Quan some clothes, and more importantly, one of his hunting rifles. Chenda and the other nuns had prepared food for the trip. Quan selected some key Chinese medicines from the stock that he had confided to Chenda. She would sell the rest and send him the proceeds. It would take five days to reach Montreal—three thousand miles across mountains, plains and forest. Five days for Voang and Quan to recount every aspect of their seven years of separation as they discovered the vastness of their adopted homeland.

Chapter Twenty-Nine

Gaza

Mathieu Hibou looked at the sparsely furnished UNDP office in Rimal. He was the first UNDP international staff member to be assigned to it. The day after the discovery at Dom Bosco, he had walked into the UNDP office and tendered his resignation. Fletcher, the UNDP Country Coordinator, had talked him out of it and convinced him to take on the assignment to open the new office in the Gaza Strip. It would get Mathieu out of Rwanda and the challenge of the new assignment would hopefully break the endless loop of remorse over *their* deaths. Mathieu agreed, but first he would put in order the photographic evidence of the genocide. Kagamé, now in Kigali, had asked him to do so. Then he would return to New Carlisle to give Denise and Etienne a proper funeral at Uncle André's church, far, far away from this nation of murderers.

For two weeks, Mathieu had buried himself in his work, refusing to look at the faces on the streets of the capital. Which ones had wielded the machetes? Which ones had stood by? Which had ended Denise's and Étienne's lives? He had loved Hutus and Tutsis alike, giving everything he could for eleven years to help both groups rise out of poverty. He had never understood the animosity between the two groups, and he had never seen the malice in their hearts. Now he would bid farewell to the madness of it all, and would with two small urns continue his voyage through life.

"Hello Mr. Hibou. I am Khaled Abdelnour," said the tall handsome Palestinian, who was to be his deputy coordinator. "Pleased to meet you."

Abdelnour came from a well-established Palestinian family. His father Yassin had headed the Palestinian delegation to the Madrid peace talks. Both father and son had reputations for competence and independence from Yasser Arafat's new Palestinian Authority and had little sympathy for the increasingly strong Islamist movement.

Mathieu had left Rwanda two months earlier. He visited his family in New Carlisle. His uncle André said mass for Denise and Étienne in his parish church. All the Hibou-Prud'homme-Bonté clan turned out.

Marie-Christine and Thomas Smith flew in from Washington. With Marie-Christine, he rowed out to the point to re-unite a few of their ashes with the sea—the final resting place of his parents. In the boat, Marie-Christine told him of Minh Chau's depression.

He phoned Voang from New Carlisle. An answered instead. Her father was in British Columbia looking for Quan. Could he speak to Minh Chau? An warned him that there might not be a response from her sister, so deep was her depression. She took the cordless phone to Minh Chau's room. As always, she was standing next to the window, her face motionless. An told Minh Chau that it was Mathieu on the phone and put the receiver to her ear. Mathieu tried to engage her, but there was no response. An asked him to just sing "Voilà le bon vent." Mathieu softly sang the song. Still no response. An thanked Mathieu and hung up. Just then, soft words in Vietnamese, the first in weeks came from her sister. They were tender and sung beautifully in Minh Chau's child-like voice.

Been a long time they say
That you do not truly love
Silently each day is a lie ...

An's heart leaped at the sound of their engagement song for Mathieu and Denise. She had recognized Mathieu's voice, even if she had not understood a word he said. She held her sister in her arms and joined in.

Love him
Then you go away
His own helplessness to stay

Minh Chau turned to her sister and changed the song. "Soldier, lily, peace and pearls. All together in one world." Her eyes opened wide, "Quan?"

"Yes, Minh Chau, he will come." promised An, as joy jumped in her heart and tears flowed down her cheeks. She held her sister tight in her arms and danced around the room, singing again and again "Soldier, lily, peace and pearls. All together in one world."

***

When Mathieu hung up the phone, he thought of the two young Vietnamese girls. He had not seen them for years, but their faces were engraved in my mind. He looked at the hair bracelet that he had taken from Denise's body. He had sworn to wear it until his own death. It brought back the memory of young Minh Chau—her vivacity and kindness. He felt powerless that he could not help her now. His own reserves had been exhausted by the death of his family. He pledged that he would write the Thieus soon and every month after that just as Han had written to Denise and him for so many years. Suddenly Mathieu felt terribly alone. He had never questioned his place in the universe and now he wondered whether his existence was worth more than just debris. His chest constricted. His shoulders slumped, and his head weighed down heavily. He looked at his open suitcase, straightened himself up and placed a call to the UNDP office in Jerusalem. He would be on the Tuesday flight as scheduled. Yes, he was looking forward to his new duties in Gaza.

"Mr. Hibou, I have read a lot of your articles on agricultural development in Rwanda," said Khaled Abd-al Shafi. "We have a lot to do here in Gaza. Your expertise is very important to us. We need to rejuvenate the land."

"Thank you. It won't be easy. These preliminary analyses of the aquifers are not promising. Our experts in New York are proposing to decrease agricultural production here in order to save water for urban consumption."

"That would kill our people. Most people in Gaza are refugees. Their parents and grandparents had fled from farming communities in central and southern Palestine during the 1948 war. Despite the concrete jungle of the refugee camps where most still live, they are still *fellaheen*—farmers at heart. The oranges from the orchards, the strawberries from the fields and even the tomatoes and cucumbers from the greenhouses connect them to the land. This gives them a sense of belonging and identity."

"Don't worry. I have a few ideas, especially in the use of Dutch glass house technology, and some West African water-harvesting techniques. There are also a few tricks in urban agriculture that I learned from my work in the *bidonvilles* of Kigali."

With Khaled, Mathieu soon visited every inch of Gaza, from the sprawling Jabalia refugee camp to the orchards of Beit Hanoun. While the Israeli army had withdrawn from the population centres in the strip, they still controlled all the main roads and protected the eight Jewish settlements, which occupied some of the best agricultural land in Gaza and which used a disproportionately high percentage of the groundwater. The Israeli soldiers had no love for the UN, but respected UNDP's right to travel uninhibited within Gaza and between Gaza, Israel and the West Bank. With a little advance notice, Mathieu was usually able to obtain a travel pass for Khaled to accompany him on his trip to the Jerusalem office and onward to the West Bank. As time passed by, the two became close friends. Khaled's family welcomed him into their lives. They were cultivated people, who could cite Sartre as well as they could Omar Khayyam. It was not easy speaking about the occupation, and less easy speaking about Rwanda, but as their confidence grew, they overcame these taboos.

"Mathieu, do you think that we will ever triumph over the evil of human nature?" asked Karin, Khaled's German wife.

"What is evil?" asked Mathieu.

"What do you mean," injected Saleh, Khaled's brother. "You documented the Rwanda genocide with your photographs. Was that not evil?"

"Saleh, please do not raise that!" implored Karin, thinking immediately of the fate of Mathieu's family.

"It is okay," said Mathieu. "I cannot deny that what happened to my family and hundreds of thousands of Tutsis and moderate Hutus will always be with me, but I do not believe in evil. It took me some time to come to some way of dealing with it."

"How do you deal with it?" asked Khaled. "We have suffered from almost half a century of dispossession and occupation, but our death toll has only been in the thousands. I understand that 90% of the Tutsis were exterminated, mostly by machetes."

Mathieu braced himself. Khaled was his friend, but the bluntness of his words hurt him just the same. Mathieu's natural stoicism enabled him to summon his inner strength to remain rational, despite the pain deep inside him.

"I met a man not long ago who practiced Zen Buddhism. He told me something that has helped me understand human nature. He told me that the 'sense of self' is at the bottom of nearly all the problems that we have. The 'selves' that we create—'false selves,' as he put it—

make us each characters in each others' novels. We are protagonists in our own novels and, often, antagonists in the novels of other people. We attribute mostly positive qualities to ourselves, and negative qualities to our antagonists. The more we buy into the existence of these qualities, the more 'real' we feel to ourselves and others feel to us.

"All the petty little grievances, all the jealousies, and yes, all the wars and evil behavior we humans have exhibited throughout history are part of an effort to make this false 'sense of self' real. And this is what happened to the Hutu extremists – their false idealization of themselves and their demonization of the Tutus led them to exterminate people who spoke the same language and had sprung from virtually the same genetic heritage. It was all based on delusion, and from it sprang cruelty on a scale that humanity has seldom seen."

"And what of us and the Israelis?" asked Saleh.

"I cannot tell you how to feel, how to deal with the injustice that you feel toward the Israelis. Nor am I here to rationalize their behavior towards you. What the Zen Buddhist taught me is that we are all the creators of our own reality. When we allow our egos, our sense of self, to grow and solidify, we lose our sense of reality—the sense, almost mystical, of our commonality. There is a real sense of self, quite different from the usual one, in which we can only feel tenderness towards our human brothers—but that perception is buried, almost always, beneath the delusions of everyday life."

"And this is what you believe?" asked Karin.

"Yes and no. I see value in containing the ego, but what I want to believe in is the driving force of kindness. It is only kindness that can dispel fear, hate, envy and all the other things that collectively others see as the baseness of human nature."

"And kindness will bring you peace and happiness?" asked Saleh with mild sacrasm.

"Not necessarily, but that is not the point. People who commit atrocities can also be happy. For them, their distorted narratives lead them to live in a fantasy world where their killing, raping and abuse are justified. To the degree that they succeed in their perversions, they are happy."

"And you, are you happy?" asked Khaled.

"I am happy to be in your company. I am happy for your friendship. I am happy to be here to help the people of Gaza. But no, I am not happy."

"Mathieu, I am sorry. We should not have raised this. It is just that it is hard to be pacifists when innocent people are humiliated every day by Israeli soldiers and settlers."

"I understand. I am the way that I am. I have seen too much bloodshed to justify any more killing," said Mathieu.

At that moment, Hanna, Khaled's sister, came in with a portable radio. She turned it up. Tens of worshippers at the Ibrahimi mosque in Hebron had been gunned down by a crazed Israeli settler, who was finally overcome and killed by the surviving worshippers.

Mathieu excused himself. It was easier declaring his belief in displacing hatred with kindness than putting it into practice.

Chapter Thirty
The Awakening

The trip from Vancouver took six days. It was the first time that Quan and Voang had seen the mountains flatten for a thousand miles into the Canadian prairies. Then the black flies of northern Ontario took over, making it almost impossible to stop along the highway. It was August, and the sun was scorching. They took Highway 11 across Northern Ontario, dropping into the small franco-ontarian town of Kapuskasing. For the first time in years, Quan spoke French. Minh Chau had been an excellent teacher, and it all came back naturally. The young waitress in the roadside café flirted shamelessly with Quan, complimenting him on his French and returning to offer re-fills of coffee three times. Voang had to smile. Quan had certainly become a handsome man, especially now that his hair was growing back and he had dispensed with his ugly glasses.

"Dr. Thieu, what did Leyna say about Minh Chau's condition?"

"She called it an acute form of post-traumatic stress disorder. What is unique is the almost catatonic state that it has induced in Minh Chau."

"Does Leyna really think that I can help?"

"It does not matter what Leyna thinks, I know that you will be able to save Minh Chau."

"Why?"

"Because you are Bao. Remember that please."

"Yes, father."

Quan saw himself back in Pulau Bidong. It was the responsibility of protecting Minh Chau that had bonded him with the Thieus. It was that which had given him a new family, new parents. He remembered fondly the rice dishes that Han and his sister Hue would prepare for the family. They did not have much in Pulau Bidong, but they had been happy there. He thought of his year in Quebec City, of how Minh Chau's coquettishness had almost gotten him into real trouble.

The sixteen-year-old waitress was back to ask if they wanted dessert.

Her milk-white complexion and winning smile would make her an irresistible woman in a few years. Her youth reminded him of Mali at that age and of his life in Bangkok, now an eternity away. He recalled Mali's words "Customber gave me big, big tip" as she stuffed the two hundred baht into his shirt pocket, and then Quan handed the waitress a ten-dollar tip. As they were leaving, she walked Quan and Voang to the door of the restaurant. When he shook her hand goodbye, he felt a small piece of folded paper go from her palm to his. "Manon 878-5533, call me if you are back in Kapuskasing." Quan smiled at the girl's boldness.

Hamas had decided to take on the Jewish settlers in the Gaza Strip with armed night-time incursions. The Israelis retaliated with frequent raids into the city and refugee camps, ending in bloody stand-offs between the Israelis and Islamists and, sometimes, the Palestinian police. Islamic Jihad, a smaller resistance group, was even more daring and introduced a new tactic, suicide bombing. First, they used it against the border guards at the Erez crossing into Israel. The Israelis promptly closed the crossing, preventing tens of thousands of Palestinian labourers from reaching their jobs inside Israel. Their incomes were the mainstay of the Gazan economy. If it were not for the dramatic increase in greenhouse vegetables and urban poultry production, there would have been widespread malnutrition.

Under Mathieu's leadership, UNDP pumped millions into rural and urban agricultural projects. Mini egg and poultry farms and plastic greenhouses began to crop up on every available piece of land. At the same time, donors' funds were directed toward water and sanitation projects. The Gazans were skilled construction workers, and underemployed civil engineers, mostly trained in Egypt, were plentiful. As Israeli middlemen in the clothing industry still were allowed to subcontract with small Palestinian suppliers, UNDP began an ambitious small-scale credit program to enable women to buy sewing machines to meet the market demand for top quality garments sold in high-end boutiques in Paris and London. Ironically, even as the noose tightened around Gaza, it experienced a spurt in economic development.

Salwa Barghouti was one of Mathieu's women income-generation experts. She had been married at 18 and widowed at 19 when her twenty-year-old husband and cousin was gunned down in the crossfire between the Israelis and the Palestinian resistance. No one really knew whose bullets had cut down Mohammed, but it did not matter, he was celebrated as a *Shahid*—a martyr. Ten years later, Salwa was still the martyr's widow, and had no intention of re-marrying, at least not to another Gazan. She was a vibrant woman with a sense of purpose in life. There was no question as to her intelligence. Mathieu enjoyed her company, and she his. His quiet manner, with the frequent retreats into dark and seemingly uncontrollable brooding, drew Salwa to her Canadian boss.

While Mathieu's pacifism rubbed some of the staff the wrong way, Salwa opened her mind to his views and understanding of world philosophies. She had always lived in Gaza, had been educated at the Islamic University, and except for the occasional trip to the UNDP office in Jerusalem or to visit a cousin in Hebron, she had never been outside of the strip. Despite that, she was well read and had an excellent command of micro-credit theory and practice. But it was through her conversations with Mathieu that she liberated herself from her temporal existence. Mathieu's breadth of development experience enriched her, and his near poetic observations of human follies and passions breathed new energy into her own love for life.

Mathieu made a habit of visiting projects with all of his staff, and it was always a pleasure to accompany Salwa on her visits. Today, they were going to visit the al-Awdah Palestinian Handicrafts Centre. When they entered the sewing room in the back of the centre, all the women rushed to put on their hijabs. Showing their hair to a man outside of their family was considered flirtation in conservative Gazan society. Salwa showed Mathieu the intricate stitching that went in each embroidered dress. One of the women asked Salwa in Arabic if Mathieu was married. She told her no, to which the woman added, he is handsome, Salwa, try your luck. Salwa thought true, but Mathieu is not Muslim. He could become Muslim though.

"Mathieu, don't you have someone special in your life that you could buy one of these dresses for?" asked Salwa.

After a moment, Mathieu answered, "In fact, there are two special people."

Salwa's heart dropped. Two! This was too much competition.

"Salwa, would you model these two dresses for me," asked Mathieu. The women in the sewing centre giggled hysterically.

"Mathieu, we don't model dresses for men in the Gaza Strip."

Soldier, Lily, Peace and Pearls   *167*

"Oh, I am sorry. I didn't mean to offend you."

"No offense taken. Hannan, could you bring the mannequin, please."

The young girl wheeled out a mannequin and placed the first dress on it.

"How big are your friends," asked Salwa.

"One is one metre 55 centimetres and 43 kilograms and the other is one metre sixty and 50 kilograms."

Salwa smiled at the preciseness of Mathieu's answer. On this, she could not fault him. He had a sharp eye for measuring the physical world, but was sometimes blind to the subtle body language of those around him. Or perhaps, he just did a good job at pretending so. Salwa, who was tall and well-proportioned, then thought at least the competition are midgets.

Salwa helped the Hannan make the adjustments to the two dresses— one with intricate blue embroidery and the other in crimson red.

"What do you think of these two, Mathieu?"

"Absolutely beautiful, I'll take them."

***

When the postman delivered the parcels, An opened the door. Quan and her father Voang had also just arrived and were sitting in the kitchen, discussing the best way to approach Minh Chau. An had called cousin Leyna, who was on her way. She then opened the parcels and admired the fine handiwork.

"Papa, I want to show these dresses to Minh Chau and tell her they are from Mathieu. When he spoke to her on the phone, it helped. Maybe these gifts from him will also help. She went up to the bedroom and stroked the slender arms of her sister and coaxed her to undress and put on the embroidered blue dress. Minh Chau looked stunning in it. She looked stunning in everything she wore. An then whispered into her sister's ear, "It's from Mathieu." For a nano-second, there was a hint of understanding in Minh Chau's eyes and then nothing.

"Sister."

An and Minh Chau turned in unison to see Quan in the doorway.

"Sister," he repeated, "I brought my treasure." Quan walked over to Minh Chau and raised her into the air and danced her around the room. When he put her down, he pulled out a handful of hard candies in tiny wrappers. Minh Chau looked cautiously at them, and then chose one. She did not seem to know what to do with it. An took off the wrapper, and placed it in her sister's mouth. The sweet familiar taste of the candy brought life to Minh Chau's eyes. She turned to Quan, "Quan? Is that really you?"

"Yes."

"I don't understand. I thought you were dead. Am I dead?" She turned around, looking in all directions to reassure herself of her own existence.

Quan took Minh Chau by the shoulders. "You are alive. You are here. I am here. Everything is going to be all right."

Energy rose in Minh Chau's body from toe to head. The biggest smile that she ever had, came out like a camera flash. And then she kissed Quan. Not a sisterly kiss, but a full bodied embrace. Quan to his surprise kissed her back with passion. An stood, her mouth agape. Just as she was about to protest, her father took her by the arm, "It is okay. It was always meant to be between Minh Chau and Quan, and now she is a woman."

"Papa, do you think that this is right?" whispered An. "Minh Chau is still unwell. Does she know what she is doing?"

"You can trust Quan. He will know what to do," answered Voang, as he closed the bedroom door.

***

Salwa stopped the car 50 yards from the Kfar Darom checkpoint to wait for the Israeli soldiers to give her the signal to advance. The checkpoint was flanked on both sides by a small but heavily guarded Jewish settlement which effectively cut the Gaza Strip in two. There were only sixty families who lived in the Kfar Darom settlement. They had been earning their living from growing organic vegetables since 1989 when the Labour government had turned over the military outpost to the deeply religious settlers. The handful of inhabitants tenaciously held onto maintaining a Jewish presence in the middle of the Gaza Strip because Kfar Darom was named in the Talmud. The families were later reinforced by even more devout students who came to research religious laws related to agriculture at the settlement's Torah and the Land Institute.

Tensions were running high in Gaza after the Ibrahimi mosque massacre. Everyone knew that Hamas and Islamic Jihad would eventually retaliate. Elements of Yasser Arafat's Fatah movement were also advocating revenge. The Israeli soldiers guarding the checkpoint were probably no older than 18 or 19, conscripts from Tel Aviv, Haifa and Ashqelon. Like most Israelis, they were secular, and despised the religious extremism of the settler movement, but they feared the Palestinians even more. Their unwritten orders were to, at the first signs of a serious threat, shoot first and ask questions later. Salwa felt at least reassured by Mathieu's presence with his flaming red hair and the hint of Asian traits in his face. No one would mistake him for a Palestinian. She regretted though her decision to take her personal car to Khan Younis instead of a clearly marked UNDP vehicle.

Jamila, her sister, was preparing lunch for them in her modest apartment in Khan Younis. Salwa had thought that a UNDP vehicle would attract too much attention from the neighbours. Although, as the widow of a *Shahid* and the employee of an international agency, Salwa was largely beyond reproach, she was still an unmarried Muslim woman in the company of a non-Muslim foreigner on her day-off.

These same concerns had put off Mathieu's decision to accept Salwa's invitation to lunch on two previous occasions. By now, he had been to all his male employees' homes for lunch and he could hardly refuse Salwa a third time. It was not that he did not find Salwa attractive or was oblivious to her thinly veiled attraction to him. Despite himself, he had even fantasized sexually about her in his dreams. And it was not just that she was his employee. Mathieu had never been one for political correctness and knew that he could distinguish between work relations and social relations.

Mathieu was caged in by the haunting memories of Rwanda. When he was alone at home, he sang the soft melodies that the RPF fighters had taught him and visualized himself with Denise and Étienne eating a lunch of cassava and corn in their garden in Nyarutarama. Sitting under the shade of the maple tree from New Carlisle that had been given to them by Father André as a wedding gift, Étienne would ask him about Canada. Mathieu would tell him about his childhood in New Carlisle. Denise would show him the hair bracelet that Minh Chau had given her and promised Étienne that one day soon, he would meet his beautiful Vietnamese-Canadian cousins. Six-year-old Étienne smiled and then said "And mama, I will give them one of my hairs too so that they can come to visit us in Kigali!"

Theirs was the only maple in Kigali. He and Denise had nurtured it tenderly in the foreign soil of Africa and sheltered it from the continent's voracious insects. Étienne had always reveled in showing off his Canadian tree to his friends, who often brought their parents over to marvel at this unique transplant from the land of snow and ice. When he returned to his Nyarutarama home after discovering Denise and Étienne at the Dom Bosco school, the maple had been chopped down for firewood by the squatters occupying his house. They were Hutus who had fled before the advance of the RPF and were frightened of what would now happen to them with the fall of the Hutus from power. Mathieu looked at their anguished faces and, even though he knew that there was a good chance they had been coerced into participating in the genocide, he gave them his house key and told them to stay. He then scooped up some of the ashes from their open fire to add to Étienne's urn. His son would always have his tree from New Carlisle.

One of the young Hutu boys ran up to Mathieu as he was leaving and pressed a half-eaten piece of plantain into Mathieu's palm. "Merci, monsieur, merci." In the boy's face, he saw Étienne. He dipped his thumb into the maple ashes and pressed it against the boy's forehead, repeating the church Latin that his uncle André had taught him *cinis ad cinerem.* The young boy smiled back—he was no longer Étienne, but just a child rising from the ashes of a country destroyed by its own people.

***

Salwa's heart was beating fast, but it was not from the danger of going through the Kfar Darom checkpoint. It was because of Mathieu. The intensity of his quietness exhilarated her. Increasingly, her dreams were long sexual fantasies about being with him. But she was a mature woman who knew how to navigate her emotions through the obscure and dangerous waters of a society under the dual occupation of the Israelis and Muslim male chauvinism. Her sister Jamila's place in the Tal Sultan neighbourhood of Khan Younis was the ideal place to get to know Mathieu outside of the office. None of Jamila's neighbours were related to her family. Most were returnees from the Egyptian side of the border, evicted from Gaza in the 1970s by General Ariel Sharon when he bull-dozed much of the Canada Camp neighbourhood of Rafah. Under the 1979 Camp David Accords, Israel and Egypt had agreed to their repatriation to Gaza, mostly to the new Tal Sultan housing project.

Salwa and Jamila had grown up in the Shati Refugee Camp in Gaza City. Their camp was inhabited by refugees from Jaffa, Ashqelon and the other southern coastal towns of 1948 Palestine. The camp's inhabitants married within their family circles, passing on from generation to generation land deeds and keys to the homes that they had left behind inside Israel, thereby keeping alive the dream of eventually returning. Those, who could, moved out of the camp to the adjacent Rimal neighbourhood, often after slaving away for years in Saudi Arabia where they could earn enough money to buy a small plot to build on back home. Many also adopted the fundamentalist practices of their Saudi hosts, particularly the stringent control of women in their extended families. While Shati Camp and Rimal were teeming with Salwa's relatives, none except Jamila lived in Khan Younis. This guaranteed Salwa a degree of anonymity in Tal Sultan. At least, there would be no prying uncles, aunts and cousins to dampen her efforts to strike up a relationship with Mathieu. Besides, Tal Sultan was dependent on a lot of UNDP funding and Canadian development aid so Mathieu was already in good standing with the local community leaders.

Jamila was also well connected in Palestinian political circles. She was a convinced Communist, a member of the Palestinian People's Party, and had studied medicine on scholarship in the Soviet Union. She had revolted against her parents' wishes for her to marry her cousin Sa'ad, a semi-literate labourer with a dull look in his eyes. This had earned her respect among Gazan feminists, including in the Islamist movement. Working for a UNRWA health clinic also protected her from conservative Hamas members who wanted to police the morality of the women in Gaza. Known only to her sister Salwa, Jamila had a longstanding relationship with a Circassian engineer in Moscow. As frequently as they could, they would meet secretly in Egypt or Jordan.

Salwa had confided her interest in Mathieu to Jamila, who whole-heartedly approved. Salwa was perplexed at how little she knew of Mathieu. At least, she had sorted out that the recipients of the embroidered dresses were only family friends—and thank God, no competition for his affection. Mathieu's development work in Rwanda was internationally recognized, and already he was invigorating the UNDP program in a way that had not been seen before.

She knew that the genocide in Rwanda had deeply affected him, but neither she nor anyone else in the office knew the specifics. As far as she could tell, he was unmarried and had no children. She wondered about this, as he was an extremely handsome man, and had speculated about his sexual orientation. Her gay colleague Fuad had assured her that Mathieu was definitely heterosexual.

It was his pensiveness that drew her deeply to him. He was not morose or introverted, but rather projected a sense of non-threatening sorrow underpinned by the most acute acts of consideration for the feelings of others.

When Fuad's lover, Abdullah, had been detained by conservative members of the new Palestinian police force on suspicions of immoral behaviour, Mathieu, without asking, drafted up a consultancy contract, back-dated it and went to the police chief to insist that he release Abdullah so that the latter could get to work finishing a project proposal for the renovation and equipping of the security forces' headquarters. That this was a bogus proposal was immaterial. Later, Mathieu would explain to the police chief that the proposal had been rejected by the UNDP project approval committee because of ongoing concerns about the arbitrary detention of homosexuals by the Palestinian police. Fuad and the now released Abdullah became Mathieu's biggest supporters, and encouraged Salwa to take the initiative to express her interest in him.

Had Salwa not been so absorbed in thoughts about Mathieu, she would have noticed the Peugeot taxi pulling up beside her and the thickset woman in a *Niqab* crouching behind her own car. Suddenly, the car raced toward the checkpoint. The soldiers fired at it, killing the driver, but were unable to stop the car's momentum. A huge explosion sent metal and human debris everywhere. Salwa ducked just before her own car's windshield shattered from the force of the bomb. Mathieu, who was in the passenger seat, threw himself down colliding with Salwa. Just as the Israelis began to regroup and tend to their injured, the heavy-set woman behind their car darted forward with a definitely masculine gait toward the remains of the checkpoint. Before the stunned teenage soldiers could react, she or he detonated a vest full of explosives and nails.

Mathieu opened the side door and rolled out to the ground. The soldiers' bodies were everywhere. As Mathieu stood up, the only surviving Israeli soldier staggered toward him with blood dripping from an arm severed at the elbow. He was looking wildly about him, swinging his Galil rifle in all directions, perhaps blinded from the earlier bombing. Mathieu was about to step forward to assist the soldier when the latter raised his rifle toward the car. Mathieu dove back into the passenger seat, as the wounded soldier sprayed the car with with lead.

Salwa had looked up to find out what was going on. A 30-calibre bullet pierced her throat just above the neckbone. The shooting ceased as the soldier slumped exsanguinated to the ground. Salwa was soon drowning in her own blood as it filled up her esophagus. Mathieu grabbed her and put her prone on the back seat so that the blood would flow out and not into her respiratory system. He ripped his shirt to make a temporary bandage to stem the bleeding.

Looking around him, he realized that they were the last persons alive at the checkpoint. He could hear men in the adjacent settlement barking orders in Hebrew at one another. They would soon be at the scene and would undoubtedly fire first and ask questions later. Returning to Gaza City would take too long and there were at least three Israeli checkpoints before reaching the city's al-Shifa Hospital. Instead, he decided to gun the Renault toward Tal Sultan. He knew the way to Jamila's place and she was known to be an excellent surgeon.

***

While Minh Chau's reaction to Quan, with her father's approval, had just disturbed An the evening before, when she awoke the next morning and realized that the two had actually spent the entire night together, she was truly furious. Minh Chau could be impetuous and her father Voang indulgent, but this was very dangerous behaviour.

An feared the long-term impact on her sister from going from a deep depression to a love affair with a man whom both she and An had always seen as a brother. Well, perhaps that was not quite true. An herself had developed a deep attraction to Quan when he lived with them in Quebec City seven years earlier. Unlike Minh Chau who had stirred up a tempest with her immature assertion to her classmates that Quan was her boyfriend, An had kept her feelings to herself. When she had "banished" Quan after the killing of the Triad gangster, she had put the interests of her family before her feelings for Quan. In any case, she had never expressed them to him, and she was only seventeen at the time.

Quan had confided to her during that year in Quebec City many things about his life in Bangkok. While An was understanding of his frequent sex with prostitutes and even his manipulation of western tourists to run drugs into Europe, Quan's stories of punishing abusive johns disturbed her. It was the dispassionate description that he gave of meting out punishment that was the hardest to take. While it did not dent her attraction to him, it was a factor in her request for Quan to leave.

An abhorred violence, even when it was done to protect the people she loved or herself. The death of Cong had also lived on with her. In some ways, she had wished that the burly passenger had slit her throat and thrown her overboard to make room for Cong on the boat. At least, this would have spared Minh Chau the painful guilt of having taken the man's life. Now could Quan's return expose Minh Chau to violence again? Had the Triad given up their search for him? Could he inadvertently put her sister and the whole family in danger again? Doubt and fear raced through An's mind.

An had always harboured a deep affection for Quan, and had been deeply grateful for what he had done for Minh Chau and all of the Thieu family when they were in Pulau Bidong. Still, she loved Minh Chau more. She would throw no glass bottle at Quan to drive him off, but she would speak to him and her father about what had happened during the night.

An's resoluteness dissipated when she entered the kitchen. Minh Chau was in seventh heaven, flipping over gigantic French pancakes, as she had learned to do while working at the Casse-Crêpe Breton restaurant one summer in Quebec City. An had not seen her sister so happy since Mathieu's and Denise's wedding. Minh Chau threw her arms around An and sang Mai Yeu Nguoi Thoi's love song, dancing An around the kitchen table. For a moment, An was transported back to their minuscule apartment on Hamel street. They were again children in a world of love and happiness, singing in Vietnamese the tender lyrics:

Been a long time they say
That you do not truly love
Silently each day is a lie ...
Love him
Then you go away
His own helplessness to stay

Voang entered the room with the biggest smile possible and sat at the table, gazing at the wondrous sight of his two daughters oscillating to the sound of their own voices, and to a song that had he and Han had taught them twenty years ago.

Mai Yeu Nguoi Thoi's lyrics woke Quan. Minh Chau was no longer at his side, but her scent permeated the room. He lay back in the bed, reflecting on the night before. They had exhausted each other with their love-making, but even as Quan finally fell asleep, he could feel her fingers gently exploring every inch of his body. Confusion governed his consciousness. He had responded physically to Minh Chau's advances and, as was his nature, had combined energy and tenderness in every twist and thrust of his body. The return of Minh Chau's passion for life, for love, had invigorated him. Her closeness had given him reassurance, and he had become Quan again and not Paul Marois or Paul Nguyen.

Now as he lay awake, looking through the window at the late summer clouds, his emotions toward Minh Chau swam in obscure waters. They were not the emotions of lust or of a convinced lover. He had known Minh Chau since childhood and the six-year age difference had been an important barrier to anything but a sense of duty to protect her as he would his own sister Hue. When he last saw her, she was 15 and not yet a woman. He had taken her teenage infatuation with him in stride. If anything, he had been drawn to An then 17, but had checked his desire out of respect for Voang and Han. At 22, Minh Chau had become a woman of incomparable beauty. Her minuscule stature, her skeletal body, made her no classic beauty, but her long, flowing hair, her eyes of jade and brown coal, and her mouth exquisitely traced on a face of mother of pearl were entrancing.

"Sleepyhead, come down, I have made *crêpes*," sang out Minh Chau from the foot of the staircase.

At the kitchen table, Voang sat proud and reassured. He had done his mission. Han would be proud of him. Their family was now complete, and Minh Chau's and Quan's happiness was now assured. He would buy a store for Quan and make him a successful businessman. Maybe a pharmacy where Quan could put his knowledge of Chinese medicine to good use. Minh Chau had told him of her desire to start law school in two weeks. She wanted to be the best lawyer possible before starting a family. A family? Voang envisioned already the toddlers who would come from the union between his daughter and Quan. They would have Minh Chau's charm and Quan's strength. For once, kindness was really bringing happiness to his life.

When Quan entered the kitchen, he knew from Voang's glowing look that his future was sealed, but all his reticence evaporated when Minh Chau sauntered flirtatiously over to him, nibbled at his ear, and asked, "Do you like maple syrup, my love?"

"Of course," he replied, shyly blushing at his companion in the gilded cage of their future.

Thirty-One
Crossing Bridges 2007

Mathieu sat across from Minh Chau in Chez Lucien. They were celebrating the departure of a colleague Marie-Louise. As usual, Minh Chau was in an excited state of conversation with Marie-Louise and the other guests. He began to reflect on the incredible vitality of this beautiful Vietnamese-Canadian woman in his presence. He had first known her as a small child and now almost thirty years later as a mature albeit spontaneously crazy woman. Returning from almost a quarter of a century of working for NGOs and the UN in Africa and the Middle East, Mathieu had joined the Canadian International Development Agency (CIDA) only to discover that Minh Chau was one of his colleagues as the legal counsel to CIDA's President.

Minh Chau was more than just a legal beagle. She was passionate about development and defended her at times radical views as a member of the agency's policy and programming board. Her office was just down the corridor from Mathieu's, and she made a point of dropping in on him at least three times a day. Her incredible ability to combine zany humour with a knack for out-of-the-box thinking breathed new life into the agency's otherwise bureaucratic blandness. The aloof professional career woman was definitely not her thing and teasing Mathieu became her new vocation.

However, beyond the theatrics that she was so adept at, there was a sense of loss, perhaps imperceptible to the world around her, and yet somehow, Mathieu felt it from the first moment of their renewed friendship. Today, she was different. Her long hair framed her petite body. It was her exuberance of grace that was so intriguing—an uncommon beauty that radiated from within and without.

"Mathieu, you look lost in your thoughts," asked Minh Chau. "Are you dreaming of Ethiopia again?"

"No, not this time. Something much nicer than mountains, deserts and jungle, but now I am all yours."

"Really. Well, I am a lucky girl! What did I do to deserve it?"

"MC, you are making Mathieu blush!" interjected Marie-Louise.

"I know, and that's the way I like it. You know that Mathieu was always my inspiration for working in development. We would sit endlessly, listening to our mother read his letters from Africa when we were young."

"Minh Chau, you are very kind. I am not sure that what I have been able to do more recently is so inspiring to anyone. But on another subject - how was your meal?"

"Beautiful. A lovely steak. And yours?"

"Great. Nothing better than a Greek salad on a warm spring day."

The clinking of a fork against a glass brought them back to the group. Marie-Louise stood with her champagne flute in hand. "Everybody, it was wonderful that all of you came to see me off. It has been fantastic working with you."

"Here, here."

Slowly the group got up, put on their coats, embraced Marie-Louise for one last time and headed out into the warmth of the May day. They hailed down two cabs.

"Mathieu will you share a cab with us?" asked Marie-Louise.

"Thanks, but it is a beautiful day. I think that I will walk."

Minh Chau then softly whispered into his ear, "Mind if I join you on your trek?"

"Sure. How could I refuse such pleasant company? It is a long walk though."

"Marie-Louise, see you back at the office," sang out Minh Chau and then in a whisper, "Mathieu, they are going to talk about us back at the office, you know."

"Is that a problem?"

"Not for me. I am a big girl."

"Shall we take the Alexandra Bridge?"

"Why not."

As she walked along at Mathieu's side, Minh Chau thought long and hard about the attraction that she felt for him. It was unnatural in a way. It wasn't the age difference of 15 years. She was already 35 and at 50, he was in top shape. Both were now in that time in life when you live closest to your emotions. Mathieu's hair had thinned and grey had replaced the red that had thrilled her as a child. She believed that beauty came within, but with Mathieu, it radiated from all directions. With age, the subtlety of Mathieu's maternal Korean heritage came out, giving him an exotic look that he had not had in his youth. His charms were not lost on her co-workers. Several had tried to flirt with him in the last three months. He was always polite enough to respond with pleasant conversation, but gave an air of general disinterest except for Minh Chau's teasing of him. He was the perfect straight man for her jokes and pranks. Gossip had quickly spread around the office that Mathieu had been one of her former lovers, and that they had even been lovers when she was under age. She did her best to keep private their long but interrupted relationship because, in explaining it, she would have had to explain Denise, and knew that this part of Mathieu's life was still an open wound.

Since the first day on the job, Minh Chau had taken Mathieu in tow to acquaint him with the byzantine world of CIDA politics. She was a superb networker and he was a doer, with an unchallenged wealth of overseas development experience. They had offered him a position as director general, but Mathieu declined, preferring instead to take on a horizontal role as the agency's Chief Agricultural Development Advisor. It felt strange to Minh Chau to have someone who had always been in her life but had hardly ever been physically there to now become so close to her on a daily basis. Her sister An worshipped Mathieu as did her father Voang. Quan, who had once been destined to be Mathieu's responsibility in Quebec City, had ironically never even met Mathieu.

Quan, saying his name in her mind still cut deeply into her. It had been a year and no news of him. After twelve years of living together, Quan had vanished and why? Simply because a relic of her past had shown up unexpectedly one day. How many of his affairs had she tolerated, seeing them as unimportant to the love that she felt for him. She had given herself totally to him, and he had abandoned her.

Now, with Mathieu, she was living for the first time emotions of affection and trust that grew stronger not weaker every day. Emotions based on respect and admiration, not just on the need to feel safe. Wasn't this better?

As the cool breeze cut through the steel of the bridge and swept up Minh Chau's hair, Mathieu gazed upon her as if it was the first time he had ever seen her. The age difference and the role that Minh Chau had played in his earlier life at first had blocked him from feeling anything more than friendship toward her. After all, she had been a flower girl at his wedding. He had been a responsible young adult and she a child when the Thieus had arrived in Canada. But Minh Chau was no longer a young girl, and Mathieu suddenly saw her as the woman she had become. By all measures, she was a beautiful woman, although her radiance was no longer that of the 22-year-old girl who had enslaved Quan with her delicate soft skin and unending lust for his touch. Instead, what attracted Mathieu was her incredible aura of youthful energy. Minh Chau's was a woman who simply refused to watch the clock tick forward the externalities of her existence.

"Mathieu, could you go a little slower please," asked Minh Chau. "I do not really feel like going back to the office so soon."

Mathieu threw his arm around her and pulled her tight, "No playing hookey today. We are going back to the office and finishing the Haraghe proposal."

"Ah gee, Mathieu, you are no fun!" she complained, and then for the first time placed a fleeting kiss on his cheek.

Both Mathieu and Minh Chau knew that the Alexandra was not the only bridge they were crossing.

Chapter Thirty-Two
Voang

The meeting was packed with CIDA's top brass. It was a real opportunity for them to hear what Canada's leading expert on agricultural development in Africa had to say, or so they thought. Mathieu advanced to first slide in his PowerPoint presentation.

"The agricultural rehabilitation project in Haraghe, eastern Ethiopia is composed of four components: water harvesting and conservation, crop diversification, community credit for farm-level agricultural investments and the commercialization of *chat* as a cash crop. *Chat* is a mild narcotic in popular demand in Somalia, Djibouti and Yemen. It is legal in most of the world, including the U.K., but is prohibited in Canada. While it may be controversial for Canadian development aid to support the cultivation of a narcotic of any type, the cash benefits of exporting *chat* are fundamental to transforming the rural population of Haraghe from subsistence, famine-prone farming to a much higher level of economic security."

Mathieu took the audience painstakingly through his thoroughly coherent, albeit rather tedious, presentation on bringing food security and socio-economic progress to 300,000 Ethiopian peasants. His efforts were to no avail—only one word stuck in everyone's mind—*narcotic.*

Minh Chau thought Mathieu has got a lot of guts to push this project, which in the eyes of many Canadians is a licence to turn tens of thousands of African farmers into drug dealers. I wish though that he had shown it to me earlier. Now, I am going to have to contradict him on the issue of the legal acceptance of *chat*. Sure enough, Barry Watson, CIDA's President turned to Minh Chau and asked, "What is our legal position on assisting *chat* production?"

Minh Chau swallowed hard before answering. She knew that her answer however carefully crafted would torpedo Mathieu's proposal, given CIDA's risk adverse nature. "Well, it is a grey matter. We will certainly not be breaking any laws in Ethiopia or those of the main *chat* importing countries like Yemen and Somalia. However, last year as part of the Canada-US-Mexico pact to fight narcotic trafficking globally, Canada committed to ensure that no official development aid would go to support the production of any crop that is considered illegal by any of the signatory countries. And of course, *chat* is considered illegal in Canada."

"Minh Chau, that is a Northern American issue. What has it got to do with African development?" asked Mathieu.

"I am sorry, Mathieu, the obligations of the agreement are global in nature. We simply cannot fund *chat* production while opposing peyote production in Monterrey State in Mexico."

"Well, I guess that solves that," said Watson. "Mathieu, we like your proposal, but can you substitute *chat* production support activities for let's say almond tree production?"

Mathieu rolled his eyes, "Well, that is basically a non-starter. First there is no local market demand for almonds and, second, no one in the region can compete in quality and quantity with Iranian almond production."

"Well, maybe we can market the Ethiopian almonds in Canada as a fair trade product, like we do for coffee," chirped in Mary Somerset, CIDA's director general for communications.

For a brief second, Mathieu considered handing in his resignation. No one around the table had more than a couple of years of overseas experience and yet they had risen in CIDA's ranks to occupy the agency's key positions. Substance had ceded its place to spin long ago in the agency, and Mathieu, who had just finished his third month on the job, was just realizing how absurd this had become.

Before he could make a career-ending remark, Minh Chau tactfully popped in, "Mary, of course that is a very avant-garde idea, but the Canadian market is already flooded with organic almond production from California. However, what we could do is substitute the word *chat* in the project proposal with the wording *appropriate dryland cash crops*. Mathieu, would not the agricultural inputs and rural infrastructure work be the same for any of these types of crops, including *chat*? Besides, the farmers themselves will be providing their own *chat* seeds, won't they?"

Mathieu turned to Minh Chau, somewhat stunned, and uttered, "Yes, that's right."

Soldier, Lily, Peace and Pearls   *183*

"Good, that is settled. Do a find and replace in your project proposal to put in *appropriate dryland cash crops* instead of *chat*," said a cheery Watson. "And add the purchase of a number of almond, apricot and fig seedlings, and Bob's your uncle. It does not matter to us that the trees don't actually get planted as long as the peasants have the tools, fertilizer and rural infrastructure to market what they really want to plant."

"A brilliant idea," chirped up Mary Somerset. "We will prepare a communications roll-out of the project for October."

Mathieu looked startled at the acquiescence by the entire programming board to the disingenuity of the compromise. And then, there was the most beautiful glint in his blue-green eyes as he realized that he had seriously underestimated Watson.

As the loyal CIDA senior managers filed out of the room behind President Watson, Minh Chau hung back. As Mathieu packed up the laptop, she slithered up to him in the empty room and whispered flirtatiously in his ear, "What's my reward for saving your butt, big boy?"

Mathieu smiled, "A drink and *chat* at Café Soup'Herbe in Chelsea followed by a stroll in the Gatineau Park?"

"My, my, Mr. Hibou, that is a very tempting offer. I see that you like to live dangerously—beer and bears?"

As Mathieu's Honda Fit navigated out of the rush-hour traffic into the sideroads of Old Chesea, Minh Chau leaned back to enjoy Evora Cesaria's deep African voice sing Ausencia.

"Do you know what the lyrics mean, Mathieu."

"Actually yes, I spent two years in Mozambique and picked up Portuguese there."

"So tell me, Mathieu, what is she singing?"

"It's a love song in the Cape Verde dialect about a woman who wakes up one morning to discover her lover has disappeared. She walks through the city, looking for him and bumps into a mutual friend who tells her that her lover has taken a ship for Portugal to escape Cape Verde's poverty."

"Can you sing it for me, Mathieu?"

"Minh Chau, you know that I can't sing well."

"I love your voice. It has always given me a great feeling of security. It doesn't matter if you don't remember all the words or get all the notes right. Just sing it in your voice."

E nunca mas ausencia
ta ser nos lema
ma so na pensamento
um ta viaja sem medo
nha liberdade

And the absence no more,
would be our reality
But it is only in my thoughts,
That I can travel fearless,
and my liberty

Minh Chau closed her eyes to listen to Mathieu's imperfect but seductive voice. She marveled at his vast culture and lamented the dark moments he still lived when he thought she was not watching him, but she had been watching him now for days without respite. With the tenacity that she had learned from her mother, she determined at that moment that she would make him happy again.

***

As the waitress brought them their *Dubonnets,* Minh Chau turned to Mathieu and gently stroked the back of his hand to catch his attention. "I have been meaning to ask you why you left Ethiopia. You seemed so enamoured with your work there."

"It was hard leaving. Working for UNDP there was the high point of my professional life, but I felt frustrated by the willingness of the agency to compromise on sound development work to accommodate the pet projects of donors and the political agenda of the local government."

"Their loss, our gain."

"Our gain?"

"Yes, <u>our gain.</u>" Minh Chau smiled shyly at her not too subtle statement of attraction, and then straightened herself out as the professional woman that she was. "I would love to work with you abroad. You have such passion."

The ringing of her Blackberry interrupted her before she added another overture of interest. "Sorry, I have to take this. It is from An in Montreal."

"Hello An. What! When! I will come right away."

"Mathieu, I am sorry. I have to go to Montreal right away. Can you take me to the bus station in Ottawa? It is, it is ... my father. He has had a stroke. I have to get there as fast as I can."

"I will drive you to Montreal. Waitress, the bill please."

"Really? To Montreal?" Tears swelled up in her eyes.

"Yes, but please don't cry. Voang will be okay."

Minh Chau's head fell gently on Mathieu's shoulder as she dozed off from emotional exhaustion. She had spent the first hour talking about her father and the death of her mother thirteen years earlier. In that hour, he discovered more of Minh Chau that he had ever known. In her outpouring of apprehension and pent-up grief, there were still moments when she would smile at him and thank him for his kindness. Mathieu held back from telling Minh Chau what he had learnt about her mother's death from Dominic Leblanc many years before. It did not matter any longer. Now she slept like a child in his car, as they raced to Montreal, hoping to find her father completely recovered from his stroke, yet dreading the worse.

As he pulled up to Notre Dame Hospital in the east part of the city, Minh Chau awoke, startled that she had slept so long with her head and hand on Mathieu's shoulder. She felt the dampness of his suit jacket, drenched from her tears. "Oh I'm sorry. I didn't mean to."

"It's okay. We are there. Would you like to go straight to see your father?"

"No, let me wash my face first. If he is conscious, I do not want him to see that I have been crying. It would make him feel bad. He needs to see me strong, not weak."

"You will never be weak, Minh Chau. Not in my eyes."

The emergency room was as jammed as hospitals are in Africa. Quebec's health system, once one of the best in the world, was straining from decades of underfunding.

"Do you have a patient by the name of Voang Thieu?" Mathieu asked the pretty young nurse at the reception.

"Yes, he is just out of intensive care, but can only be seen by relatives."

"I have brought his daughter to see him. She will be here in a minute."

"Mr. Thieu is in Room 208."

At the moment, Mathieu felt the light touch of Minh Chau's fingertips on his shoulder, "Mathieu, what did she say?"

"Voang is out of intensive care. We can see him now. Let's go."

"Excuse me, Monsieur, only relatives," interjected the nurse.

"Monsieur is my husband," proclaimed Minh Chau, catching Mathieu off-guard.

As they moved away from the reception desk, Mathieu quirped, "A very good catch there!"

"Or maybe it was a Freudian slip and you are the *good catch*," replied Minh Chau in a saucy voice.

Then just as they reached the door, she pulled Mathieu aside. "Wait Mathieu. I have to tell you something. My father thinks that I am still with Quan. We have not been together for a year, but I have not told my father."

"Don't worry, I won't say anything."

"No, but you don't understand. I want to tell him about Quan. I want to tell him about *us,* but just not now."

"About us?"

"Yes, Matthieu, about us. Don't play innocent with me. About us! "

The quantum leap in their relations took Mathieu by surprise, and to

Soldier, Lily, Peace and Pearls   *187*

his own astonishment gave him a shot of adrenaline that he had not expected.

As Mathieu stood at the door, still under the shock that his life had taken an incredibly happy turn for the better, Minh Chau rushed into the room and embraced her sister An.

"An, how is papa?"

"He is out of danger, but he is sleeping. Mathieu, you are here. How wonderful. My father will be so happy."

A faint voice came from the bed, "Minh Chau, is that you?"

"Yes, and Mathieu is here too."

"Mathieu? Mathieu, our old friend?"

"Yes, papa."

"Hi Voang. How are you feeling?"

"Not too good, but the doctors said that I will be all right in a few days."

"That is great news," said Mathieu.

"And where is Quan?" asked Voang.

"He could not come. He is traveling this week." Minh Chau lied.

"I did not understand the doctors when they told me what happened." said Voang. "What did happen?"

"Papa, you had a stroke, but the doctors say that you will soon recover," An explained. "They want to keep you here to run some tests."

Just then a young Haitian doctor entered the room. "I am afraid that Mr. Thieu will need some rest before we conduct some additional tests in about an hour," she explained. "You can all see him tomorrow morning."

"Thank you, doctor. Bye papa. We will see you tomorrow."

Just then Voang reached out to Minh Chau to grab her by the wrist. "Tell Quan that I must see him. It's important!"

Minh Chau turned away from her father with a terrified look. Mathieu stepped between them to distract Voang in a brief conversation and then joined the two Thieu sisters in the corridor.

"Mathieu, will you be heading back to Ottawa tonight?" asked An.

"I suppose I should."

"You are not going anywhere, Mathieu," commanded Minh Chau. "Papa's house has lots of room."

Her sister's peremptory tone puzzled An, who then suggested that they all eat at the Red Dragon Restaurant. Mathieu's presence at the hospital had surprised An. She had called Minh Chau just two hours earlier. They must have been together when she called. How else could they have made it here so fast? And why won't Minh Chau come clean and tell everyone that it was over with Quan? It had been a year.

On the way to the restaurant, Minh Chau thought how glad she was that Mathieu was here, but worried about what An might think of their relationship. Already for her, it was a relationship. Did Mathieu feel the same? She decided that tonight she would find out. She also worried about what An might say about her to Mathieu. Would she warn him off, with tales of fragile mental health. Would she even tell him about the *boat?* It did not matter. Minh Chau was determined that at the restaurant, she would send the right message to An about Mathieu.

The Red Dragon was filled to the brim with its regular Friday night patrons. The owner, Tommy Lee, was a friend and one-time business partner of their father's and was only too pleased to bring out another table to accommodate them, although he expressed concern over the news of his friend's health.

"Let's raise a glass to papa. He gave us quite the scare." proposed An. "And to Mathieu, our first and best friend in Canada!"

"Yes, to papa and Mathieu the oldest and newest men in my life." chirped in Minh Chau.

"Really?" asked a very surprised An.

"Really," replied Minh Chau, mockingly sticking her tongue out at her sister.

"And Quan?"

"Don't speak his name in my presence!"

"You should tell papa about Quan."

"No. I will tell papa what he needs to hear. Remember he is sick."

"Mathieu, I am sorry," apologized An. "We should not be arguing in front of you."

"Look, it is okay. I understand. If there is any way to be helpful, I would like to help, but I do not want to interfere. Excuse me, but I need to check my Blackberry for messages. I will be back shortly."

"He is very considerate," said Minh Chau.

"Do you love him?"

"An, we both love Mathieu."

"You know what I mean."

"I know. I just don't know if he loves me more than just as a sister."

"If you love him, never hurt him. You owe that to Denise."

"I will never, ever hurt Mathieu."

"And Quan?"

"Quan hurt me. He was unfair to me. I will never forgive him."

"Minh Chau, you are too harsh. Everyone makes mistakes."

"Maybe, but with Quan, it is over. I don't want to tell Papa just yet. He had such hopes that we would spend the rest of our lives happily together."

Both sisters watched Mathieu return toward them. An felt like a young girl waiting for the return of their Canadian friend and protector, but Minh Chau felt only the accelerating pounding of her heart—the heart of a woman—as she studied his handsome face and lost herself in his smile.

Chapter Thirty-Three
Red Magic

Quan looked across at his new girlfriend Françoise. She was young, barely twenty. At forty, he was twice her age. Her pristine beauty lay across the bed as an adornment to the night that they had just spent together. Quan had not lost his looks. If anything, he had become more attractive to women than ever before. Over the last year in Paris, he had waltzed from one erotic experience to another. For a time, he thought that this would be the cure for the deep pain that he felt inside.

It was not leaving Minh Chau that hurt him. He thought of her every day and in every one of her manifestations—from the child who followed and worshiped his every step in Pulau Bidong to the teenager in Quebec City who wanted to leapfrog her youth to embrace him in intimate love, to the loving and devoted partner of twelve years, whose love he had always short-changed. He wondered where she was now, what she was doing.

His eyes turned to the small bedside table where the note from Leyna lay. He had cut all communications with the Thieus, but Leyna on a trip to visit her relatives in Paris had stumbled across him two months ago at a dinner party hosted by Françoise's parents. Leyna did not judge or take sides. She knew and loved both Quan and Minh Chau equally. As a psychologist, she had treated Minh Chau many times, and intuitively she knew the causes of Quan's inability to respond fully to her younger cousin's love for him. Leyna had told Quan of her worries about Voang's health. The strength that he had demonstrated after the death of Han was now being sapped away. He spoke often about returning to see Vietnam one last time.

Leyna offered to act as a conduit for Quan, should he want news of the family, news of Minh Chau. He took her e-mail address, but refused to give her his. At first, she felt offended that he did not trust her, but then, as only Quan could, he gently caressed the cheek of her disfigured face, and said, "It will be safer for you this way." Leyna looked into his eyes, their softness washed away the scars of nineteen years, and she felt beautiful again.

Leyna had kept her promise to be Quan's conduit to the world that he had left behind. The note had arrived only yesterday via Françoise's parents. Voang Thieu was ill and at the hospital. Quan decided that he must see again the man who saved his life from crime and self-destruction and enabled him to have a new life in Canada, but how would he explain to Voang that he had left his daughter in a jealous rage, and worse that he did not intend to return to her. Quan packed his bags quietly as Françoise slept soundly. He booked a ticket on his computer for Montreal that afternoon, and slipped out of the apartment, leaving behind a short note for Françoise.

Chérie,

I am leaving for a while, but I will be back. Don't worry about me. I will dream of the sweet bonjours of happiness you give me every morning. I love you deeply.

Quan

Of all the women whom Quan had loved in his life, Françoise was the purest, the least complicated and the most fulfilling. It was not just her youth. It was her openness to him in all ways. She had sought him out after noticing him read his newspapers at the Café de la Rotonde in Montparnasse. At first, it was a physical attraction and then intellectual curiosity as she unraveled the layers of his identity—Paul Marois, Paul Nguyen and finally Quan. In Paris, he had taken on a new identity—Daniel Jing, an importer of modern Vietnamese paintings. His work was done completely through the internet and his growing clientele soon included Françoise's wealthy parents, both surgeons at Hôtel-Dieu Hospital.

The speed at which Quan had reestablished himself in Paris and the phenomenal pace of his new love for Françoise surprised even him. But today, his mind was not on his new life here. Montreal was calling.

By the time that the taxi pulled up to Charles de Gaulles Airport, he was buried in memories of his life with Minh Chau. Scenes of Pulau Bidong, Quebec City and Montreal passed through his mind like horses on a carousel. He saw her at fourteen teaching him the conjugation of French verbs. At twenty-two, she was shaping his life with her own desires, but how could he forget the sweetness of the first time she had made love to him when he was still in doubt. The gentleness of her touch had banished those doubts, if only for a few months. He recalled the deep sorrow in her heart that at times he managed to heal, but never fully. He was Minh Chau's protector and she and her family had always been his saviors. Their fates were intertwined, but now he loved Françoise.

The hustle and bustle of the airport terminal forced him to concentrate on the practical matter of checking in luggage and passing through security. There was always a degree of apprehension about that. The identity of Daniel Jing, born in Réunion, a French island in the Indian Ocean, and raised in Canada, was as good as it could be, and a real Daniel Jing did exist unnamed in the crematorium on Mont-Royal. Purchasing the man's identity had been easy enough. In exchange for $20,000 to be left to his family, Daniel had sold it to Quan just a week before cancer took his life. That was two years ago. Quan had purchased it as insurance should the Canadian immigration authorities ever catch up with the twenty years that he had illegally lived in Canada under different aliases and earning his living off the grid. Voang had set him up in business, but his name appeared nowhere in the company records. Voang, the titular owner of the business, simply transferred monthly payments to a Swiss-based supplier of Chinese medicines and more recently of Indochinese art and artifacts. After electronic transfers became possible through the internet, Quan carried on the transfers with the password to Voang's account.

"Monsieur, you are a resident of France?" asked the immigration agent.

"Not quite, but as you can see, I am a French citizen living in Canada."

"Very well, but if you stay in France for more than two months at a time, you should really get a bio-metric national identity card."

"Certainly. I will look into that," said Quan, wondering how long he could still be Daniel Jing, what new identity he might need to seek out.

On the plane, he took his place beside a women in her late fifties. She spoke a beautiful French with only the hint of a Canadian accent. Daniel Jing's French was a similar hybrid of Canadian and continental French. The woman had lived in Vietnam until the fall of Saigon. They discussed the war. The folly of the violence. The crimes that all sides had committed. Quan found in her a reassurance of humanity.

She came from the Gaspésie and had studied in Quebec City. When Quan introduced himself as Daniel Jing and she responded with Marie-Christine Labonté, Quan went into a panic. One part of him wanted to reveal himself to her, the woman who had tried so hard to save him in Pulau Bidong. The other part preached caution. Travelling under a false identity could land him in prison in Canada and eventual deportation, and to where?—Cambodia, a country that he had not seen in almost thirty years. Instead, Quan chose subterfuge once again. He explained that he had heard her name from the Thieu family, who were close friends of his in Montreal. She was delighted. She had lost contact with them after the death of Han, and after her own life took a turn for the worse with the tragic death of her husband Thomas and her daughter Andréa in a plane crash ten years earlier.

"Did you ever meet Quan, Minh Chau's boyfriend?" asked Marie-Christine. "I knew him as a boy in the refugee camp in Malaysia, and tried very hard to have him sponsored to Canada, but failed. Eventually, he turned up in Canada and got together with Minh Chau after her mother's death." Marie-Christine had a thousand questions to ask.

"I know Quan very well and have for a long time. He told me about you and all the kindness that you extended to him and his sister Hue. Madame Labonté, you are a very good person."

Marie-Christine's eyes moistened at hearing Daniel Jing speak this compliment. He sounded so sincere, almost as if he was Quan himself. Physically, he bore a remarkable resemblance to the boy whom she had once known. When the passenger across the aisle asked Quan in English if he had a pen, the lilting Malaysian accent that Abdul Hakim had instilled in all his students, came out in Quan's answer. Marie-Christine was shocked. Could this really be Quan sitting beside her, trying to impersonate someone else? Why would he do that? She remembered Quan's hands. On the palm of his right hand, there had been a minuscule birthmark. She remember well because Denis Prud'homme had to take note of it in Quan's immigration file and because Hue had the same birthmark. It was shaped like an owl, an *hibou*. When Marie-Christine first saw the birthmark, the idea came to her mind of asking her cousin Mathieu Hibou to assist in bringing Quan and his sister to Canada.

"Mr. Jing. Would you mind if I read your palm?" asked Marie-Christine.

"Read my palm?"

"Yes, it may sound superstitious, but every once in a while, I like to do this with someone whom I have just met."

"I hate to confess this, but I too am a little superstitious, so why not?"

When the owl appeared in the middle of Quan's palm, Marie-Christine took his hand in hers and said, "Quan, you have nothing to fear from me."

Quan's heart jolted at the sensation of being discovered, but the touch of Marie-Christine's hand and the confident reassurance of her voice calmed his surprise.

"I am sorry. I did not want to deceive you. It is complicated, and I have to be careful."

For the duration of the six hours in flight, he related the last twenty-five years of his existence to Marie-Christine. He opened up to confessing his loves and his inability to fully love. Finally, he sketched out the circumstances that had led him to abandon Minh Chau the year before, and the illness of Voang which was now drawing him back to a world that he thought he had left for good.

Marie-Christine listened sympathetically to every detail of Quan's story. She was not horrified by his criminal past in Bangkok or his killing of the gangster in Quebec City. She knew already of his violent temper. His adventures with prostitutes and his multiple affairs when he was with Minh Chau slid effortlessly into the context of his real albeit uncompleted love for only four women in his life: Mali, Melissa, Minh Chau and now Françoise.

At the end of Quan's narrative, she asked, "Now do you want me to really read your future?"

"Yes."

"You will see Minh Chau and tell her how you feel about her. You cannot escape seeing her. What happens after that is between you and her."

"And Françoise?"

"Let her be, Quan. She is only twenty. She will love again and soon. It is not your destiny to live in France. Canada is your country."

Marie-Christine's words stirred within him the need to check the silver locket around his neck. He opened it and saw Denis Prud'homme's single red hair was still there. When he showed the hair to Minh Chau in Quebec City when they were first reunited, she was ecstatic. "I told you so, Quan. This magic hair brought you to Canada. Never lose it." She then went out and bought him the locket that he now wore.

Marie-Christine and Quan parted at Pierre Elliot Trudeau Airport in Montreal. She embraced him, holding him tightly as if he was still the child in Pulau Bidong, and then kissed him on the forehead. Somehow, she knew that she would not see him again, but felt an inner peace that she had at least found him again after so many years.

Just after Quan took his taxi to the hotel near the hospital, Mathieu drove up to pick up his cousin. True to her word to Quan, she did not reveal their chance meeting on the airplane. She gave her cousin an endless hug. Her mind fled through the images of her life in Southeast Asia, all the wonderful people whom she had met and had helped, and who had helped her. Now she was back in Canada, holding in her arms the man that she mothered after the death of Tae-Ok. The man who had himself lived in Rwanda the most tragic event that could happen to anyone. And in her moment of abandon, she plucked one of her cousin's few remaining red hairs and put it in her pocket. He was surprised by her gesture, but said nothing. She could have all his hair if she wanted. The single hair would do. It would be her lucky charm to bring her back to Canada when the cancer that was devouring her body had run its course.

"Mathieu, we should go right away. My appointment with Dr. Leblanc is at 11:00 a.m."

In the car, she stroked the red hair and then admired her handsome cousin—the boy she had loved in New Carlisle and the man who had convinced her, when she had given up hope, to try the revolutionary treatment that Dominic Leblanc was pioneering based on Han's research.

"Marie-Christine, I have something to tell you," smiled Mathieu.

She sensed his happiness and asked, "Are you in love?"

"Yes."

"Do I know her?"

"Yes, you have known her all her life. You sent her to me."

"Mathieu, really? I can't ..."

"Minh Chau and I are in love."

"Han's daughter?"

"Yes."

Marie-Christine swallowed hard. What had she done? What would happen now that Quan had returned?

If Greek tragedies were still written in the 21st century, the story of Quan, Minh Chau and Mathieu would have figured among them. But their story is life—life in all its cruel and happy twists.

Chapter Thirty-Four
Love is the Counterface of Suffering

The fundamental Buddhist belief that Minh Chau adhered to, despite all the efforts of the Ursuline sisters to cleanse her Catholic soul of foreign influences, was that there is no happiness without suffering. In her world, love had always come as a byproduct of her greatest pain. When love ended, her soul drifted quickly back to misery. Suffering was the constant, and happiness from love was the interloper. Minh Chau was determined to end this vicious cycle and the soft and gentle love that she now felt for Mathieu would be the balm to heal the wounds from the past. Mathieu was the reincarnation of gentleness. She knew this for a fact. But he too suffered deeply from his own trauma, and Minh Chau was determined to be the elixir to in turn heal him. Never had her mind or her determination been stronger. She would soon be approaching forty. She wanted to live out her life with someone who would always care for her. Someone whom she in turn would always love and respect.

Minh Chau and An prepared for Mathieu the guest room in her father's house. It was really just a charade to calm down An, who was already fretting that her sister was about to leap into another doomed relationship, and this time with someone whom An also loved and respected. Minh Chau should come to her senses before she hurt Mathieu. And there was the age difference. Mathieu was 50 and she was 35. Minh Chau mocked this point. Fifty perhaps but the body of a young buck. Believe me, An, I am not the only woman in the office to see his beauty, even the twenty-year-old coop students give him a once-over. In any case, Minh Chau cut short her sister's argument. No, they were not lovers, and well, if they became lovers that was their business and not An's.

As she tucked in the sheets, she thought how neat they would be in the morning. She had no intention of letting Mathieu spend the night in the guest room. Even if it took summoning all of her inner strength, she would ensure that Mathieu knew her tonight.

Minh Chau felt a little anger at An's interference, but mostly she felt envy. For almost twelve years, An had been happily married to Marc, her carpenter who now owned a thriving contracting business on the West Island. Many of his clients were prosperous Vietnamese who had moved from small apartments in the city centre to suburban bungalows and duplexes in quiet neighbourhoods where the residents spoke English and French interchangeably and lived the Canadian dream of an ever expanding cultural mosaic. Voang had used his influence in Montreal's Vietnamese community to steer customers in his son-in-law's direction. When Voang was elected president of the South Vietnamese veterans' association, Marc's business picked up even more. Ironically, Voang had never seen combat as a soldier. There were always lots of teeth to yank in Saigon to keep him away from the front lines. Nonetheless, Voang had been an officer in good standing and had survived the re-education camps without ever turning against a fellow soldier. Some of the association members had been his patients in the Danang re-education camp before his hand was shattered. Others knew of the leadership that he had shown in Pulau Bidong. So they rallied their comrades and friends to vote Voang into the coveted presidential function.

It was not enough that An had a loving husband, but she was also blessed with three children—Huynh, Dao and Lan. Minh Chau had insisted on the name Huynh. An had gone along and added the other names of kindness from their childhood. All three children were now attending the primary school where An had started as an art teacher and was now its principal.

Her life was simply perfect. Even her three pregnancies had not damaged her sensual figure, and age had not tarnished her mother of pearl complexion. If anything, An was more beautiful now than she had ever been, and Marc, her husband, was attentive both day and night to her every need.

When Quan had left her in his fit of jealousy, Minh Chau became bitter. The world had turned against her once again. How stupid he was. How petty and hypocritical Quan had become. How could she have known that out of the blue, a ghost from her past would simply walk in and make him look like a cuckold in front of so many in Montreal's Vietnamese community. It had been more a comedy of errors than a tragedy. Their friends Robert and Jocelyne Leblanc had invited them to spend the weekend with them to attend the Montreal International Film Festival. As a special surprise, they were invited to attend the gala premiere of a new German film, on the condition that Quan and Minh Chau not look up on the internet or in the newspaper the name of the film.

Robert was now a successful oncologist and worked with his uncle Dominic at Notre Dame Hospital. He had plenty of patients from the film industry, some of whom literally owed their lives to him. It was not too hard to swing the coveted fifth row seats for the premiere and arrange to sneak their party in by the stage door entrance so that Quan and Minh Chau would not see the publicity about the film. Yann Charpentier, the director of the festival, took them to their seats.

"You are really going to enjoy this. I have arranged for the German film director to sit right beside you after he finishes his introduction."

"Fantastic, why don't we put him between Minh Chau and Quan," replied Robert. "They are the real guests of honour and Minh Chau speaks German."

"It has been a long time," protested Minh Chau. "But yes, let's do that."

Minh Chau looked around the theatre and noticed a very large number of Vietnamese-Canadians, and even recognized two or three who had been in Pulau Bidong with them. She looked at her watch and registered that it was April 30, exactly thirty-one years since the fall of Saigon. There were two young girls with flowers and small Republic of Vietnamese flags sitting in the front row. Wait, what would a German film have to do with Vietnam? This was confusing.

Just then a giant of a man sauntered past them on his way to the front of the theatre. Yann Charpentier greeted him with a bearhug and then turned to the audience.

"Mesdames and Messieurs, it is a great pleasure to introduce you to one of the most innovative film directors of our age, Wolfgang Schwarzfeld."

Minh Chau's gasp did not go unnoticed by Quan, who asked her quietly if she was all right.

"Yes, my love. It is nothing."

Then Wolfgang took the microphone and said the words that she had been dreading.

"Ladies and Gentlemen, the film that you about to see, *The Boat,* is not entirely a work of fiction. Many of the facts are real and were related to me by the most beautiful Vietnamese woman whom I have ever known. She was as passionate in life as she was in making love, and she came from your city Montreal. In the stolen moments between our love-making, she told me much of the story that you are about to see. One day she vanished and so did my script for this film. Her disappearance devastated me so I put all my efforts into my other work, producing the documentary films that you may already have seen. It was a colleague of mine also from Vietnam, Minh Khai Vinh, who convinced me that the story that you will soon see is not about one person, but rather about the millions who fled to freedom at great risk to themselves and their families. I hope that you will enjoy this film. It is the *work of love* of my life, and I know that I will never make another film like it."

To the applause of the audience, Wolfgang walked beside the festival director to take his seat in the fifth role.

"Wolfgang, allow me to introduce you to my dear friends Robert and Jocelyne Leblanc and their guests Minh Chau and Quan, who like the characters in your film also lived in Pulau Bidong refugee camp."

Wolfgang looked directly at Minh Chau, and she knew that there was no escape. As Wolfgang sat down between Quan and her, she whispered in German, "If you say a word, I will kill you." Quan looked quizzically at them. From his seduction of young German tourists, twenty years earlier, he had learned enough to recognize the word "kill."

The first scene of the film took place in a bedroom. A young half-clad Vietnamese woman sat on the bed speaking to her German lover about her escape from Vietnam and the long boat ride to Pulau Bidong. As she described the role that a certain General Dang had played in their escape, Quan got up. He had heard from the Thieus a hundred times the story of their escape. His face was beet red. He glared at Minh Chau, who noticed the turned heads of several of the Vietnamese in the audience. Within seconds, he had vanished.

Wolfgang turned to Minh Chau. "Your husband?"

Her long fingernails gashed his cheek as she slapped him. "Arschloch!"

She ran out of the cinema toward their parked car. Quan had already started it and sped by her, without even turning his head. Robert Leblanc was soon at her side. She turned to him, and placed her head on his shoulder as she had done thirteen years earlier in the bus from Mirabel. He held her in his arms and let her tears soak his shirt.

Minh Chau tried desperately to call Quan on his cell phone. No answer. It was too late for the train or bus to Ottawa. Robert offered to drive her, but she turned him down. The next morning, she tried again to reach Quan but without success. By the time she got to Ottawa that evening, his suitcases and clothes were gone. The photo of their last vacation in the Gaspésie was torn in pieces. On the kitchen, he had left a note.

You betrayed me, Minh Chau. I now know what you did on your vacation in Europe four years ago. I saw it in your eyes, and I saw it in his. Give my respect to your father and to An. Live a happy life, but without me.

Minh Chau was stunned. He had not even given her a chance to explain. And she was with Wolfgang before they were together, *not* during that short European vacation. How selfish he had become! All the affairs that she had silently put up with, and now on the mere suspicion of infidelity, he had abandoned her. She would not let him get away with this. She would find him and tell him what she thought.

After six months, Minh Chau abandoned her efforts to track down Quan. She had exhausted every avenue to find him. She had even hired John Shaw, one of Canada's best private detectives. Through him, she learned much about Quan's life in British Columbia, about his love affair for seven years with Melissa Wong. How he had constantly been on the run from the Chinese Triad and needed to change his identity. How his affairs since they had been together had always been of short duration and how he had broken them off when the women became serious. Despite the amazing skills of John Shaw, the detective was utterly incapable of finding Quan's new whereabouts. Just as adroitly as he had remained hidden from the Triad, Quan had now disappeared from her life.

* * *

Minh Chau folded the fresh towels in the bathroom. She would prepare a nice bath for Mathieu, just like Mary had done for her so many years ago. She would bathe him from toe to foot. She just needed to send An on her way first.

After many assurances that everything was okay, An finally bid goodnight to her sister.

"Mathieu, you look tired. Can I run you a bath?" asked Minh Chau.

"That's all right. Please don't trouble yourself."

"No, I want to. Remember the lovely bear-claw bathtub in Madame Lau's house in Hamel Street? My father had one just like it installed here last year. Let me run you a bath, please?"

"Why not. That would be great."

Minh Chau could sense victory in her grasp. Mathieu would not just enjoy the pleasure of a bath, but much more tonight.

She slipped into her father's bathrobe and ran the steaming water almost to the brim. She then called Mathieu to the bathroom and left him there to undress.

The water scalded Mathieu's skin, but he liked it that way. Hot water always drove away the persistent nightmares of his past. He dunked his head below the water's surface and repeated the simple Arabic poem that he learned from Jamila many years ago.

Life is a shell,
That we must fill,
With kindness,
Only love brings us,
Out of the shell,
Only death,
Closes it on us,
For eternity.

Was he in love again with this beautiful woman from his past? Did he have the right to see in her gestures the signs of interest in him or was she just returning the kindness that he had shown toward her so many years ago? When he surfaced, he felt a hand on his shoulder. Minh Chau was offering him a glass of champagne. His nakedness did not seem to bother her at all. He took the glass and sipped it as she lathered his back with soap, and then his chest. "Mathieu, you have the beautiful body of a twenty-year-old," she unabashedly proclaimed. Her slim but perfectly formed legs peeked out of her father's bathrobe. He stroked them tenderly, sliding his hand between them. She moaned as he touched her womanhood, and then shook off the bathrobe and slid into the water. The nipples on her nubile breasts were hard and hardened even more as he bent forward to kiss them. She could feel his manhood beneath her. She looked into his eyes for the reassurance of his desire. When her jade eyes melded into his, she knew that she wanted him more than anyone else before. She tried to straddle him, but he raised her up and said, "Not yet, let me bathe you first." She nodded in agreement at the postponement of her desire.

Mathieu's hands had the gentle touch that is not learned, but comes from within. Like everything about him, he was authentic. As he applied the soap to her flawless skin, she felt the bitterness and anger of the past year wash away. Quan had been a skillful lover, an ardent lover, but she had never felt this way with him. When her hands began to wrinkle and the water became lukewarm, Mathieu lifted her in his strong arms and ritually dried her from head to toe. No sooner was her skin dry than he moistened it again with his lips and hard tongue. Her body quivered as he tasted her all over. When she could not take it any longer, she took his hand in both of hers and led him to the bedroom.

Over the bed hung a large oil painting of a woman looking wistfully through a window, enclosed by dark shadows. Minh Chau glanced at it for a moment and then looked at Mathieu who seemed entranced by the painting. She touched his arm and he returned from his moment of silence. Their brief enthrallment with the portrait had chased its shadows away and unchained their desire. Minh Chau pulled herself to Mathieu and kissed him passionately on the mouth. He was hard and his heart was beating strongly against her breasts. She kissed his body, taking every part of it in her soft mouth, and then stood, turned her back to him and leaned forward. It pleased her to feel his thrust from behind, his hands on her hips. She controlled his movements with her body in the start of an endless night of sexual exploration.

Chapter Thirty-Five
Demons from the Past

Robert Leblanc looked at the patient's chart. The man was 69 years with advanced lung cancer for the last three years. It seemed that he would never give up on life, but Robert as a physician knew that the cancer had entered its final stage. He had only agreed to see the patient from Hong Kong because of the insistence of Paul Wong, his uncle's lawyer. Paul had successfully defended his uncle, Dominic Leblanc, against a vicious malpractice suit launched by the wife of a patient whom he had unsuccessfully treated with Jing Zi's herbal cancer cures.

"Nurse Lafleur, please ask Mr. Tao to come in."

Robert knew that western medicine would be of no avail to this patient, and decided that he would explore the possibility of testing Jing Zi's remedies. He took his research very seriously and had even spent six months in Laos where with a translator he poured through Jing Zi's medical library, still intact in the shop that the old healer had abandoned thirty years ago. To his surprise, he discovered that Jing Zi was well versed in western medicine and wrote up extensive notes on his own medical trials in much the same way that a western medical researcher would. Although it still remained unclear why, over the last three years, one of Jing Zi's remedies appeared to have statistically significant results in halting the progression of cancer in at least half a dozen patients.

"Hello, Mr. Tao, how do you do?"

The old man whispered to Paul Wong who translated for him. "Not very well, I can't walk very far before I lose my breath."

"Mr. Tao, let me be very clear with you. Your lung cancer has progressed too far for any western treatment that I know of. However, I would like to put you on some Chinese medicine that seems to be effective for at least some patients."

Again through Wong, Tao said, "I know of Jing Zi's medicine."

"How do you know the name of Jing Zi?" asked Robert, surprised as that name did not appear in any of the half-dozen scientific articles that he and his uncle had published since the first article by Dr. Han Thieu some thirteen years earlier.

"I just know," said the old man.

"Okay, I have some release forms that I would like you to sign before we begin the treatment. I should warn you, though, that part of the treatment involves poisons that when taken in a slightly higher dose than what I will prescribe can kill. It is difficult to determine each patient's resistance to these poisons. The best results have been obtained when we push the patient's resistance to its limits."

"I do not have much to lose anyway." acknowledged Tao.

"Okay, we will start tomorrow."

After thanking the doctor, the old man got up and went to the door, followed closely by Paul Wong. When they reached the corridor, a familiar-looking Asian man passed by them and knocked on Robert Leblanc's open door.

"Quan, please come in," said an astonished Leblanc.

The name Quan rang in Tao's ears. He turned around and glared at the young Asian's face. It was him! He turned to Paul Wong, "Have that man brought to me."

Paul Wong immediately took out his cell phone and called the Triad.

It was just then that Melissa Wong passed by the old man and his lawyer. Paul Wong was a distant relative, but Melissa had avoided contact with him since she had joined the Leblancs in their research six months earlier. Paul Wong did not recognize her, but she knew who he was and then, to her astonishment, she also recognized Tao Tsao who had frequently visited her father, and who had put a bounty on Quan's head.

She thought of Quan. After he had disappeared thirteen years ago, she still received letters from him every month for a year. His last letter finally told her what she feared the most. He would never return and he was committed to another woman. Ironically, he had written "committed" and not "in love." Had she not loved him so deeply, she would have hated him for that. Over time, she learned to reconcile life with deception and moved on.

She knocked on Robert's door. He opened it briefly. "Melissa, I am sorry. I am tied up."

Through the crack of the door, he saw him. There was no mistake, even thirteen years later. For seven years, she had woken up by his side and etched into her memory every scratch on his body. She pushed the door open, and marched in.

"Melissa," protested Robert Leblanc.

"Out of my way, Robert." She walked right up to Quan and stood face to face. Her voice quivered as she asked only one question. "Why?"

Quan bowed his eyes in repentance. He had abandoned her, and there was no going back on that. He had decided that he would return to Minh Chau. The years had eroded the feelings he still had for Melissa.

She stood defiantly, waiting for an answer.

Finally, in Mandarin, Quan recited a poem that he learned from one of the Chinese Buddhist nuns at Cultus Lake.

Autumn breaks the leaf,
From the birch tree,
It floats in the air,
And gently settles among the others,
And can never return to the tree,
Which lives on and on.

Melissa stood aghast. "Fuck you!" Her slap on his face was designed to banish his Asian soul to hell. But she could not hold back, and collapsed into his arms, sobbing with anger and joy at having finally found him again, and alive.

When she regained her composure, she asked quietly, "Just tell me why you left. No poetry or Buddhist mantras. In straight language, tell me what happened."

Quan stood there motionless. He remembered why he had loved Melissa. It was her honesty, her frankness, her ability to forgive the transgressions of others. She was the most Canadian woman he had ever known. He suddenly felt a deep sense of failure. In his relations

Soldier, Lily, Peace and Pearls   *207*

with women, he had been failing all his life. His conversation with Marie-Christine in the plane had made him realize this more than ever. He had abandoned women in a constant search to change his life. In leaving Mali, he had turned the page on his life in Bangkok. In leaving Melissa for Minh Chau, he had given up seven years of bliss out of a sense of duty mixed with the intoxication of Minh Chau's charms. Finally, in abandoning Minh Chau last year, he had given in to his ego, his misplaced sense of pride. And Françoise, what reasoning could make him understand why he was leaving this exquisite soul?

"Melissa, I left you first out of fear at what could happen to you and then because I fell in love with someone whom I have always loved in one way or the other."

"Do you still love her?"

"Until five minutes ago, I thought that I did."

"And me?"

"Are you saying that you still love me?" asked Quan.

"My poor indigent Buddhist scholar, what do you think?" said Melissa hopefully.

Robert Leblanc stood there unsure of whether there was a role that he should be playing as a friend to Quan, to Melissa and to Minh Chau. No, the loyalties were too confusing. Finally, he said, "Melissa, can I speak with you for a couple of minutes? Quan, here is the room number for Voang. Let's all of us meet in the cafeteria in fifteen minutes."

"Robert, what are you doing?"

"Trust me. Please trust me." He then took Melissa by the arm and walked with her to her office. Quan watched them depart and then glanced down at the slip of paper with the room number.

"Robert, how do you know Quan? What was he doing in your office? I need to get back to him before he disappears again!"

"Don't worry. He won't disappear. He has come back for a very special reason."

"Yes, to be with me."

"No."

Robert sat across from Melissa in her tiny office, and recounted the story of Minh Chau. Melissa had met Minh Chau on a couple of occasions at Robert's house. She admired her stunning beauty and zany character, but was put off by her slipping into deep brooding when Robert or his wife Jocelyne mentioned some get-together in the past. For some inexplicable reason, Melissa felt an antipathy toward Minh Chau, almost as if they were rivals. Melissa also felt resentful of Minh Chau's constant adulation of her father Voang and her deceased mother Han. Melissa loved her father despite his ruthless criminal activities, but could not bear to speak about him to others. As for her mother, this was a scar that ran too deep to discuss. In studying Jing Zi's medicine, she had recently pieced together the cause of her mother's premature death. Unlike the extroverted Minh Chau, Melissa was an introvert, made worse from years of self-imposed celibacy. She was the opposite of Minh Chau and now she discovered that they had loved and still loved the same man.

Still she was touched by Robert's description of Minh Chau's return from the darkness, and remembered her own mother's long bouts of standing at her bedroom window. Emotionally, Melissa thought of herself as the Rock of Gibraltar and had little use for stories of sentimental roller-coasters, but Minh Chau's story brought out a different reaction in her. She suddenly understood the trap that Quan had fallen into. As Robert finished his narrative with the sudden and angry disappearance of Quan the year before, Melissa looked at her reflection in the office window. She was now 41 and thought she was still attractive, but Minh Chau's beauty seemed to her to be ageless.

"Robert, am I still pretty?"

"Of course, you are. Why do you ask?"

"Am I as pretty as Minh Chau?"

This was an area where Robert was unwilling to go. He had been captivated by Minh Chau's beauty when he first saw on the bus thirteen years ago. For years, he had been silent about his own deep attraction to her, but had endeared himself to both Quan and her, just to be near her. When he married Jocelyne, he swore that he would obliterate his feelings for Minh Chau, but had proven unable to do so. Still he had never expressed more than friendship toward Minh Chau and had become a loyal friend to Quan. After Quan had left, he had struggled with the idea of telling Minh Chau how he felt. Out of loyalty to Quan, he refrained, but the conflict with his emotions had made him aloof in his relationship with Jocelyne and they had gone through a bad time.

Finally, Robert said, "Melissa, you are a beautiful woman in all ways. We have only known each other for six months, but I see you as a very close friend. However, I've known Minh Chau for a long, long time and she and Quan are my closest friends. I do not want to get involved in this. I just wanted to explain why Quan had left Minh Chau and what the situation is now. I respect Quan, Minh Chau and you for whatever decisions you will take. There is one thing though. Minh Chau's father Voang is gravely ill, and that is why Quan has returned. We all have to be careful not to put Voang under additional stress."

Melissa, as a physician, understood exactly what her obligation to Voang was, but needed to raise one more question. "Does Minh Chau know that Quan is back?"

"I do not think so."

On this, Robert was wrong. Three minutes after Quan had found Voang, Minh Chau pulled into the hospital parking lot. Mathieu would be joining her shortly from a meeting he was wrapping up in downtown Montreal. She was anxious about her father's health, and hurried to his room. Mathieu had been a darling. He had literally taken over her life so she could be free to focus on her father's health. He brought down laptops from headquarters and set both of them up to tele-work from her father's house. From the first night in the house, every morning was a struggle to let him leave her bed. She caressed him before he woke and made love to him as soon as his eyes opened. He in turn fixed her breakfast with the tenderness of genuine care, introduced her to *Foul Mudammas* with onions to start the day, fed her olives and *Baba Ghannoush* at noon, and in the evening, he prepared the *Injera Wots* from Ethiopia. She travelled the world through his cooking, and she took him around the world in her nocturnal embraces.

Had it not been for her concern for her father's deteriorating health, Minh Chau could not have been happier in her life. No, that was not true. She had never been as happy as she was now.

Chapter Thirty-Six
Encounters and Memories Settled

The two Triad gangsters watched as Quan left Robert's office for Room 208. They kept a safe distance. He was a big prize. In his obsession with finding Quan, Tao Tsao had over the years continually raised the bounty on Quan's head. It now stood at a cool million. This was still peanuts for Tao Tsoa who was now on his way to becoming a billionaire.

Tao had succeeded in pushing out many of his competitors in Canada and the United States. He had successfully displaced John Wong in Vancouver, reducing him to an errand boy. His ruthlessness was legendary. He had coerced Chung Fat in California into handing over one-half of his real estate empire in exchange for the lives of the real estate mogul's two grand-daughters. Chung Fat had at first refused, but when Tao Tsao had sent the older of the two girls home with a torn vagina, lacerated breasts, and carrying a backpack with the heads of the three ex-special forces commandos whom the businessman had hired to rescue the children, Chung Fat immediately put have half of his empire into escrow in Tao's Panamanian bank account. Chung Fat was no angel, but he had never known this level of brutality.

The thugs watched Quan enter Room 208. They knew that they had him cornered, but they were also equally aware that their presence was gathering attention from the medical staff. One nurse had already approached them to ask if she could help them. They concocted a story that they were waiting for their sister before visiting their uncle. They felt that the nurse had not bought the story and it would only be a matter of time before hospital security showed up. Besides, kidnapping Quan from a crowded hospital was simply too risky for them. The leader of the two, Jackie Leung, decided that it was time to subcontract the kidnapping. He pulled out his cell phone and phoned the Nomads. They would do anything for $5,000.

"Hello J.F., it is me. I have got a package for you to pick up from Room 208 at Notre Dame Hospital. Can you come now?" asked Leung.

"Sure, how many delivery men should I send?"

"At least three, it is a heavy package."

"Usual postage?"

"No, this time, we pay express mail."

"Usual destination?"

"Yes."

Leung turned to his partner Hong. "Let's beat it. We will wait for the delivery at the restaurant."

"Should we tell the boss?"

"No, J.F.'s crew is efficient. Dead or alive, the package will be delivered."

Chapter Thirty-Seven
New Life

The Power Point presentation by the *Société de développement international Desjardins (SDID)* was really dragging on. These guys might be the best micro-credit organization in the world after the Grameen Bank, but their communications strategies were still from the dark ages. Mathieu was already late for his appointment with Minh Chau at the hospital, which was luckily only ten minutes away by car. He quickly sent her an e-mail from his Blackberry—*Stuck in the meeting. Should be done in ten. Love you, Hibou.*

"And ladies and gentlemen, that is our strategy for Ethiopia. We hope that you will consider us for the credit component of the Haraghe Project," wrapped up Jean-Marie Gauvreau, one of Mathieu's oldest friends from Laval University and now vice-president of SDID.

"Thank you, Jean-Marie. We will get back to you on your project proposal as soon as we can," declared Mathieu as he furiously shoved documents into his briefcase. He did not want to appear impolite, but every minute apart from Minh Chau seemed now an eternity.

On the elevator down to the underground parking, Mathieu began again to dream about this woman whose features danced before his eyes every waking moment of the day and night. It had only been four days, and he had been totally unprepared for the intensity but complete harmony of their relationship. It had quickly displaced the grief that he had felt since the deaths of Denise and Étienne. He knew that Denise would have approved of this relationship. She had always had a tremendous affection for Minh Chau. Now that the child had become a woman and the most important thing in Mathieu's life, Denise would have seen this relationship as the most natural thing possible.

He looked at the hair bracelet on his wrist. When Minh Chau had discovered that he was wearing it on the first night of their love-making, she recoiled and said, "Mathieu, I am so sorry. Is this right what we are doing?" It was the only time that she had expressed any doubt. His tender touch banished her doubts, and the next morning, he spoke for the first time about how he had found Denise and Étienne. Minh

Chau took him in her tiny arms as if to lift his soul from the abyss. "You will always have Denise and Étienne, Mathieu. I only ask you for a small place in your heart."

Minh Chau's place in Mathieu's heart had no boundaries. She filled him now with a sense of completeness.

As if to clear his heart of all competition for Minh Chau, Mathieu's mind raced back to his love affair with Jamila, Salwa's sister. When he had arrived in Jamila's Tal Sultan clinic, it was too late for Salwa, who had drowned in her own blood. He and Jamila had heard Salwa stutter the words, "Bahibbak Mathieu—I love you Mathieu" before she died. For months afterwards, he tried with Jamila to clear Salwa's name from any association with terrorism. Every member of Salwa's family was called in for questioning by the Israeli authorities. Three were detained for six months. They even threatened to expel Mathieu if he did not refrain from repeating the truthful version of events.

The one-armed dying soldier was the son of an Israeli Brigadier-General close to the Peace Now movement. He did not want his son's memory tarnished by a last act of firing on an unarmed civilian. Even when Mathieu explained to the general that his son had probably lost so much blood that he was surely delusional or even blind during the shooting spree, this was not enough. The general insisted that the official version of the story would be that Salwa had tried to ram the checkpoint as a diversionary tactic before the main assault by the suicide bombers. Lies born of paternal love are the most resilient.

Jamila had come to admire Mathieu's tenacity in defending the true story of her sister's death. In their mutual grief, they came to share the same bed. It was love without happiness, a bond based on sorrow and perhaps a sense of duty or surrogacy. Mathieu did not fully understand why he had responded to Jamila's sexual advances. Did he see in her Salwa and feel that he owed her the love that he had almost had with her sister? Jamila accepted what Mathieu had to offer, and when after six months, he asked that they end their relationship, she embraced him as a friend. It was the only time since Denise's death that he had known another woman until Minh Chau.

His thoughts returned to Minh Chau. In many ways, she reincarnated the intelligence of Jamila and Salwa and the purity of Denise's soul. He thought also of Étienne. His heart stopped. He held the bannister of the stairway to the basement to stop himself from stumbling head-on against the concrete steps. His years of stoicism collapsed in a river of tears and sobs as he sat on the cold steps, his hands propping up a near lifeless face. Anger soon displaced his tears. How could they have killed a boy so gentle, so kind? What drove this evil in the minds of men? For a moment, he lost all control over his emotions. For years, he had not shed a tear. He had stood up to the world, defiantly trying to make it a better place, and now hatred filled his being. In the silence of the concrete, he heard music. It was the love song that Minh Chau and An had sung in Quebec. Minh Chau's voice metamorphosed into a vision of her tiny, slender body walking in its naked splendour from their bed to the window. He followed her every moment, and dwelled on the slight curve of her belly. A smile returned to Mathieu's face as he picked himself up and marched to his car, determined to start life anew.

Chapter Thirty-Eight
Reckoning of Accounts

J.F. sent his two stupidest gang members. If they got caught, it would be no loss for the motorcycle gang. There were times when he wanted to take Bruno and André out to the woods and waste them. How many times had their drunken debauchery landed the club in deep water. And their violent rape of the niece of a Colombian drug lord had nearly started a war. The convenient knocking-off of the drug lord by one of his rivals had saved their butts that time, but it had also forced the Nomads to ally with the Triad to ensure their survival against a future onslaught by the dead man's followers and friends.

J.F. hated the alliance. He saw the Chinese and all Asians as a cancer that was killing Quebec society. Before the Asians and the Colombians, life had been easier. A bit of selling marijuana, the odd high-end car theft and the weekly take from a few of the club's girls walking the streets, and the gang was happy, boozing away the nights and criss-crossing the province on their hogs on the weekend. Now, the Nomads had to compete in the big time, pushing heroin and cocaine and smuggling starving illegal immigrants to the sweatshops of New York and Chicago.

Upping the ante meant taking risks. Half of the Nomads' membership was now behind bars in New Bordeaux Prison, and the club was vulnerable to a possible take-over by their rivals, the Banditos. The Triad had sent the Nomads a life-line by supplying them with Belarusian-built AK-47s and RPGs. There would be a nasty welcome for the Banditos whenever they made their move. Still, J.F. could not but bitterly note that not a single Triad member was rotting away in New Bordeaux Prison. The Chinese were tough, but they knew how to get others to take the real risks. That was fine. The time would come when the Nomads would again be strong enough to fuck over the slick Chinese gangsters with their Armani suits and tight-ass whores.

Bruno and André were already high on coke when they reached the reception desk of the hospital to ask for Room 208. They had brought along Ti-Jean, an 18-year-old crack addict who would do anything to become a Nomad member. As they made their way toward Room 208, they saw a beautiful slender Asian woman rush by them. They lusted after her, admiring the hint of a dragon tattoo across the small of her back where her t-shirt did not reach the top of her jeans. Then they ducked into a laundry closet to find three orderly smocks.

When Minh Chau entered her father's hospital room, Quan was in deep discussion with him. She froze at the sight of Quan. All the anger that she wanted to unleash upon him would have to wait until they were alone. But she no longer felt the same anger toward him. Mathieu had cleansed her of that emotion. She needed only to tell her father that she and Quan were finished. She only needed to turn the clock back thirteen years and wish Quan a good life.

"Minh Chau, come in," called out her father. "Quan has just told me the good news."

"What good news?"

"That you and Quan are finally going to get married!"

Minh Chau summoned all her strength to suppress glaring at Quan. This was not the time to upset her father. "Chéri, can I see you out-side for a second."

Quan dutifully followed Minh Chau into the corridor and out of earshot from her father.

Trembling with anger, she pounced on him. "What the fuck are you doing, you asshole?!"

"Minh Chau, he asked when we would get married, and I realized that you hadn't even told him that we were separated. Besides, I love you and I want to marry you!"

"You can fuck yourself!"

She was so excited that she was about to land her nails into his face when three orderlies walked by, bumping her into the wall. Quan grabbed one of the men who brushed him aside. Minh Chau pulled Quan away to avoid a fight.

The three men marched into Room 208. Minh Chau and Quan looked at each other surprised. They followed the men into the room. One of the men was plunging a syringe into Voang's neck while the other

Soldier, Lily, Peace and Pearls   *217*

held him down. The third man pulled a knife on Quan, who easily kicked it out of his hand and knocked him down with one blow to the layrnx. The two other thugs pulled revolvers out of their jackets, pointing one at Quan and the other at Minh Chau. The thug that Quan had decked rose to his feet and smashed a vase against Quan's head. Minh Chau jumped the attacker, but was thrown against wall, falling unconscious to the floor.

For good measure, the Nomad leader re-filled the syringe and injected the sedative into Quan's neck. They put Voang into to a wheelchair and headed for the hospital's exit.

Mathieu turned the corner just as the Nomads came wheeling Voang down a ramp. From the corner of his eye, Mathieu recognized his old friend. The orderly smocks deceived him. Where were they taking Voang? Then he heard a soft moan coming from Room 208. He rushed there to find Minh Chau raising herself from the floor. Beside her, an Asian man lay, his head in a small pool of blood.

"What has happened? Where are they taking Voang?"

"I don't know. It happened so fast. They had guns and knocked out Quan."

"Quan?"

"Yes, Quan. That's him. Please help him."

Mathieu checked Quan's pulse. He was fine. The blood was only from a scalp wound.

"He's alive. Minh Chau, I have to go after them. Will you be okay?"

"Yes. Go. Go now. I will take care of Quan. Call me on my Blackberry."

Mathieu kissed her quickly, and ran in the direction of the kidnappers. From the entrance, he saw the Nomads put Voang into a dark blue van. He ran to his Nissan, just in time to follow the van before it was out of sight. Keeping a safe distance, he followed the van through the city to the crowded streets of Montreal's Chinatown. The van pulled into the back parking lot of the Green Door restaurant. As the Nomads dragged Voang through the back, Mathieu called Minh Chau, gave her the name of the restaurant and asked her to inform the police. He then parked his car in the alley and sneaked up to the restaurant's back door. When he opened it, he felt the nuzzle of a 38-calibre in his neck. Ti-Jean grabbed his hair and pushed him forward inside the restaurant. The Chinese cooks did not even bat an eye as Ti-Jean marched Mathieu past them into the cellar. At the bottom of the stairs, Voang was already strapped to a chair. An old Chinese man was screaming at Voang. "Who are you? Where is Quan?"

Voang realized that only his silence would keep Quan safe. He thought of the beatings in the Hue interrogation centre before he was sent to the re-education camp. They hadn't broken him then. They wouldn't now. When he saw Mathieu marched down the stairs, his heart sank. He knew what these thugs would do to Mathieu.

"Who is this white demon," asked Tao Tsoa.

"He was hanging around outside," answered Paul Wong.

"String him up," ordered Tao.

As Mathieu hung from the low basement ceiling, the Triad and Nomad thugs took turns beating him with tire irons and baseball bats. First, they cracked his ribs. Then they began on his legs.

Tao continued to interrogate Voang. "Talk, old man," ordered Tao, but Voang remained silent. He knew that Mathieu and he were already dead, and was determined not to betray Quan or put Minh Chau into danger. By now, he had recognized Tao Tsoa, and the hatred for the man who had left them as prey for the Thai pirates surged within him. He would tell this man nothing.

"Bring the knives," shouted Tao.

Quan recovered quickly from the sedative. As he heard Minh Chau give the name of the restaurant to the police, he leaped to his feet.

"Quan, where are you going? The police will handle this."

"Minh Chau, if we wait for the police, your father will die."

"Quan, you don't have to go. Mathieu is already there."

"Then Mathieu is a fool, and they will kill him too. I am the one that they want."

"Quan, don't go. It is too dangerous. They will recognize you."

"Minh Chau, remember Pulau Bidong. I am your Bao. I am your father's Bao. I must go."

Quan raced to his car in the parking lot, and gunned it toward China-town. His life now made sense. He knew Tao Tsoa. There was only one way to save Voang and Mathieu. He thought of Minh Chau shad-owing him in Pulau Bidong in the hope of finding candied treasure, of Mali's last sensual gift of her body before he left Bangkok and of Melissa's outburst of love barely an hour earlier. Finally, he thought of Françoise whose youthful love had never put him in doubt. He was at peace with himself and with his decision.

When he arrived at the restaurant, he double-parked outside, went in through the front door and approached the kitchen. He barked in his best Teochew dialect at the cooks to get out of his way, turned to the guard at the cellar door and told him that Tao was waiting for him. When the guard tried to stop him, he kneed him in the groin and took his gun from him. He thundered down the stairs and pointed the gun directly at Tao. Immediately, five guns turned on Quan.

"Tao, let them go, and you can have me. If not, say goodbye to this world."

Tao smiled wryly. "Let those two go. We now have what we want."

Voang helped Mathieu stagger up the stairs. The pain was unbearable. As soon as they reached the top, they heard a hail of bullets. Tao lay dead on the floor with a bullet to the brain, and Quan's body quivered before it collapsed from multiple wounds. In the kitchen, the cooks pulled out large knives to prevent Voang and Mathieu from leaving.

Suddenly, the front and back doors were crashed in under the heavy boots of the Montreal SWAT squad. The cooks dropped their knives and put their hands in the air. The Triad and Nomad thugs were cor-nered in the basement, but that did not stop them from carrying on a futile ten-minute gun battle with the police. When it was all over, two of the three Nomads lay dead on the floor and two Triad members propped themselves up against the walls, bleeding profusely.

Voang asked to go to Quan. The police agreed once they had taken the remaining gang members into custody. Voang knelt beside Quan's body, kissed his head and whispered, "My Bao, my dear Bao, forgive me." Voang tried to lift Quan's body, but he couldn't. He felt Math-ieu's hand on his shoulder. Despite his injuries, Mathieu had drawn on his inner strength to follow Voang to the basement. He now looked down on Voang and his son. Quan's face was twisted in a grimace of anger. He had seen the face only thirty minutes before for the first time in his life. Yet, Quan had been part of his life for almost thirty years. Mathieu knelt down beside Voang. "Let me," he asked. As Voang stood back, Mathieu took Quan's lifeless form into his arms, and carried him from the dark, damp cellar to the brightness of the day, just as the ambulance arrived. He stood there before the medics, unsure whether to hand over Quan's body or not. He looked at Quan's face and saw that of Étienne, Denise and thousands and thousands of victims of the genocide. The voice of Robert Leblanc woke him from his reverie.

"Let the medics take him." said Robert Leblanc who had ridden in with the ambulances. At Robert's side was a beautiful Asian doctor with red eyes and tear-stained cheeks. From the corner of his eye, he then saw Minh Chau helping her father into the back of a police car. Their eyes met and sealed their souls into one in an instant of confusion and grief before his legs buckled under him.

Epilogue

La Galaxie des lumières tardives

In the shade of the pagoda in Suoi Tien Park, two elderly men focused intently on their game of Da' Ngu'a, as a third looked on. A sixteen-year-old girl played with a toddler.

"Grandpapa, Grandpapa. When will mama and Auntie Dao come back?"

"Soon, Quan, soon. Please let me play, your Uncle Phuc is going to beat me if I don't concentrate."

"Don't worry, my old friend. We can always play another game," piped up Phuc.

"Where are they?" asked little Quan.

"Our mothers went to buy some lychees, mangoes and plums at the fruit festival. You like lychees, don't you?" asked Cousin Han.

"Yes, but I want treasure too."

"What treasure?" asked the third old man.

"Huynh's treasure, Uncle Nguyen."

"Of course, of course. Will you dance for it?"

"Okay, but first the treasure."

Just at that moment, little Quan felt a hand on his head. He turned to see his mother Minh Chau's amazingly beautiful face beam at him. "We only have fruit, darling."

Quan pouted. "Then no dancing for you."

Minh Chau and her cousin Dao began to cut the pieces of fruit into bowls for the old Da' Ngu'a combatants. Quan's cousin Han did her best to cheer him up. Just as grandfather Voang threw up his hands in joy, proclaiming victory, a Eurasian man accompanied by a Vietnamese man of a similar age and a young girl turned the corner of the narrow path to the pagoda. The Eurasian man limped forward, but with a confident gait.

"Papa, papa, papa." cried the toddler who raced to the newcomers.

"Did Uncle Huynh bring the treasure?"

"I really don't know. Did you bring it, Huynh?"

Huynh turned to his new friend and shook his head.

Quan again began to pout.

Auntie Dao leaned over and whispered into the toddler's eye, "Why don't you check out your cousin Hue's pockets?" pointing to her eight-year-old girl standing with her father and Mathieu.

"Okay, Auntie Dao."

Little Hue was engrossed in staring at her Canadian uncle's face. She had never seen a man like him before and thought that he was very handsome. Suddenly, she felt a tiny hand in her pocket, fishing out the hard candy that her father had just given her. "Hey, you little red-haired devil, leave that alone!"

"Ah, ha, I have got the treasure. I've got the treasure."

"And now you must dance for us," commanded Aunt An, who began clapping her hands.

As the little Hue took her cousin's hand in hers to dance on the paving stones, all the women joined hands and began to sing a song that she had never heard before.

Soldier, lily, peace and pearls,
All together in one world,
When the owl comes out at night,
He will make everything all right.

Mathieu looked on at his son, his beautiful wife, her sister, cousins and nieces, and then at the old men whose victories at Parcheesi exiled their memories of war. Sometimes, the lights of the galaxies shine late in life, but their soft glow is as beautiful as the young comets in the night's sky.

www.ingramcontent.com/pod-product-compliance
Lightning Source LLC
Chambersburg PA
CBHW060804120626
46557CB00001B/87